WHO SHE WAS

'A cracking story with a wonderful style of writing that draws you in and keeps you hooked till the last page.'
Heidi Perks

'Tony Parsons is channelling Daphne du Maurier with his latest thriller, a haunting Gothic romance set in Cornwall. Gripping and beautifully written, with atmosphere you could cut with a knife, *Who She Was* will stay with you long after you turn the final page.'
Alex Michaelides

'Vividly drawn and utterly engrossing.'
Tom Hindle

'It's a brilliant book.'
Piers Morgan

'An intriguing du Maurier-ish Cornwall mystery . . . a story of twists and turns.'
Peterborough Telegraph

'Parsons' command of narrative grows from book to book . . . *Who She Was* is quite possibly his most assured outing yet.'
Crime Time

'Clever, tricky stuff from a master of lad lit.'
SAGA

'Expertly plotted.'
Choice Magazine

Also by Tony Parsons

Man and Boy
One For My Baby
Man and Wife
The Family Way
Stories We Could Tell
My Favourite Wife
Starting Over
Men from the Boys
Catching the Sun
The Murder Bag (Max Wolfe #1)
The Slaughter Man (Max Wolfe #2)
The Hanging Club (Max Wolfe #3)
Die Last (Max Wolfe #4)
Girl on Fire (Max Wolfe #5)
#taken (Max Wolfe #6)
Your Neighbour's Wife
The People Next Door

Max Wolfe Digital Shorts
Dead Time
Fresh Blood
Tell Him He's Dead

TONY PARSONS

WHO
SHE
WAS

PENGUIN BOOKS

PENGUIN BOOKS

UK | USA | Canada | Ireland | Australia
India | New Zealand | South Africa

Penguin Books is part of the Penguin Random House group of companies
whose addresses can be found at global.penguinrandomhouse.com

First published by Century in 2023
Published in Penguin Books 2024
001

Copyright © Tony Parsons, 2023
Excerpt from *Murder for Busy People* copyright © Tony Parsons, 2024

The moral right of the author has been asserted

Printed and bound in Great Britain by Clays Ltd, Elcograf S.p.A.

The authorised representative in the EEA is Penguin Random House Ireland,
Morrison Chambers, 32 Nassau Street, Dublin D02 YH68

A CIP catalogue record for this book is available from the British Library

ISBN: 978–1–804–94104–1

www.greenpenguin.co.uk

MIX
Paper | Supporting
responsible forestry
FSC
www.fsc.org
FSC® C018179

Penguin Random House is committed to a
sustainable future for our business, our readers
and our planet. This book is made from Forest
Stewardship Council® certified paper.

For Yuriko, who walked the coastal path with me

Two days at home
Eight days at sea
But when he sleeps
He dreams of me.

Anonymous

WHO SHE WAS

PART ONE

The Lobster Pot

1

A bonfire was burning down on the beach.

Somewhere in the night I was dragged from my sleep by the flames on my bedroom wall, or rather by the shadow of flames. I watched them flicker and change shape for a while and when I knew for sure that sleep would not find me again, I got out of my bed to have a look. I was watching the fire on the beach from my bedroom window when Bet Farthing called.

'Surfers, my lovely,' Bet said in her soft Cornish burr, and it made me smile.

There was no surfing on our side of the coast. But by *surfers*, Bet meant folk who were not local. And like Eskimos with snow, in St Jude's we had multiple names for people who were not local. Emmets, in-comers, upcountry folk, outsiders, strangers, second homeowners, tourists, stag parties, *moryons* (the old Cornish word for ants), rich wankers, and, yes, surfers. Call them what you like, outsiders were the only people who would start a fire down on the beach in the middle of the night. People from outside the county, or more likely their drunk and stoned and overexcited teenage children, enjoying the first rumour of summer, feeling all wild and free so far from their private schools.

'He's going down there to sort them out,' Bet said, meaning her husband Will, and my smile faded, because Will was over seventy now, and this could get messy. 'I can't stop the old fool, Tom. He's already getting his boots on.'

It wasn't the fire on the beach that Will Farthing and the other locals objected to but the crap that the outsiders so casually left behind. Broken bottles that hurt the dogs and the little kids with their crabbing buckets and nets, the litter that someone else would have to pick up from our small but pristine and beloved beach.

When the hour was late and the Bad Apple Cider was flowing, they brought the thin-skinned belligerence of the city and the suburb with them on their holidays.

They could get aggressive, start showing off for each other, too young and dumb to realise how easily a shouting match can escalate into real violence. *They don't like to be told*, as Bet Farthing said. And now that he was getting his boots on, nothing on earth was going to stop Will Farthing from telling them.

'I'll go down there with him, Bet,' I told her. 'Don't worry.'

I began pulling on some clothes.

I had a one-bedroom flat above my restaurant, the Lobster Pot. It was one of those semi-secret places that you could drive past and not even notice, perched high above the esplanade. The Lobster Pot was nothing fancy – a restaurant of old wooden tables and day-caught fish and a great view over the water, the inside lit by candles and the deck overlooking the water strung with fairy lights – my idea of a classy touch when I opened ten years ago. The menu mattered to me, and our customers usually came back for more, and that was what the business was built on. But the Lobster Pot wasn't one of those Cornish restaurants – and there are plenty of them – that get raved about by the outside world. I had been in business for ten years and had yet to see my first restaurant critic. And that was fine by me. The Lobster Pot wasn't much but it was good, and it was mine, and owning it was a dream that came true.

I came down the stairs from the flat, went out to the sea-view deck of the restaurant at the back and down some steep wooden steps and onto the esplanade, smelling the salt of the sea and all the things that live in it. The water hissed and moaned and moved in the night.

Bet and Will's cottage was on the other side of St Jude's, our fishing village, directly above the small beach where the fire was burning. But even the far side of St Jude's was only a short walk away.

I went down the esplanade, parallel to the water, a street so narrow that a passing car meant pedestrians had to flatten themselves against the wall of the white stone fishermen's cottages, many of them second homes or rentals now, fishermen's cottages that had not seen an actual fisherman since the last century. Will Farthing was close to the last of the line.

At the end of the esplanade, the street started winding steeply down towards the Platt, which is what locals called the harbour.

It was April now but still felt out of season as I passed the closed signs of the surf shop, the fudge shop and the ice-cream shop.

But the six months of Sundays were ending soon, and I passed the places that were open all year round. The bakery – Pasty Master – and the pub, the Rabbit Hole, with its black-and-white bunting, the colours of the flag of our Cornish nation, the interior warmly glowing like a honey-coloured cave, and the church, the boathouse, the icehouse where the catch was stored when it could not be sold immediately, and the Loft – which wasn't a loft at all, but the quayside shack where the dwindling tribe of St Jude's fishermen kept all their kit.

I went up what we called the downalongs – the cobbled alleyways and streets that formed the old town, hardly wide enough for a man to pass, let alone a car, where generations of tin miners and their families had lived and died, but not for a hundred years or so – and then down to the end of Pudding Bag Lane, where my friends the Farthings lived.

Bet and Will's front door was open, and Will was in the hall, sitting on the bottom step of the staircase, struggling into his boots, Bet watching him with her arms folded in weary marital disapproval.

Will and Bet Farthing were both large people, tall, hard and hefty, too big for the small cottage where they had spent their entire married life, and they filled the hallway. An old black Lab stared up at them with wonder at all this activity in the middle of the night. Will was a pot fisherman, catching lobster and crab for as much of the year as he could and then mackerel with hook and line when their winter schools came and the lobsters were gone. He had been doing it for more than fifty years and it was starting to wear him out. He was breathing heavily as he pulled his boots on.

Bet glanced at me, both of us glad that I was going down there with him.

'I don't know why we can't just get the law on 'em,' Bet was saying. 'I don't see why *you* have to go down there. Bloody Clint Eastwood here, he is.'

'Skipper's not always right,' Will said, standing up, winking at me. 'But he's always skipper.'

'And sometimes skipper's a silly old fool,' Bet said.

Will looked at me with a sly, snaggle-toothed grin, and winked, as if we were going to have some fun sorting out these surfers. There was a lifetime of weather etched on his smiling face. He clapped his hands. His silver hair was cropped close, and it gave him the look of an elderly skinhead, always up for some mischief.

Will and I walked down a short narrow street to the far end of the quay and then down a slope to the beach.

But there were no surfers around the fire.

There was only her.

DETECTIVE CHIEF INSPECTOR GRAVES:
The jewel in Cornwall's crown, they call St Jude's. A picturesque fishing village, they call it. I went crabbing there on that little beach when I was a kid.

And so it just goes to show, doesn't it?

Murder can happen anywhere.

2

She sat cross-legged by the fire, warming herself on this freezing night, a hoodie pulled over her face, giving her the look of a character from Tolkien, or the lady from the Scottish Widows commercial.

Will and I stood at a respectful distance.

I cleared my throat.

'We saw the fire,' I said.

'Thought you was surfers,' Will said, with an embarrassed chuckle.

She looked up quickly, staring at us for a moment through the flames.

'I'm sorry to have disturbed you,' she said, her accent what my mother would have called 'well-spoken'. Not quite posh, dialled down from the old-school cut glass, but near enough to read the evening news. There was also a hint of the north in there somewhere, the trace of an earlier accent, and a poorer place, that she had discarded somewhere along the way.

Will and I stood there on the other side of the fire, abashed and surprised.

The sea crashed against distant rocks, sighed in the night, withdrew. She rubbed at her hair inside the hoodie with her hand and I saw it looked wet.

I stared out into the roaring blackness.

She hadn't actually been swimming, had she?

Will looked at me for a lead, but I hesitated, still not understanding who she was or what she was doing here or why she had started a fire on our beach. She wasn't homeless. She wasn't a camper wandering the coastal path.

'I have to wait until morning,' she said. 'For the estate agent? He's bringing the keys. It was *so cold* in the car. And it was such a long drive.' She stretched her arms above her head.

It was true. St Jude's was a long drive from anywhere.

Will understood what was happening before I did.

'Grandma Jo's place,' he said. 'You're waiting for the keys to Grandma Jo's place.'

Grandma Jo had been one of those much-loved elderly relatives who wasn't really anyone's elderly relative. Her home was – had been for a lifetime – a small cream-and-blue cottage that overlooked the harbour.

I remembered Grandma Jo's funeral at the end of last summer, the hearse edging through the narrow, crowded streets, the tourists with their ice creams and takeaway pasties pressing themselves against the walls of the esplanade, gawping at the mourners, and our tears. The cream-and-blue cottage had been empty since then.

Grandma Jo had moved into the cottage as a young bride half a century ago, when the fishermen's dwellings were all still full of men who really did fish for a living. She had never had children but had doted on the sons and daughters of her neighbours. After the death of her husband, decades ago, Grandma Jo had lived alone. I stared up into the blackness above the beach. In the daytime, you would be able to see her cream-and-blue cottage from here.

There was luggage scattered around the bonfire. Not much. A couple of suitcases, some smaller bags.

'You're moving in,' I said, aware of just how lumbering and awkward I must seem to her.

'Second home?' Will said politely, making conversation. 'Holiday place, like?'

She shook her head, and a stray tendril of long damp hair slipped from under the hoodie, and I didn't know it then, because you could not tell by the light of the fire and the thin sliver of moon, but her hair was dark red, like copper.

She tucked the rogue tendril of hair behind her ear.

'No,' she said. 'It's my new home. I've got a year's lease.'

Will and I stared at each other, and I could tell he felt it too.

Like we were the ones who were intruding.

Will lifted his chin to sea.

'Tide's coming in,' he pointed out.

The woman followed his gaze. Will cleared his throat.

'You might want to move yourself before the estate agent chap gets here,' he told her. 'Beach will be gone by then, it will.'

She briefly nodded, and we mumbled our good-nights, and she smiled beneath her hoodie, warming her hands on the fire. It was made up of wood with stripy scraps of blue-and-white canvas attached, clinging like the little flags of some defeated army. I realised it was the tattered remains of a deckchair she was burning.

That was – odd. That was – not quite right. Who burns a deckchair?

Will and I mumbled our farewell, turned away, going back up the slope to the village, and the night closed around her.

'Don't understand the tides, do they?' Will said, not unkindly. 'Townies, I mean.'

Townies. That was another one of our words for outsiders. Townies. Ten years ago – another lifetime – I had been a townie in St Jude's.

And it was true. Will was right.

Townies did not understand the way the sea ebbed and flowed, as regular as sunlight and moonlight. There were two high tides and two low tides every day, and they didn't get it, all those townies.

The moon pulls the sea.

And the sea can do nothing to resist.

There was a little Japanese sports car parked outside Will and Bet's cottage, its hot engine still clicking and ticking from a fast drive back from the bright lights of Padstow.

Charlie – Bet and Will's grown-up son – was in the kitchen, dressed for a night out, slightly dishevelled, reeking of craft beer and cologne. Charlie Farthing was a good-looking young man around thirty, touchingly self-conscious about his thinning fair hair, big like Will and Bet but with a polish about him which he had brought back from university. We were old friends – in fact, Charlie had been my first friend, and my best friend, when I came to St Jude's ten years ago with wild dreams about opening a restaurant called the Lobster Pot, and Charlie was a student on his long summer holiday. I must have been around the age he was now. Charlie had been the only local who seemed genuinely interested in someone who had left his life in the city to open a restaurant in St Jude's. I realised later that our friendship was based on a kind of benign envy. I envied Charlie Farthing's deep, lifelong roots in the place I had fallen in love with, while he envied me for what he imagined was the glamorous urban life that I had left behind. For Charlie's dreams were all of getting out.

He smiled at me now as his father frowned at him.

'No work in the morning then?' Will said.

Charlie leaned against the table. He was a little tipsy. 'Late start tomorrow, Dad.'

'Five generations of fishermen,' Will muttered, 'to produce a tour guide.'

Charlie grinned at me, rolled his eyes, flashed his even white teeth. He had a glamorous sheen about him that was wasted in St Jude's.

Bet was looking at her husband, waiting for an update on the crazy bonfire-starting surfers.

'It's . . . a maid,' Will said, dumbfounded.

'A woman?'

Will nodded. 'Aye, a maid. A girl. A woman. All by herself.'

'Not surfers then?'

'No.'

Bet stared at the kitchen window. 'A woman, you say?'

'Renting Grandma Jo's place, she reckons,' Will said, as if there was an element of doubt. 'Waiting for the estate agent chap to bring the keys first thing.'

We all looked towards the fire on the beach.

'And you pair of doughnuts just *left* her out there? A woman all alone in the middle of the night on *our* beach, and you *left* her there?' Bet was looking from her husband to me and back again, furious with us both. 'What's wrong with you?'

She bustled out of the house, not shutting the front door behind her. The black Lab ambled after her. That's the other thing about these people and this place. Despite all the names we have for outsiders, and all the things we say, and all the resentments we nurture, the locals are kind. They truly are. If you can pierce the thin skin of hostility, the veneer of indifference and hard shell of commercial cynicism, then you will discover a world of kindness among the people of Cornwall like you have never known.

Bet soon returned with the woman from the beach, the pair of them struggling with her luggage. Will and Charlie and I rushed to help.

'I'll put the kettle on, my lovely,' Bet said, smiling shyly. 'You'll have some tea and toast, Clementine.'

Clementine. Her name was *Clementine*.

And Bet enjoyed saying her name, she relished it. Exotic, sweet and perfect. Like a fruit, like a song.

Clementine.

The woman in the hoodie – Clementine – turned towards Bet and the boiling kettle. She was rubbing her hands, shivering, and now she was standing I could see that Clementine was quite tall, and very slim, and that made her seem taller than she really was. Like a model, I thought. Like a girl in a magazine who meets you with her level gaze and makes you think – What is her life like? Who loves her? And who does she love?

'I don't want to trouble you,' she said to Bet, tucking another tendril of hair inside her hoodie. I saw that it was a kind of habit, or nervous tic that she had, this fiddling with her hair when it actually required no fiddling whatsoever.

'No trouble at all, my lovely. Sit.'

Will and Charlie hurried to find Clementine a place at the head of the kitchen table. She sat down, stared around her, and then she slowly pulled back her hoodie, shaking out her hair. And she shone. That's the only way I can describe it, despite everything that happened later and all the tears and the grief and the horror.

Clementine shone, and I could do nothing to resist that light.

Age? It was hard to tell, for she was one of those women who will look beautiful at either end of life's journey. That night, she was just out of her middle twenties, still young but no longer a kid, and she had that Celtic colouring, the pale skin and the dark, dark red hair with a spark of green fire in the eyes.

I looked toward the window.

The sky was getting light.

You could smell the toast. The kettle was whistling its merry tune. Bet took the butter from the fridge and the black Lab licked his lips. It felt like a new morning was already here.

And then she smiled.

It was one of those smiles that pull you up, and stop you in your tracks, and knock you off your feet, so wide and white and open it was, so good-natured and natural and glad to be alive.

It started slowly, Clementine's smile, like the sun coming up, but then suddenly it was all I could see, and it was dazzling, blinding, and I wanted to look away, but I found I could not.

LISA: *I knew she was trouble from the start. Why? Because I could see she was fake. That's what I thought when I saw her for the first time, when I was on my way to work at the Lobster Pot — you know, Tom's* restaurant? — and she was all smiles and collecting the keys to Grandma Jo's old place. I watched her, and I could see it as clear as you like. Fake. The way she acted with the young estate agent chap from Truro, fluttering her eyelashes at him, turning on the charm, like butter would melt. Fake. What do I mean? I'll tell you what I mean. I mean bogus, counterfeit, phoney. Fake, all right? Are we clear? Fake accent. Fake smile, fake teeth, fake tits. Probably. Was she even really a redhead? I suppose Tom could tell you. Ask him. And a few others, if you get my drift. What? Oh no, no, no! There's those that'll tell you I was jealous of her from the start. But that's just not true. I had nothing against the woman. In the end, it turned out she treated me with great kindness when I had my trouble, my bad trouble, the worst of my trouble. I liked her. Even though everything about her was fake. And those broad shoulders — I thought she might be a bloke. It crossed my mind. So if everything about a woman is fake, you have to ask yourself the obvious question.

Who is she really?

3

At dawn I stood on the deck of the Lobster Pot and watched Will Farthing go out on the falling tide on the *Bonnie Bet*, the 25-foot-fishing boat he had named after his wife. Will stood in the wheelhouse, staring out to sea, heading for the mouth of the estuary and the open water beyond, and the clothes he wore – yellow oilskins and red beanie – were as brightly coloured as a small child's on his first day in a primary school playground. Rain clouds rolled and churned out at sea, about one hour from St Jude's, where the lobsters were waiting. You could taste the saltwater on the fresh spring wind and the sea was the colour of wet cement.

A storm was coming in.

My restaurant was a dark wooden cave of a place. A small cave – four tables inside, and four tables out on the deck. The deck overlooked the esplanade and the estuary, the very start of the sea. As Will reached its mouth, the waves broke bridal white against the ragged black rocks on either side. The *Bonnie Bet* already looked very small.

On the far side of the estuary there was another fishing village, Polmouth, a seven-minute ferry ride away – somebody timed it – but it was mostly holiday homes on that side now, a cascade of cream-coloured houses rising on the steep hill, and they were shuttered and still, hibernating for the long closed season. There were still working fishing boats on our side, St Jude's, but the rotten weather meant the other fishermen were staying home today.

Only Will Farthing was going out.

The bigger boats in the deeper harbours could be out for four or five days before they landed their lavishly iced fresh fish – which really wasn't that fresh at all, by the time they brought it to market. But on his 25-footer, Will could land his catch the same day. Will Farthing's day-caught lobster was what I had built my business upon.

When I could see the *Bonnie Bet* no more, I went up to the flat and did my morning exercises. Weights, press-ups, burpees. Nothing too demanding, but four sets of 25 reps that were done every day, baked into my routine. I would be forty soon, and nothing could stop that, but I was never going to be one of those old men you see displaying their gut as if it was a prize watermelon. I showered, checked the only news that mattered to me – the weather report – and went back to the deck.

I was outside watching St Jude's waking up when Lisa – my chef, my friend – came to stand beside me, two mugs of instant coffee in her hand. She handed one to me and we watched the world in silence. Then she inhaled and looked at the rolling sky out at sea.

'Old Will's taking a chance with this weather, isn't he?' she said.

I nodded. 'But either he takes a chance or stays tied up in dock with the rest of them,' I said. 'And then he earns nothing.'

I turned to look at her. Despite her approximation of a West Country accent, Lisa was Italian, mid-thirties, small but compact, pretty and tough. She smiled up at me and brushed a sweep of her glossy black hair from her face. The toughness was something she had had to learn.

Fifteen years ago, Lisa had been an art student in London when she met a young St Jude's fisherman called Jack Bates when she was on holiday with some mates in Padstow. Now Jack was gone and Lisa was a single mother who bought fish, cooked fish, served fish and did the accounts for the Lobster Pot. Her son, Paolo, one year into big school, was sitting alone at the bar of the Lobster Pot, frowning over some last-minute homework. Paolo was a good-looking, dark-haired kid in glasses, like a half-Italian Buddy Holly.

'All right, Paolo?' I called.

He gave me a jaunty thumbs-up, not looking up from his homework.

'So today's menu is going to wait, is it?' Lisa said.

I nodded. 'Going to have to,' I said.

We only served day-caught fish at the Lobster Pot. When they caught it, we bought lobster, crab and mackerel from Will Farthing and the other local fishermen. And when they didn't – when the weather was too bad to go out of St Jude's, or when the fish were hiding – Lisa and I would drive to market in Mevagissey, or other fishermen would come to us. And on those days, we would serve salmon, trout, cod, turbot, brill, bream, scallops, king prawns, red mullet, mussels and Thai fish cakes – Lisa's specialist dish that could accommodate a multitude of fish. But when your restaurant is called the Lobster Pot, the customers don't really come for your Thai fish cakes.

'Paolo and I saw someone collecting the keys to Grandma Jo's place,' Lisa said, her accent hovering somewhere between Maranello and Mousehole. 'Been empty for too long, that place. It's going to make a good little holiday home.' She chuckled ruefully, as if we were in this together. 'Upcountry folk, eh?

Can't live with them, can't afford to live without them.'

'Clementine's staying,' I said, just a little too quickly. It was only a year's lease. Probably a break-clause at six months. But to have her here for a full year! Was that too much to hope for? 'The woman who's renting Grandma Jo's place, I mean,' I said. 'Her name is Clementine. And she's moved here permanently.'

Lisa stared at me curiously, and I was horribly aware that my face was burning like a teenager's with a crush too strong to hide.

'She told me and Will that she was staying,' I said, shrugging as if none of it mattered very much to me, nodding to where the estuary flowed into the wild open sea.

But of course the *Bonnie Bet* was long gone.

Another boat was about to put out from the harbour.

Unlike the *Bonnie Bet*, this was a sleek, glossy motorboat, three times the size of Will's fishing boat, designed for catching tourists not fish. The *Pleasure Dome*. A sign on the dock advertised its wares: *Seal watching. Dolphin watching. Sunset booze cruise. Family fun time. Singles mingle. The best boat rides in St Jude's.*

Charlie Farthing, the *Pleasure Dome*'s skipper, was on deck ushering on board what looked like a stag party. There must have been a dozen of them, subdued and hungover after a night overdoing the local vodka and craft beer. They were not lads – these were men in their thirties who could not recover quickly as they once did from a night on the tiles, and they shuffled miserably onto the *Pleasure Dome*.

An elderly backpacking couple already on board, sitting in the stern and wrapped up sensibly in the fresh spring morning, eyed them warily.

'What Charlie should do,' Lisa mused, 'is get some plastic fish and some nets and a fisherman from central casting going *ooh-ar, ooh-ar!* That would pack in the punters.'

Down on the esplanade, a Porsche Cayenne had stopped. Even out of season, when the roads were quiet and the second homes were shuttered, the visitors never really stopped coming.

A man got out and stretched his arms above his head, his face contorting with relief, and I felt it again – St Jude's was a long drive from anywhere.

I watched as the man came up the steps to the Lobster Pot's deck. A tanned, slim man with rimless spectacles, he had the look of London money about him. Polo shirt and chinos, as if he wouldn't really be on holiday unless he was dressed for a round of golf.

He yomped up the steps that led to the deck of the Lobster Pot. His family were milling around his Porsche Cayenne down on the esplanade. Two teenagers, a boy and girl, their bored, pouty faces buried in their phones. Their mother was staring across the water at Polmouth, stunned by the beauty of this place. The man appeared, breathless from the climb.

'How do you do your lobsters?' he asked.

'Thermidor, Newburg or grilled.'

'Got plenty for tonight?' He eyed me suspiciously. 'Fresh ones, I mean?'

'We don't know yet.'

'You don't know?' He looked around, quietly amused. 'This place is called the Lobster Pot but you don't know if you've got any lobsters tonight?'

I thought of Will Farthing all alone out there on the *Bonnie Bet*. Will's game was a hard, dangerous life with no sick pay, no pension and no money if you didn't go out and bring back some fish. There were no guarantees of anything.

'If we have lobster, it will be day caught,' I said. 'As fresh as you can get it. But we don't know if they're biting.'

He booked a table anyway. Lisa put their name in the big leather book that sat by reception. The Winter family. The booking was twelve people, the Winters and two other families, friends who were meant to be driving down, which would mean three tables pushed together out on the deck of the Lobster Pot, overlooking Polmouth and the estuary and beyond. Booking a table wasn't really necessary this far out of season, but Mr Winter wanted to make sure he had the best table in the house.

Everybody wanted the table with the view of the sea.

There was no lunch trade so Lisa and I put up our closed sign – a cartoon lobster in a top hat and monocle mouthing the words *Gone fishing – catch you later!* – and we went down the steps to the esplanade and off to the Rabbit Hole, St Jude's only pub, for some lunch of our own.

It was raining quite hard now, the wind picking up, the sea boiling. One of those late spring mornings when you can feel the six months of winter trying to last forever. We met Bet Farthing on her way down to the quay, wrapped up in her winter coat. She nodded briefly at us, her face set in stone.

'Going out in this bloody weather,' Bet said. 'Silly old bugger.'

Lisa squeezed her arm.

'He'll be fine, Bet,' she said, and something passed between them without words, these women who had both loved men who went off to sea for their living.

Inside the Rabbit Hole, there was a man in his six-ties sitting at the bar sipping a sparkling water. In his smart leather jacket, clean jeans and patent leather shoes with no socks, he looked like a different species to the fishermen killing time over a pint of draught Korev lager until the weather turned. The man was talking to a small, busty blonde – Sandy, the landlady of the Rabbit Hole, a rural Barbara Windsor. Sandy nodded a welcome and drifted further down the bar to take an order. The man looked up at us and smiled.

Anton.

Anton had a restaurant – Le Poisson Imaginaire – on the north coast, on a beach near Padstow. And Anton had a wife – Michelle, who sometimes acted as hostess at Le Poisson Imaginaire, greeting diners as they entered, which always caused a stir as Michelle was one of those strikingly gorgeous middle-aged French women, not necessarily who you would ex-pect to welcome you to a Cornish restaurant, for Michelle was more Boulevard Montparnasse than Bodmin Moor. Le Poisson Imaginaire was a far fan-cier gaff than the Lobster Pot, the kind of restaurant that had white linen on the table and a serious wine list and reviews from critics who ate in restaurants for their job. But Anton revered Will Farthing's lob-sters and that's why he was often in St Jude's.

'He's not still out there, is he?' he said.

'He's still out there,' I said.

Anton shook his head and said nothing.

We ordered some lunch from Sandy, and we were still waiting for it to arrive when the door opened and Clementine walked into the pub.

She was with her estate agent. He was the only man within a ten-mile radius wearing a suit and tie, not quite as tall as her, but he had the shiny look of money that Mr Winter had, and the urban glamour about him that my friend Charlie Farthing aspired to. Clementine and the estate agent were laughing, a little drunk, it seemed, or maybe just happy that their business had been successfully concluded.

I felt a sudden stab of jealousy. What was wrong with me? It was crazy, and I knew it was crazy, and yet I could not dial down the crazy, not when Clementine walked into the room.

I smiled – a hesitant, self-conscious smile that collapsed in on itself before it had even really begun – and Clementine just stared back at me without changing her semi-amused expression – still tickled by something that the slick man-boy beside her had said. I was not even sure she recognised me from last night, and I felt like a fool.

They took two seats at the bar and stared up at the dozens of photographs that covered the wall of the Rabbit Hole.

The photographs went back sixty years. It was an impressive display. There were tiny black-and-white photographs of grinning men, curling at the edges, and the faded colour photos taken in the late twentieth century, and rough printouts from photos that had been taken on phones.

The men – and they were all men – were of all ages. The photos were taken in their place of work. They were taken down on the harbour, or outside the boathouse, or on the decks of their boats, on the open sea.

They were the faces of St Jude's lost fishermen.

Clementine half-swivelled on her bar stool and addressed the room.

'What do you have to do to get your picture on the wall?' she said.

Silence fell over the bar.

Sandy, with a landlady's instinctive diplomacy, quickly glanced at Lisa, swabbed a non-existent spill on the bar top, and looked away.

Lisa cleared her throat, then she raised her chin and smiled, keeping it light.

'To get your photo on that wall,' she said, 'you have to go out fishing on the falling tide, which is either around midnight or around dawn.' It was totally silent in the Rabbit Hole. 'And then you never come back,' she said, indicating the faces on the wall behind the bar. 'That's the really important bit – the never coming back bit.'

Clementine and Lisa smiled at each other and something I could not read passed between them.

And Lisa didn't have to say that one of the men on the wall had been her husband, Jack. The faded colour photograph must have been around ten years old now because Paolo had been a toddler the last time Jack went out on the falling tide.

The door of the pub banged open.

Bet Farthing stood in the doorway, her weathered face wreathed in smiles.

'Will's back,' Anton said.

4

In the icehouse beside the harbour, a dozen sea-fresh lobsters stirred on a bed of ice.

'I will cook for you one day, my friend,' Anton promised Will. 'At Le Poisson Imaginaire.'

Will chuckled. 'You bring the wine, Anton, mate, and I'll bring us a few o' these beauties.'

'I will open a good Macon-Villages for you and your beautiful lobsters, Will.'

Will and Anton cackled in perfect harmony.

They both thought that the other one was a bit of a character.

People thought of our county as split in two – the authentic fishing folk like Will Farthing, keeping the old ways intact, and the fancy Dans like Anton, with their posh restaurants by some golden beach, all major credit cards accepted. But the two worlds totally relied on each other for their existence. That's why Will had gone out today. Because there was Anton – and me – waiting for him to bring home the lobsters.

Will Farthing stood there grinning in the icehouse, still a strong man, and happy and proud that he had won his bet with the weather.

Bet Farthing stood by his side, staring thoughtfully at the lobsters on their bed of ice, visibly shaking as the relief came off her in waves.

The weather was still rubbish but we had a good night at the Lobster Pot.

The Porsche Cayenne family came in – the Winters, I remembered – and their children looked a little happier and their friends had made it down from London, both families arriving within minutes of each other, hugging and kissing and laughing out on the deck, and it was like a party.

And late in the evening, when the Winters and their friends were on coffee and dessert, Clementine came in alone and took a table inside.

'You got your keys then?' I said.

I didn't know if she recognised me, and it made me off balance, unsure of myself. Then her eyes screwed up with something like ecstasy.

'My keys! Yes! I *love* my keys! And I love my new home!'

I laughed. That's the way people feel when they move down here for good. As if life is beginning again, as if they have another chance to get it all right.

At least that was the way it had felt to me.

I handed her a menu. She watched Lisa moving around inside the kitchen.

'May I ask you a question?' she said.

I waited. A burst of laughter came from the big table out on the deck. It was too windy and cold to be eating outside, but the Winters and their pals had kept their coats on and were making the bad weather part of the fun.

'Your colleague,' she said. 'The one who spoke to me in the pub?'

'Lisa,' I said. 'My friend.'

'What happened to her husband?'

I looked across at Lisa. She gave me a grin and placed two coffees on the counter.

'Service!' she called. Our waiter, a long-haired local teen in double denim, Ryan, came over to get the coffees. Ryan was the son and grandson and great-grandson of fishermen, but he dreamed only of surfing, and he worked for me as a way of staving off the life at sea that he had been born for. Lisa had disappeared inside the kitchen.

'Lisa lost her husband at sea,' I told Clementine. 'Everyone in these fishing families around here has lost someone out there. And I do mean every single one of them, because they've all been doing it for generations. But when they lose someone, they never really know exactly what happened. It's like Lisa said – they go out on the falling tide, and they never come home. Jack – Lisa's husband – had this sky-blue boat – *Moon River* – and then he went out one day and he didn't come back.'

'No body? No boat?'

I shook my head.

'When Lisa was younger, she was down here with some friends from her uni, and she fell in love with a local lad, a fisherman – Jack – and then they were married, and she was pregnant with their son, and they were just getting their life started, and then Jack was gone.'

'You weren't born here either, were you?' she said. 'Why did you stay?'

I thought about it. I wanted to get it right.

'It was my chance to try a different way of living, I guess.' I remembered the life I had left behind ten years ago and shuddered. 'I was a journalist, back in my old life.'

'Anything I might have read?'

I shook my head. 'I was on what they called the backbench. It's more on the editing side. A backroom boy. But the industry was dying. That's what happens in most jobs, I realise now. You think you have a job for life and then suddenly you discover you're a milkman and nobody wants a bottle of full-fat gold top left on their doorstep anymore. And you're lucky if you even have a milk round. My old trade just got harder and harder – lower budgets, more redundancies, more stress, always wondering if you were going to be next for the chop, always wondering how you would manage if – when – it came to the end. And my marriage broke up – my fault entirely. And I burned out. Quite badly, actually. A bit of a breakdown.'

I was talking far too much. Who cared about my old life? I took a breath.

'So all this' – I took in the Lobster Pot, the storm-blown spring night, the smell of grilled lobster coming from the kitchen and the bottles of white and rosé and champagne and beer stacked high behind the bar – 'all this looked good.'

'It is good,' she said.

'And how about you?' I said. 'What's your story?'

'My husband died,' she said simply. 'He died on a zebra crossing.' She shook her head as if it was still not quite believable. As if it would never be believable. 'A cop killed him. A drunk driver. A pissed, off-duty policeman, funnily enough. He slowed down but he didn't stop, because he was looking at something on his phone, this drunken cop, and he just kept coming. And I saw that he wasn't going to stop and I took one step back onto the pavement.

And my husband – Alex – did not step back, and then Alex was under the drunk cop's wheels, and then he was gone. Not immediately, but twelve hours later. In the hospital, in the night.' A long pause. 'And I got to the point where I knew that I just couldn't be there anymore, on those same streets. I thought I could see the stains of his blood still on that zebra crossing. And I don't know if that was my imagination or if it was real. But I needed to be away from there, as far away as possible. I need to be *here* at the end of England, the end of the country, the end of the line.'

All of this was told dry-eyed, her gaze level and her chin raised, with no sense of self-pity but on the edge of furious disbelief. As if all the tears had been shed, but the cold rage remained.

I said nothing. I could think of nothing to say. But I think it was at that moment that I realised I was falling in love with her.

'Miss? Excuse me, miss?'

It was the man from the Porsche Cayenne. I remembered his full name on the reservation. Oliver Winter. He was somewhere in his forties, I saw now, although it was hard to tell exactly because he was so well preserved. I had not seen him smile before.

'Will you join us?' he asked Clementine.

I looked across at his table, at his glossy wife and their friends – more outsiders with money and teenage children who were not really children any more. The adults were all looking towards Clementine, their smiles as fixed as an ice skater at the end of her routine.

And I got it. Clementine was a stunning woman, and she was eating her dinner alone. I suddenly felt enormously protective towards her.

But she didn't need my protection.

'Will you join us?' Winter repeated.

Clementine nodded, half-smiled, as if it was no big deal one way or the other, as if she was neither grateful nor offended by the invitation, and moved across to their crowded table. Winter poured her a glass of champagne as the introductions were made and they laughed as the bubbles rose too quickly and spilled on the bare wooden table to mix with the pink shells of the lobsters.

Even out of season, you could have these good nights.

'She makes friends so quickly,' Lisa said, handing me a Korev beer, the best Cornish lager, and we stared out at the night in silence. Lisa and I had been friends for too many years to feel the need to make conversation. I read the label on my bottle of Korev. *The coast is our compass*, it said. *Born in Cornwall*.

Across the river, Polmouth was black and silent, but the lights still glittered all across the small, steep fishing village of St Jude's. Beyond the esplanade, there were some kids down on the beach passing around a spliff and kicking round a ball.

And then there was the sound of motorbikes.

Two of them, driving fast. The sound split the night as they came up the tight winding road out of the harbour, drowning the noise being made by the Winter party out on the deck. The two motorbikes rolled more slowly down the esplanade.

It was two cops.

That was an unusual sight around here.

We never really saw the police.

Their two motorbikes took the high winding road for all outbound traffic out of St Jude's, speeding up as they passed the kids down on the beach. But the two motorbike cops did not even slow down to look at them. Whatever the police were looking for, it was not surfers smoking weed on the beach.

And drifting to me on the wild night air, as I drank from the cold bottle of Korev, I heard the sound of Clementine's laughter.

BET FARTHING: *It is strange who we love. When you stop and think, it makes no sense. My Will – when* we were courting — he always told me, 'I like your eyes.' But they are ordinary eyes, really. There's nothing special about them. Not even when I was young. But that is what he liked, or what he thought he liked, and why he wanted to take me to the Odeon in Truro. Because he liked my eyes! And I do think — is that all it takes to love someone? It's got bugger all to do with how good someone's heart is, or if they are kind, or if they are nice. Or how they treat you, even. What matters more is — the curve of their face. The shape of their body. Their perfectly ordinary eyes. The way they look and the way that makes you feel. I don't know. It just seems to me that it's not much to build your life on, is it?

5

I stood on the deck of the Lobster Pot watching a young seal sunbathing. He was out on the rocks where the estuary meets the open sea, stretching his great glossy bulk out on the black rocks as though they were a feather bed, sleek and fat and happy, digesting his breakfast as the waves swelled and broke beneath him. The sea was choppy, restless, moving through the darker shades of grey.

Down on the Platt the fishermen went about what they called their windy-day chores, mending nets and fixing pots and chopping bait, the jobs they did when it was too rough to go out on the open sea but quite not rough enough to sit in the Rabbit Hole nursing a pint of Korev and cursing the weather. One of them was painting the hull of his boat with a lazy, loving delicacy. They chatted as they worked and their laughter drifted up to me. I could see Will Farthing standing in the middle of them, the centre of attention by the look of the grin on his face, a constant splash of colour in his bright yellow oil-skins and red beanie. I guessed they were talking about yesterday, teasing Will and each other because the old man had been the only one of them with the nerve to go out and fish. They had already turned it into a yarn, a story they would tell again and again down on the Platt and in the Rabbit Hole and on the days and nights out at sea.

From the deck of the Lobster Pot, I could look up at the storied cottages rising above the harbour and see Grandma Jo's cream-and-blue cottage. A workman was taking metal grilles out of his white van. He had already installed one of them in the ground-floor windows.

Lisa came out on the deck and stood beside me. She followed my gaze up to the cream-and-blue cottage and then looked back at me. She raised her eyebrows at the new security measures, and said nothing. But I felt it too.

What's she scared of?

We were not big on security grilles in St Jude's.

Then something seemed to change in the air as the front door of the cottage opened and Clementine stepped out. She was wearing a red one-piece bathing suit, like a modest Olympian, her copper-coloured hair piled up high on top of her head, a beach towel draped around her broad shoulders.

My breath caught. With her hair piled up like that, she looked different. Uncovered, vulnerable. As if this was the real Clementine. There was something about the way her ears stuck out that nagged at my heart. I knew that when you had earned one of her smiles, you would see a pink flash of gum above her teeth. On such random accidents of birth, we give our hearts away.

The locksmith unloading the metal grilles looked up at her, grinning foolishly, and she gave him some unsmiling, murmured instructions. He nodded obediently and watched her as she began walking down to the Platt.

And we all watched her. All of us.

Will Farthing and the other fishermen, glancing up from their banter and windy-day chores to watch her progress down the winding streets that led to where they worked on the harbour.

And Charlie Farthing watched her from the deck of the *Pleasure Dome* as he loaded a scattering of early tourists, ravenous for the sight of seals and dolphins.

And Lisa and I watched her from the deck of the Lobster Pot.

Some of the party from last night's big dinner at the restaurant were coming down the esplanade. Two of the Winters. The man – Oliver – and his teenage son. When they saw Clementine strolling onto the harbour, they stopped talking to each other, and they watched her too. Even the seal out on the rocks seemed to lift up his massive slug-like bulk and bat his enormous eyes at the sight of Clementine walking down to the harbour in her red one-piece swimsuit.

She walked down to the sea and it was like that old song, the girl walking to the beach at Ipanema, and the men all respectfully step aside to watch her pass but she does not even notice.

'Bloody funny weather for a dip,' Lisa grumbled, sipping her coffee.

And I saw that Lisa envied her. Clementine's freedom, and the way we all stopped what we were doing to look at her, all of it. And suddenly it was important to me for Lisa to know the truth about our new neighbour.

'She lost her husband,' I said.

'What?'

'Clementine lost her husband.'

I didn't say — *too*. I didn't say — *just like you, Lisa*.

But I wanted Lisa to see that every life has its tragedies that the world doesn't guess at.

'He got hit by a drunken off-duty policeman on a zebra crossing. That's why she's moved down here. To start again. To get away from it all.'

Lisa nodded. 'She looks like she's coping quite well.'

I felt a flare of irritation. 'You don't believe her?'

She shrugged. 'I don't know anything about the woman. I'm just *saying*, Tom. She's not my idea of a widow. Look at her. I mean – she doesn't wear a ring, does she?'

'I don't know.'

'*A widow wears her ring.*' She held up her third finger, left hand, and the thin band of gold glittered in the morning sunlight. 'Where's her ring, Tom?'

Clementine was nodding good morning to the fishermen, a special smile of recognition for Will Farthing, as she walked to the small pier at the edge of the Platt. Charlie's boat idled nearby, the visitors gazing up at him, wondering why they were not on their way to see the dolphins and seals.

Clementine paused at the end of the pier, staring across at Polmouth, as if measuring the distance. She placed her towel on a bench, and turned to face the water. She rose on the balls of her feet, the muscles in her legs tightening, and then she stepped from the pier and dropped into the water below with a look of rapture on her face, like some sixteen-year-old boy on the first day of summer with Bad Apple Cider coursing through his bloodstream. She disappeared under the water, bobbed back up and took her bearings.

And then she began to swim to the other side.

Usually when someone jumped off the pier into the water, which happened all the time at the height of summer, they paddled around for a bit and then got out and did it again. But Clementine went into this steady but determined crawl, heading away from St Jude's towards the shuttered village of Polmouth on the far side of the estuary.

Lisa shifted uneasily. 'There's a wicked current out there,' she said, not taking her eyes from the figure in the choppy water.

'I know.'

'She could *drown*. Stop her, Tom.'

But nobody could stop her. And then the crazy emmets decided to join her.

Oliver and his son, Harry, were laughing as they jogged down to the Platt, saluting the fishermen who stared at them silently, and then stripping down to their underwear. Oliver, the dad, was in good shape for his age, as that kind of London money usually is. The boy was as skinny as a whippet.

They went in the water, Harry with a dive-bomb, and his dad seconds later with a clean expert dive. But when they swam after her, they could have been twins, their dark hair gleaming in the bright spring sunshine.

They went off at a furious pace, as if father and son were racing each other rather than following

Clementine. Too fast. Then the boy suddenly stopped, treading water, calling for his dad. Something had gripped him. Cramp, possibly, or more likely fear, and the realisation of just how far it was to the other side. What it would take. They exchanged a few words. Then the boy turned back and his father ploughed on.

By now Clementine was nearer to Polmouth than St Jude's.

Polmouth had a slipway, a boat ramp for access to and from the estuary, and this was where she was heading for. It was clear she was going to make it. Her stroke was measured and strong. When she rose from the water and waded ashore up the slipway, all the fishermen on the St Jude's side applauded and cheered.

But Oliver Winter was slowing as he reached the halfway mark.

Then he suddenly stopped. You couldn't see the expression on his face from this distance, but he was clearly in some distress, suddenly out of fuel, his head snapping back as if he was feeling the strength of the current, and looking around for help.

'Bloody idiot,' Lisa said. 'I'm calling out the lifeboat.'

But Charlie Farthing's engine rumbled into life and his boat took off, quickly reaching Oliver in a smooth clean curve, swooping around him to throw a lifebelt, and then idling as hands reached out to haul him from the water.

Charlie paused, clearly uncertain what to do next, looking from his wheelhouse across at Clementine on the far side. She sat on the slipway, her long legs stretched out in front of her, toes touching the water, her hair hanging in damp, dark-red clumps around her shoulders, all of Polmouth rising up behind her, all the windows of all those shuttered fishermen's cottages staring down at her.

Clementine waved to Charlie, a lazy, friendly wave that asked for nothing in return, but the *Pleasure Dome*'s engine responded immediately with a deep diesel growl as he motored over to collect her.

Lisa laughed with genuine amusement. 'You're all eating out of her hand!'

Clementine stepped on board and then joined Charlie in the wheelhouse as the sleek boat began the short journey back to St Jude's, where Will and the other fishermen stood watching, their windy-day chores forgotten.

I watched Clementine as she stood on the bridge of the *Pleasure Dome* with Charlie, one hand raised in what looked like a salute to us all and the other shielding her eyes from the morning glare.

From where I was standing, it looked like Charlie had one hand on the wheel and another one on the small of her back.

I tried and failed to look away from them.

And the thought came with a stab of pain – *Where's her widow's ring?*

Anton joined me and Lisa on the deck of the Lobster Pot as Charlie delivered Clementine back from Polmouth and she stepped ashore like the queen across the water coming home. The fishermen of St Jude's came forward to pay amused, affectionate homage.

Will and Charlie Farthing looked at each other and laughed with delight. You didn't see this father and son laugh together much these days. As a child, Charlie had been a harbour rat – one of the kids who hung around the Platt outside of school hours, all of them the sons and daughters of fishermen. When he was a bit older, his dad would let him steer the *Bonnie Bet* around the harbour. When I first met the Farthings, Charlie was still fishing in the summer holiday with his father. Charlie already had his ticket – the licence he needed to captain his own boat. The old man clearly believed his son would one day skipper the *Bonnie Bet*. But Charlie, lost in his own dreams for the future, had other ideas.

Now the gap that grows between most ageing fathers and their adult sons was getting wider with the years. Will and Charlie would routinely ignore each other when they met on the Platt. I had seen them, Charlie loading his tourists as Will unloaded his lobsters, so oblivious to each other that you would never guess that the two men were father and son.

But not today.

Today the gap between them was bridged. Clementine brought Will and Charlie back together, she made them seem closer than they had been for a long time, like a special girlfriend who had been brought home to meet the folks. Clementine stood smiling between them, all of them delighted.

Lisa turned to me with an infuriating sympathy in her eyes.

'I suppose Charlie's a bit closer to her age than you are, Tom,' she said.

It was a busy night at the Lobster Pot.

A dozen youngish men commandeered the big table out on the deck. The future groom at the head of the table and at the centre of their banter, taunts and affection. They were halfway drunk by the time they sat down, and all the way there by the time their table was a mess of empty bottles and lobster shells scattered like pink confetti.

Other diners – older couples, a young family – eyed them warily. Only Anton looked relaxed, eating his lobster Thermidor alone at the next table, Le Poisson Imaginaire left in the capable hands of his wife Michelle, sipping a big glass of bone-dry Chablis and staring contentedly out into the night.

'They're harmless,' Lisa said of the stag party. 'Rich city boys and the first of the gang to get spliced.'

And when they were gone and we were clearing up, and Anton was the only customer to remain, I stood on the deck with Anton by my side, smoking the one cigarette he allowed himself after dinner, inhaling with endless pleasure, like someone from another century, and I saw Clementine and Charlie walking from the quay up to the cream-and-blue cottage.

I watched the way they held their bodies, not quite touching, with the smell of the sea on the rising tide and the sky full of stars, and all that heavenly light blurred by the ridiculous fury in my heart.

And then I saw Anton's face.

'What's wrong?'

He shook his head.

'Anton?'

'A memory from long ago – but I am mistaken. Yes, I am mistaken.'

He was staring at Clementine, his cigarette forgotten.

Not the way other men stared at her. But as if he had seen a ghost.

'Do you know her, Anton?'

He attempted a smile. 'She's a striking woman.'

I waited. We both knew there was more.

'I thought – there was a woman I saw once in my old restaurant.' He shook his head again. 'It was a few years ago. A couple came to the restaurant where I worked in London. It was a celebration. And I remember them for two reasons. They were a beautiful couple. And they fought. A terrible fight at their table. She was – how can I say? – there was a violence in her. They were asked to leave. That's why I remember them. Because they were beautiful. And because they fought. But she – Clementine, is it? – can't be the same woman.'

'Why not?'

'Because that woman is dead.'

LISA: *Tom was my friend. Before anything else – before everything else – Tom was my mate. When I lost my Jack, my husband, there was immediately no money coming in. That's the way it is in these fishing communities, and the way it has always been. You lose the* breadwinner and the love of your life, but the bills don't stop. I thought I would struggle after losing Jack. I thought I would have to do anything and everything, just to get by. Cleaning jobs, babysitting, waitressing. Hand to mouth stuff. Whatever was going. In a way, everyone struggles here – because they are all trying to make enough money in the season to last through the winter. And Tom was new in St Jude's – just another townie looking to start again. But when he opened the Lobster Pot, he asked me if I wanted a job. And it saved us – me and Paolo.

I didn't know anything – I could cook a bit, from my mother, and from sharing a flat with a bunch of lazy girls at uni – but Tom gave me the chance to become a real cook, and he showed me how to order stock – the wine, the beer, the vegetables – and how to do the books and how to talk to the fishermen we bought our fish from. They were not all as sweet as Will Farthing, believe me. Tom needed someone to help him, it's true, but he didn't have to ask me. He could have got someone more qualified than a youngish Italian widow who still burst into tears at odd moments. And I had a kid, I had my boy, my Paolo, and so there were times when I had to be at the school gates instead of the Lobster Pot, especially when Paolo was younger and could not walk home alone. Tom was kind to me. That's what it started with – his kindness. And we became friends. And we got to know each other.

We became real mates. And I liked the way he kept himself in shape, not like some of them old boys propping up the bar at the Rabbit Hole. There were these little exercises Tom did as regular as cleaning his teeth. Press-ups and lifting weights. I would catch him looking at himself in the mirror sometimes, and it made me smile. The Lobster Pot was like his own little kingdom where he ruled the roost. And there were plenty of unattached women visitors who would have been up for drinks with the master of the house in his flat above the restaurant, but he wasn't interested. It was like he was done with all that. And I liked that, too — as if he was saving himself for something a bit more special than a quick plough with a half-cut lady from London.

The more I got to know him, the more I liked him. And a few times over the years we'd hit the Korev a bit hard after closing time at the Lobster Pot, or walk home together after a lock-in at the Rabbit Hole, and on those nights — how can I put it? I just felt like I had been alone for a long time. I missed the touch of someone else, someone you care about. There were moments when I would not have said no thank you to some slow sex with someone I liked with a flat stomach, a nice apartment, and no girlfriend or wife wondering where he was. But Tom and I never took that step, not even after some all-night lock-ins at the Rabbit Hole when everyone was a bit squiffy.

To tell you the truth, I am a bit sad about that, although it is probably just as well. Because I am not some silly kid, all right? I know it is really stupid to fall in love with your friend. Although nowhere near as stupid as falling in love with a total stranger.

6

'Listen,' Lisa said. 'It's the Rabbit Hole.' The smile spread across her face. 'Sandy's having a lock-in.'

I stared at her, my brain foggy from lack of sleep after a night and day tormented by images of Clementine in the arms of Charlie Farthing. Were they still up there in the cream-and-blue cottage? Charlie's boat had not left dock today. Outside of my jealous, feverish dreams, I had seen no sign of either of them since he walked her home yesterday.

Now it was closing time at the Lobster Pot. The diners had all gone home and we were doing our end-of-night chores – Lisa loading up the big rack dishwasher, me clearing the tables, Ryan half-heartedly sweeping the floor, our long-haired surfer out on his feet. This close to midnight the air in St Jude's should have been full of nothing but the sound of the gulls and the sea. But from the village came the distant boom of a thumping bass, drunken voices raised in exultant song and the slurred mass chorus of 'Sweet Caroline'.

'Nightcap?' Lisa grinned. 'Come on, old man. It will help you sleep. I know you have a lot on your mind.'

She knew me so well! So we finished our chores, I paid Ryan for the night, and Lisa and I locked the back door of the restaurant and went down the steep stone steps that led to the esplanade, the music in the distance changing to Sigala & Ella Eyre's 'Came Here for Love'. It was an eclectic playlist they had at the Rabbit Hole. The corny and the cool, the old and the new, the cheese and the grime all merrily rubbing shoulders. Sandy, the Rabbit Hole's landlady, played requests. Lisa texted her that we were coming down. As we came down the steps to the esplanade, we could see it glowing in the distance. The Rabbit Hole was bathed in a permanent dimly lit golden glow that did not change with night and day or the seasons. It was a lovely deep yellow light somewhere between old gold and warm honey that I never saw anywhere but in the Rabbit Hole, and it was punctuated with red fairy lights – all year round, nothing but red, glittering and twinkling in the gloaming – so the old pub looked like it was always celebrating Christmas, or some ancient pagan festival that nobody could remember.

Sandy was waiting for us.

'Quick,' she said, letting us inside then hurriedly bolting the door of the Rabbit Hole behind us. The streets were empty and here in St Jude's we never had the police sniffing around just because we were drinking after hours. The country's licensing laws were not our laws. But Sandy took no chances.

The Rabbit Hole was rocking. It was one of those nights when the pub became a party. There were locals, mostly the younger fishermen and their girlfriends, and the young men from the stag party, noticeably drunker than they had been at the restaurant.

The Winter family and their London friends sat at tables on the perimeter, sipping rosé and smiling indulgently at the shenanigans.

Everywhere there were tables covered with rounds of shots, pitchers of beer and decanted carafes of mystery wine. Someone shoved a cold bottle of Korev into my hand. I took a swig and surveyed the scene.

You got these big nights and strangely enough they often came before the season had really started. There was always a mad rush of people coming to the county trying to avoid the mad rush.

The future groom approached me. Even staggering drunk, he was an unassuming young man with a baby face and a shaven head to cover for male pattern baldness. He looked like a very ancient baby, despite the bottle of local gin he was carrying. He shouted something at me but was drowned out by Kate Bush singing 'The Big Sky'.

I shook my head. 'What?'

He leaned closer.

'I said – *I'm thinking of moving down here.*'

I nodded politely. 'Where are you now?'

'Crouch End.' A pause. 'It's in north London.'

I sipped my Korev. 'I know where Crouch End is.'

Everybody wants the holiday to last forever, I thought. Everyone wants to start again. Live better, cleaner. Get it right this time. I wasn't laughing at him. That's what I had wanted too.

Those who actually make the move down here are usually on the run from something, even if it is only the boredom and disappointment that strikes when the life you are living is not the one you were anticipating.

Usually the ones who dream of starting again have been here before – for a week, a holiday, a summer – a stag party – or in their dreams. But they all see the same thing – that glimpse of absolute freedom, that hunch the county at the end of the country is the chance to try again. And they are not always wrong.

They come down here for the simpler life, the cleaner air, the fresher food, the cheaper bills, the easy living. And they come for the sea – to surf, to swim, to fish, to sail, to paddle on some endless golden beach where there is only you and the crabs.

They come because their life is still ahead of them or because it is mostly behind them. They come because they are retired, or semi-retired, or because they have an idea for a business – to start a cafe, a craft shop, or a lobster restaurant.

They come because they are hopeful, and optimistic, and full of big plans, but they also come because they are used up, burned out, and they feel like they are done in their old life, their nerves shattered, all hope gone. And they either don't talk about the past, or they tell you far more than you want to know. And sometimes, in my experience, they lie. But they come – we all come – *to try again*. And for that game-changing shot at finally getting life right.

I felt a stab of sympathy for the hopeful young groom with the bald head. Because I knew exactly how he felt.

'I've never regretted moving down here ten years ago,' I told the young man. 'At least – not yet.'

He smiled at me, not hearing a word because the guitar solo in 'Another Girl, Another Planet' by the Only Ones was playing too loud.

And then suddenly she was there.

Clementine came into the Rabbit Hole ahead of Charlie, Sandy quickly locking the door behind them. They had heard the music up at the cream-and-blue cottage. And they had answered the call.

They looked for a space and spotted a table in a dark cranny of the Rabbit Hole known as the snug, two chairs miraculously free though the sopping table was strewn with bottles and glasses. The eyes of the stag boys were all on Clementine as she led Charlie through the crowded pub towards the snug.

She smiled with her easy grace, as though she would be at home anywhere, but Charlie's face was stiff with what looked like anxiety. A lock-in at the Rabbit Hole was not the place for smooth seduction, not the right venue for getting-to-know-you cocktails and adorably clever talk.

A lock-in at the Rabbit Hole was a night for Korev and karaoke, Kate Bush and bellowing 'Sweet Caroline' out of key, falling off your chair and dancing on a table.

'They don't look like people who just spent the last twenty-four hours in bed,' Lisa said, laughing, and my heart surged with absurd hope.

Sandy stopped dancing with a couple of the stag boys to approach the latest arrivals in the snug. She hugged Clementine, stood back and applauded.

And then others were applauding too, and then the entire pub, because of course Clementine was a local hero after swimming from St Jude's to Polmouth. It had been done before – Will Farthing had done it in his youth – but not for years, and the swim across the estuary was never a small thing. It took skill, and strength, and not a little courage. Smiling faces turned towards her, glasses were raised. Not everyone had seen her swim, but by now everyone had heard about it.

Clementine smiled with shy pride. I was getting to know her smile, the nuances of it. When her smile was dialled all the way up – when she was smiling because she just could not help herself, rather than being polite or friendly – then it was a wide-open smile that she had, just a bit goofy because of her not inconsiderable overbite, and you saw pink gums glisten above the white teeth before she self-consciously closed her mouth, and I thought that she did not see the flawless beauty that the rest of the world saw, she saw only the imperfections.

Charlie and Clementine settled at their little table. A bottle of champagne appeared. Oliver Winter saluted with a glass of white wine. His wife Tamara sipped her rosé and smiled stiffly. Clementine and Charlie grinned at each other. They were still at that getting-to-know-you stage, I saw, where you await some unspoken confirmation of something that you don't really understand. Clementine opened the champagne. She was good at it, twisting the cork rather than pulling at it.

'Dance with me, old man,' Lisa told me. 'And close your mouth, will you?'

'What?'

'You heard,' she laughed, and we danced. Me, the typical shy dancing Englishman, moving on feet that could have been cemented to the floor, Lisa losing herself in some hot-blooded Mediterranean Euro-jig.

It was 'The Hounds of Love' playing now, because we were at the peak of the Kate Bush comeback, and Lisa was singing along, pushing back a lock of that lush Italian hair from a forehead moist with sweat.

A bottle broke. One of the stag boys pushed another one in the chest, their faces contorted with anger. I turned away as Lisa took my hands, silently instructing me not to get involved, and when I looked back, they were laughing and hugging each other. Then Clementine and Charlie were dancing. Clementine a better dancer than Lisa – her long arms above her head, relaxed, swaying, in control – and Charlie even worse than me, if that was possible, jerking his arms up and down as if he was jogging on the spot.

Then Charlie was whispering something in Clementine's ear.

'*But I want to stay,*' she said, and as I read her lips I knew that nobody would ever control her. Nobody would ever make her go when she wanted to stay. Or make her stay when she wanted to go.

Charlie was making his way to the door when he saw me looking at him, and he grinned and raised his eyebrows. The gesture could have meant anything, but I thought it meant one thing.

She's a handful!

Then Charlie was gone and Sandy was bolting the door behind him, and Clementine and Lisa and I were all back at the little table in the snug, drinking champagne from icy flutes that must have been kept in Sandy's freezer.

Lisa and Clementine were deep in shouted intimate conversation.

'You feel weightless,' Clementine said. 'It's like flying. That's why I love it. Swimming in the wild. And you only ever get that feeling swimming in the wild. Rivers, the sea, lakes, ponds. You don't get it in swimming pools. They are all like some dead thing – unmoving, stuffed full of chemicals.'

Lisa was nodding.

There was a curiosity about my friend Lisa. She was still the interested outsider she had been when she had first moved down here to be with her late husband Jack, and that curiosity seemed to be getting the better of any early resentment she felt towards Clementine.

'And it kept me sane,' Clementine said, and I did not look at her. 'When I lost my husband.' She smiled, her eyes shining. 'Bathroom?'

Lisa pointed towards the far side of the Rabbit Hole's long bar.

Clementine went off to the bathroom but never made it, surrounded before she got there by admiring, elaborately courteous stag-do boys who had annexed the length of the long bar, and they raised their glasses in her honour, and clapped their hands, and offered Clementine one of the many shots they were drinking from a battered metal tray.

On the far side of the pub, voices were again raised in anger. Sandy was standing between one of the stag boys and a local lad, whose girlfriend was standing behind him, mad as hell. The stag boy – a big beefy lad – was laughing at them. Sandy held them apart until the friends of both parties – some of the younger fishermen and the stag-do boys – pulled them apart.

I lost sight of Clementine and drank more Korev and danced with Lisa to songs I did not recognise. There was a time when I knew all the songs.

Then Lisa was suddenly pulling at my arm.

'Clementine,' she said. 'We have to get her out of here. Fast.'

We pushed through the crowd to where Clementine was sitting at the bar, her eyes half-closed, her head falling forward as if it was too heavy for her neck. She seemed exhausted. Two of the stag boys stood either side of her, as if guarding her. Lisa pushed past them and put her arm around Clementine, looking into her face. Lisa sniffed the empty shot glass in front of her. When she looked up, the stag boys had gone.

'Clementine?' Lisa said. 'Give me your keys. Can you hear me?'

Clementine fumbled in her jeans, took out a set of keys, handed them to Lisa.

And still I did not understand.

'Is she sick?' I said.

'There's something in her drink. I think it's a roofie.'

'A what?'

'A date-rape drug, Tom. Something to turn out her lights so those bastards can do what they like to her. Help me, will you?'

The stag boys protested as Lisa eased Clementine from her stool. Then they were trying to take her by the hand, to make her stay.

Lisa pushed them away. A bottle smashed close by, and was sarcastically cheered. There were young men all around us now, their mouths moving, words I didn't understand, their faces flushed and sweaty. Lisa and I pushed through them, heading for the door. Iggy Pop was in his pomp, chanting 'No Fun'. I knew that one.

Then Sandy was helping us, understanding immediately, leading us to the door and unbolting it, throwing it wide open now, the cold night air and the smell of the sea hitting us.

Clementine stood between Lisa and me, her legs unsteady, her head heavy, her red hair falling forward, and Sandy turned away in a fury. Lisa and I stepped out into the night with Clementine between us and someone placed a hand on my arm and I shrugged them off. Footsteps followed us outside. Sandy had killed the music. Someone took a handful of the neck of my polo shirt and I turned around and threw a wild punch. It connected with the bony corner of someone's shoulder blade and a shock of pain ran up my arm.

And then they were in front of us, blocking our path. The stag party stared at Clementine and then back at us.

'Party's just getting started,' said the bald groom, an apologetic smile on his baby face.

They moved towards us but suddenly there was a police car turning on to the esplanade from the road into town. It paused outside the Rabbit Hole. A round pale face watched us without emotion from the squad car.

'Party's over, boys,' Lisa said, and when we turned away, Clementine a dead weight between us now, they did not try to stop us.

We slowly climbed the narrow streets towards the cream-and-blue cottage.

Then Lisa's phone was buzzing. We paused while she read the message.

'Paolo. He woke up. Thought I'd be home by now.'

'I've got her.'

'Are you sure?'

'Go to your son, Lisa.'

I lifted Clementine in my arms.

It was actually easier than trying to get her to walk, for she was slipping into a deeper sleep.

'Bastards,' Lisa spat. 'Those fucking bastards.' She stuffed Clementine's keys into my pocket. 'Don't let her sleep on her back, Tom. She might choke.'

And so I took her home.

The steep narrow streets made it much harder than I anticipated. The cream-and-blue cottage was high above us, but we kept climbing, Clementine sleeping in my arms, and in the end I stood outside her home, catching my breath, looking down at the whole of St Jude's spread out below. The lights were off at the Rabbit Hole. The police car was gone. A few stragglers were making their way home. There was only the sound of the sea and the gulls and breaking glass.

I stood Clementine on her feet and held her up while I opened the door. We went inside. The hall was crowded with unpacked boxes. I carried her into the bedroom and, as gently as I could, I placed her on top of her bed, pulled off her shoes and placed the duvet over her. I turned her on her side and watched her as she seemed to settle.

When I was sure she was safe and sleeping, and in no danger of rolling onto her back, I wandered slowly through her home, looking for signs of her old life, the husband who died, the family she had lost.

But there was nothing.

I looked around at the stacks of boxes, the suitcases, the bags. Her old life was clearly still waiting to be unpacked.

I stubbed my toe against a red-and-black Cleto Reyes kitbag, sitting between removal boxes.

I had seen it before. She had this kitbag with her on the beach that first night. It looked like something you would take to a gym. But when I lifted it, and hefted it, it was far heavier than anything you would ever take to a gym.

I hesitated for a moment. But only a moment.

Then I unzipped it and I saw rolls of cash inside, all those £20 notes in their little plastic £1,000 bags.

I struggled to breathe, wishing I had not seen what was inside for reasons I could not name. It was a heady mix of excitement, fear, and memories that were both good and bad. Very good and very bad. A cocktail so strong it made me dizzy and sick. And then came a euphoric feeling I knew from long ago.

I could double this for her, I thought. *I bet I could!*

Whatever was in that Cleto Reyes kitbag – it looked to be around twenty or thirty grand – I knew I could make it into twice as much. She would like me then! But then came a nagging doubt, as impossible to ignore as toothache.

Because you don't *know*, do you, Tom? You *believe*. You *hope*. You *think* maybe you could double it for her, with a bit of luck. But maybe you would lose the lot. And what then, Tom?

I zipped the bag and left it where I found it.

Then I went back into the bedroom and pulled out the chair from the old dresser and I sat by the bed. And I watched over her, for hours.

Her voice pulled me from my shallow sleep.

The light that comes just before the dawn, that rumour of morning, was seeping into the room. She was still on her side and it took me a moment to process her words, half-muffled against the duvet.

'Why do they cry all night?' she had said.

I looked towards the window. She was talking about the gulls.

'They cry because their chicks are about to leave the nest.'

'Oh.'

We were silent.

'How you feeling?'

'Better.'

'Someone put something into your drink.'

'I know.' A pause. 'I mean – I guessed.'

Her voice was different at the end of the night. Something had changed with her accent. It seemed more northern now, I thought, as if this was the accent she had heard all around her as a little girl.

The real her, if such a thing existed.

'It's happened to me before,' she said. 'Once or twice. Long time ago.'

I thought about that for a while, and I tried to imagine her life before she came to St Jude's.

'I'm not going to die,' she said. 'You can go now.'

Her voice stopped me at the bedroom door.

'Thank you,' she said.

I let myself out of the cream-and-blue cottage and paused on her doorstep, listening to the sound of the new morning, the whispered roar of the sea and the keening gulls locked in their never-ending duet.

How long had we been at the Rabbit Hole? How long had I sat by her bedside?

It felt like a lifetime.

I walked home as the day was breaking, bone-tired but strangely elated, as proper full-on sunrise came all at once with St Jude's bathed in a heavenly light that turned the estuary into molten gold, and when I filled my lungs filled with salty sea air, I could feel the seasons turning.

Then I suddenly saw my friend on his boat far below and I raised my hand in salute even though he was staring straight ahead, looking out to sea.

Will Farthing in his yellow oilskin and red beanie on the bridge of the *Bonnie Bet*, all alone on the estuary, chugging out on the falling tide to where the lobsters were waiting.

7

The police car was back.

From the deck of the Lobster Pot, I watched it park at the end of the esplanade. There was only one policeman in the car, which seemed odd. When he got out to suck hungrily on a cigarette, I saw him clearly. He was huge, a big man who was out of shape, as though he spent his entire crime-fighting career sitting behind a steering wheel. Even from this distance, I could see his uniform was pristine. His silver buttons gleamed. There were the three stripes of a sergeant on his arm.

Lisa came onto the deck with our first coffee of the day. Her boy Paolo was unpacking his homework at a table inside the restaurant.

'Do you think it's about last night?' she said, indicating the massive policeman. 'Maybe Sandy called them.'

'Sandy would never call them.' I thought about it. 'Nobody local would call them.'

'Or *she* could have called them. Clementine.'

I nodded, but I didn't quite believe it. If Clementine had called the police, why hadn't the big policeman gone to the cream-and-blue cottage?

'Maybe we should tell him,' Lisa said. 'Nick those bastards for what they did before they bugger off back to London for their wedding.'

She made a gesture with her hand, spreading her fingers in an expression of fury.

The angrier Lisa got, the more Italian she sounded.

'What do you think the law are going to do? Even if they can find them?'

'Nothing,' she said bitterly as the *Bonnie Bet* hoved onto the estuary. 'They'll do nothing.'

I took Paolo with me when I went down to the quay to meet Will. He had the day's lobsters covered with damp newspaper and he peeled a page back to reveal them.

'You keep your lobster *moist* but never *wet*,' Will told the boy. 'You keep him *cold* as possible but never *frozen*. They like fresh seaweed or damp newspaper. Can you remember all that?'

Paolo nodded solemnly, his large brown eyes wide behind his spectacles. Will patted him fondly on his head.

'I find the damp newspaper works better than fresh seaweed,' Will told him seriously. Then he paused for the punchline. 'And I find they prefer the sports pages.'

Paolo gawped at him.

The old man's eyes gleamed with mischief. Then they both laughed.

And when I helped Will carry the day's catch up to the restaurant, the police car was gone.

You could be alone on this part of the coast.

Even at the height of the season, when the roads of St Jude's were clogged with cars, you could walk for thirty minutes along the coastal path and feel like the last person left alive.

There were hidden coves, endless meadows cut off from both sea and land, secret beaches that you could never reach in a car, abandoned tin mines at the end of a path that led nowhere. In this quiet time in the middle of the afternoon, when the lunch trade was over and before we had to start prepping for dinner, it was my habit to walk out to a beach you could only reach by the coastal path.

There was an old abandoned cottage set back on a beach of golden sand that looked out on a sheltered bay with a narrow, rocky opening to the sea. It did not have a name on any map I ever saw, but the locals called it Maggie's Cove. And that's where I saw her.

At first, I thought I was imagining her. I thought that after the night she had just had, she would surely sleep the entire day away. But her red hair bobbed above the calm, glassy water of the bay and then was gone. She was like a dolphin, like a seal, breaking surface just beyond the mouth of the bay, out in the choppy open water of the sea now, and then disappearing again so quickly that you thought it was a trick of the light, or a trick of your mind.

But it was really her, and every time she came up, I could see she was moving further away from the beach, and then in the end she was actually swimming beyond the entrance of the bay and closer to the black rocks that massed at the foot of the steep cliffs beyond. All around her, dark waves flecked with white broke against the rocks. I called her name. It didn't matter how strong a swimmer she was, she was dangerously far out.

She came up for air, trod water, then again dived below the surface. Then she didn't come up. And I waited for a long moment, and she still didn't come up. I pulled off my trainers and socks, calling her name, then shouting her name, the panic flooding me.

Then she was there, swimming out of the rough open sea and back inside the calm water of the bay once more, swimming to the beach with that strong fluid freestyle crawl she had, and soon she was standing up and wading to where I was waiting.

I felt the mix of relief and anger.

'You shouldn't go that far out,' I said. 'It's crazy to go out of the bay. There's a riptide just beyond those rocks that will carry you away.'

I saw the flare of irritation on her face.

Then she smiled at me with what seemed like real warmth. 'My saviour,' she said. 'Thanks for last night.'

'I'm serious. Do you want to die?' I said.

She looked at me, her smile fading.

'There's something out there,' she said. 'A boat.' She pointed towards the rocks on the edge of the cove. 'At least, it used to be a boat,' she said. 'Years ago. A sky-blue boat.'

'A sky-blue boat?'

And I knew that Lisa's husband Jack had gone out on a sky-blue boat and never come home.

But it was impossible that this could be the same boat — wasn't it? They would have found the wreck by now. They would have found it when it happened. Wouldn't they? But I could hear my friend Will Farthing reflecting on the endless mystery of tides and time. Townies don't understand tides and even a lifelong lobster man can't explain everything they can do. The moon pulls the sea and the sea can do nothing to resist. Twice a day, every day until the end of time. It is like a message in a bottle. It should never be found. It should be beyond the realms of what is possible. And then it is found. Tides and time.

I ran all the way to the Lobster Pot to find my friend.

Paolo was doing his homework and Lisa was in the kitchen, prepping the lobster.

'We've got a table for ten out on the deck for eight o'clock,' she said. 'The Winters and friends again. What's wrong?'

I looked over at Paolo hunched over his books and I felt a flood of pity for them both.

She was watching my face now.

'What is it? You're scaring me, Tom.'

'It's about Jack,' I said, the name of Lisa's dead husband strange in my mouth, because we never mentioned his name. 'I think Clementine has found his boat.'

A police diver surfaced out by the rocks.

He held up his right hand in what looked like a V for victory salute.

We stood watching from the beach.

There was quite a crowd of us by now.

The fishermen of St Jude's and some of their wives. The police from Truro, who had to park their cars a mile away and walk to the bay. And a few curious tourists, including the Winters.

But not Lisa, and not Paolo.

Bet Farthing turned to a policeman, indicating the diver.

'Is your diver saying he found Jack?' she said. 'Is that what he means? Is he saying they found the body?'

'No, he's telling us he found two bodies, my love,' the policeman said.

We let that settle.

Two bodies.

'That's not possible,' I said.

Perhaps it wasn't Jack's boat. Perhaps it was a wreck from some other time. There had to be more than one sky-blue fishing boat that never came home.

Other divers surfaced. Three of them in the underwater search team. They waded on to the shore.

The policeman from Truro turned to consider us.

'Now where's the young lady who found the wreck?'

But long before the police had arrived from Truro, Clementine had gone.

*

I put the closed sign on the door of the Lobster Pot. Then I got a couple of Korevs from the fridge and joined Lisa out on the deserted deck.

There was a fresh wind, too cold for this time of year. Below us the lights of St Jude's were beginning to come on.

'We had a babysitter,' Lisa said. 'When Paolo was little. Remember her? Maybe you don't. She was gone not long after you arrived. Sixteen, she was. Denim shorts. She worked as a barmaid in the Rabbit Hole. Far too young, but Sandy does like to bend the old rules.'

I nodded. I had a vague memory of a girl I had seen briefly – and she was a girl. I had seen her a couple of times sitting on a bench down on the quay, checking her phone while Paolo waddled around too close to the edge. And I had seen her on my first visit to the Rabbit Hole, serving behind the bar with a big smile, the star of the show. It must have been just before Jack was lost, and before Lisa came to work for me. When she was still doing odd jobs to bring in a bit of extra cash, needing someone to look after the kid. As Lisa said, the girl in the denim shorts had stopped being around, but that was no great mystery. People came and went all the time in St Jude's, especially young people from outside.

'Marcia?' I said. 'Was her name Marcia?'

'Maria,' Lisa said. 'Lads in the Rabbit Hole liked to sing her that song from *West Side Story*. She lapped it up. She was some kind of runaway. Beautiful maid. Not a great babysitter. But that's who I reckon was on the boat with my Jack. That's who it has to be. It can't be anyone else. The maid in her shorts.'

'Maybe it's not Jack. Maybe it's not Maria. Wouldn't they have looked for her? The police?'

She laughed bitterly.

'A maid from outside who vanishes? They only look for missing locals. The community rallies around the fisherman's widow. Everybody else, they come and go. You know they do. Nobody missed Maria. Nobody put a picture of Maria up in the Rabbit Hole.'

She picked up the bottle of Korev but did not drink. Her eyes shone with tears.

'That cheating bastard, Tom.'

Lisa shook her head and laughed again, as if everything she had ever believed had been proved wrong.

Clementine came up the stone steps that led to the esplanade. She joined us out on the deck, sitting beside Lisa, taking her hands, saying nothing.

'They wanted to talk to you,' I told her. 'The police from Truro. Because you found the boat.'

She didn't look at me. She kept holding Lisa's hands.

'I'm allergic to the police,' she said calmly. 'I hate them.'

I left them out on the deck and went upstairs to my room. And long into the night, I could hear the quiet voices of the women, speaking of loss and betrayal and how to carry on.

I was sleeping when I heard the door of the restaurant slam.

I did not fully wake until the tap on my door.

And then she was standing there.

'No,' Clementine said.

I stared at her.

'The answer to your question is – no, I don't want to die.'

I was still waking up. I was suddenly conscious that I was only wearing boxer shorts. I rubbed my eyes and stared at her.

'I don't want to die,' she repeated. 'And I have thought about it a lot. I thought – for a long time – that I *did* want to die. That there was no point in living. The feeling you get that the best is over and done, and that nothing good is ever going to happen again. Sometimes it felt like it might be better for everyone. And just *easier*, you know? Check out early. Like a hotel. But no – I don't want to die, Tom.'

She put her mouth on my mouth. I was stunned. It felt like a perfect fit.

Then she came into my apartment, kicking the door behind her, her thumbs slipping inside my boxer shorts, and I was stunned all over again at my luck.

'When they were taking those bodies out of the water, I knew for sure,' she said. *I want to live.'*

Even as I felt myself harden for her, I was aware of sudden stage fright.

'I haven't had sex with anyone for a while,' I said.

'Me neither,' she said, and I believed her. I wanted to believe her.

'I'm sure we can work it out,' she said softly, her mouth against mine.

I have always preferred to sleep alone.

But as I awoke with Clementine in my arms, her body warm and long against me, all limbs and heat, snuggled up and totally at rest, her breathing soft as a prayer, I realised that I slept better when Clementine was in my arms, better than I slept alone, better than I slept with anyone else I had ever known, as if I was finally in the place I was meant to be, and finally with the woman I was born to be with.

I wanted her again.

A pure animal craving that I called love.

In the first light my hands ran over her body – all of her, as if I was still learning her, as if I must commit her to memory, so that I would have these moments forever, so they could never be taken away from me, as if not quite believing what was happening, and she stirred in her sleep and pressed against me as the gulls cried beyond the window and the sea whispered its secrets, and when she rolled away with a sleepy sigh and lay on her back, my fingertips traced the contours of her flat belly and I remembered another lifetime when I had laid like this by the side of another woman and these same fingertips had traced the softly rising welt of the caesarean scar. But in the dreamy dawn there were no clues to the life that Clementine lived before she came to St Jude's, and as the palm of my hand stroked her stomach it was as if her past was just out of reach, and her future was still waiting to be written.

8

She was dressing when I woke.

'I have something this morning,' she said, pulling on her T-shirt. Her eyes were wide in mock surprise. 'I nearly forgot!'

Still in her pants, I watched her go to the flat's small bathroom, wet the tip of her index finger and run it briskly over her teeth.

I sat up in bed, my hand reaching out for where she had been, and the sheets where she had slept were already cold.

She came back and sat on the bed to pull her jeans on, smiling over her shoulder at my expression. She swept a veil of long red hair from her face. Still grinning, she stood up, fastened the belt on her jeans, and then leaned forward and kissed me lightly on the mouth. She kept her face close, her eyes sparkling with mischief.

'Feeling used?' she said.

I smiled weakly. I felt . . . disappointed. Somewhere in the night, between sleeping and waking, I had the idea that in the morning I would make her breakfast downstairs in the restaurant kitchen while she watched the sun come up over the water and we would seal whatever had happened between us. But I was starting to understand this was typical of Clementine, and I could hear her chuckling to herself as she closed the door behind her.

Clementine always left you wanting more.

I went to the window and looked at the day.

Down on the quay, the Winters were loading a hamper and some snorkelling equipment and a wakeboard – like a skateboard for the water – on the back of a hired speedboat.

I saw Clementine jogging down the esplanade.

They were waiting for her. I watched the father and the son both hold out their hands to help her on board. Mrs Winter gave her a big hug, one of those overdone welcomes that fancy city people love.

Charlie watched her from the deck of the *Pleasure Dome*, the first of the day's tourists yet to show as the speedboat pulled out into the estuary, its stern tracing a long white arc as it headed out to open sea.

At the back of the boat, the Winters gathered around Clementine, delighted by her presence, and I saw her smiling face, and the sky was so blue that it burned my eyes.

*

Later that morning she sent me a text message, and my heart surged.

C U 4 dinner?

Dinner was not actually a real word in her message, but an emoji of cartoon bangers and mash. I flinched at the lazy, sub-literate phone-speak and immediately felt a stab of shame.

She's *young*, I thought, forgiving her the excruciating modern-world shorthand, ready to forgive her anything.

She wasn't talking about dinner at the Lobster Pot, I guessed. She didn't see herself sitting alone at a table for one with me joining her when the night allowed. She meant a meal shared together, like a normal couple. A date. And I found myself longing for normality, craving it.

We should go to Anton's restaurant, I thought. Le Poisson Imaginaire.

I could ask my friend Anton for a table looking out over those big north-coast beaches. Would she like that? She would like that. But that would mean leaving Lisa and Ryan to handle dinner at the Lobster Pot alone. That would be terrible, I thought, my fingers already tapping out my acceptance.

Early in the afternoon, when I was out on the Lobster Pot's deck, the speedboat returned.

It idled halfway between St Jude's and Polmouth. Masks, snorkels and fins were drying on the deck. Clementine was stretched out on the bow while Mrs Winter rubbed sunblock on her dangerously pale shoulders.

Oliver Winter and his son Harry were attaching the wakeboard to the back. When it was ready, they called out to Clementine. She left Mrs Winter with a smile, slipped easily into the water, strapped her feet to the board and signalled to the Winter boy at the wheel.

He took off, too fast, but she rose from the water, her face split in a broad grin, her body looking stiff and uncertain at first, but then getting into it, flexing her knees, shifting her weight and finally shouting out with pure joy.

There were a few fishermen down on the quay. They stopped to watch her progress. It was nothing we hadn't seen a thousand times before. Rich outsiders messing about on their hired boat.

But as the speedboat traced a figure of eight on water as smooth as glass, we all watched her as if we were seeing this grace and this privilege and this other kind of life for the very first time.

I left the Lobster Pot and walked down to the quay and stared out at the people still on the water. I did not notice the big police sergeant was standing by my side until he spoke.

'Beautiful, isn't she?' he said.

His face was flushed with the rosy glow of the committed drinker. His nose looked as though it had been broken more than once. His lopsided grin seemed to contain all the dirt of the modern world. His looks – coarse, broken, all those hard miles on the clock – were in bizarre contrast to his smart uniform. He looked like a parody of a policeman.

I looked at him for a moment, my guts twisting, and then back at Clementine.

I didn't feel he needed an answer.

'I bet she could crack walnuts with that arse,' he said. 'What do you reckon?'

I stared at him and he grinned back at me. His nose was covered with vivid red blood vessels, like a road map of alcohol abuse.

'You should have seen her when she was nineteen,' he told me, turning away.

CHARLIE FARTHING: *She was out of my league. I understood that very early on. There was a moment – when I was bringing her back to St Jude's on the* Pleasure Dome *after she swam across the water, and when we were walking back to her cottage – when I had some mad hope. But it is all about levels, isn't it? And some people are just out of your league. Too beautiful for you. Too free. Too confident. Too many other people who want to be next to them. And despite everything that happened later, I have no hard feelings towards her. I like her, and I am grateful to her, because she gave me my first taste of the world that I had always dreamed about. A world of beauty, freedom, a life without limits. That was her. That was Clementine. She did what she wanted. The anger towards her in St Jude's is because our little fishing village was never the same again after she arrived. We don't have a lot to do with the law down here. We take care of each other. And whatever else she did, she brought the police to our door.*

9

In the kitchen of the Lobster Pot, Lisa was ripping open a lobster with ferocious expertise. She had a shell cracker in one hand and a thin stainless steel lobster pick in the other. The cracker broke the lobster shell without shattering it, and the thin pick with its tiny hook allowed her to pull out the pink and white flesh inside without tearing it. The bowls for a dozen lobster cocktails were lined up before her, already decorated with their slivers of lettuce and lemon.

'We could close,' I said. 'Just for one night.'

'But we were closed *last* night.'

'Because they found Jack—'

'I'm not using that cheating bastard as an excuse for anything,' Lisa said. 'Close the doors two nights in a row? This close to the season? I do your books. We can't *afford* it, Tom.'

Ryan came into the kitchen, nodding to the tune on his AirPods.

'Just you and me tonight, Ryan,' Lisa said briskly. 'Just us, OK? So I'm going to need you at the top of your game.'

Ryan brushed his long hair from his face, looking suitably terrified.

Lisa sighed, paused with her cracker and pick, and stared at me standing there in my best clothes.

'Do what you like, Tom,' she told me, shaking her head, suddenly sounding tired.

She didn't look up from her work as I left, and I heard the steady rhythm of the Lobster Pot preparing for dinner. The clink and clutter of Ryan laying the tables, and Lisa's cracking of the claws, then the silent stabbing of the pink flesh inside, and then the cracking of the claws again.

An hour later, Clementine and I were sitting at the best table in Le Poisson Imaginaire, her face framed by the sky and the sea, and the last thing on my mind was what was happening back at the Lobster Pot.

'A hundred years ago, everyone learned to swim in open water,' Clementine told me, taking a big pull on her Chablis.

She held out her glass and I filled it.

Her face was flushed from the sunshine of her day spent out on the water.

'There were no heated swimming pools in the olden days,' she said. 'Everyone learned to swim in the sea and lakes and rivers and the village pond. Sometimes they threw you in. To see if you could float. Or not!'

Smiling, she gazed out at the huge golden beach that stretched off in either direction, a beach the size of a small planet, one of those beaches in Cornwall that equal or exceed the beauty of any beach in the world, and she exhaled with pleasure. The sea was wild and windy, for this was the north coast of the county, surfing paradise, and high waves rolled in with a lone surfer on top.

I looked around Le Poisson Imaginaire. Anton's restaurant was fully booked, even out of season. Le Poisson Imaginaire wasn't like the Lobster Pot, where there was just 100 metres from boat to restaurant and I could help Will Farthing carry his lobsters to our kitchen. Anton's place was far fancier, the kind of big, serious restaurant that could do a hundred for lunch and two hundred for dinner.

'All good?' Anton said, appearing by our table.

We murmured our thanks, heady and exhilarated from the sun and the sea, the wine and the food, and the thrill of our first dinner together.

Anton was solicitous, charming, the perfect host.

But it seemed to me that he never quite looked Clementine in the eye.

Back in St Jude's, she slipped her arm around my waist, and kissed me lightly on the face. We could smell the sea and taste the salt and the sky was full of stars. I had not been this happy in years. In fact, I had never been this happy.

And then I saw the police car parked on the esplanade. Its lights were off.

The big sergeant got out, grinning at her.

There was a parked car behind him.

A man whose face I could not see sat behind the wheel, staring at us.

'There's our girl,' smiled the fat cop. 'Had a nice night, Tina?'

He was talking to Clementine. He walked slowly towards us, in no rush at all, acting as if I wasn't there, or he had not noticed me, or I was totally irrelevant to what was about to happen.

I was struck again by the paradox of him. This leering, rough-looking, red-faced man and his pristine blue uniform, so pressed and clean he looked like he was about to go on parade. He indicated the parked car.

'Now you *know* you're going to have to talk to him, don't you?' he said. He was all reason. 'We can do it here or up at your charming little house.' He spread his meaty hands. 'Your choice. Either way is fine.'

Even then, I stupidly thought that he meant the cops from Truro wanted to talk to her about finding the wreck of Jack's boat, and then not sticking around to make a statement. That's what I thought. But then the way he acted as if I was totally invisible made me start to understand he was there for some other reason.

'I want to see your warrant card,' I said. 'I don't believe you're a policeman. You don't act like any cop I ever met.'

He looked at me now, and seemed genuinely amused.

He showed me his warrant card.

'But how do you know it's the real thing, little man?' he asked. 'I guess you're going to have to trust me!' He turned to Clementine, his face clouding. He nodded again at the parked car. 'Coming or what?'

I could feel it all slipping away.

I wanted her, and I wanted her tonight, and I wanted her for ever. I wanted this woman, the perfect stranger who would turn me into the person that I was meant to be all along. But I was also starting to understand that this perfect stranger was not quite who she said she was.

'Who are you?' I asked the fat cop.

He turned on me with ferocious contempt.

'Who am I? Is that your question? The question should be – *Who the fuck are you?* Do you think she was down here for the sea air and a fish supper, you dumb bastard?'

I took a step towards him and he placed a big paw on my chest, his eyes burning into me.

'Don't,' he said.

Then the car door opened.

A man got out. Young, I thought. Short but muscular, dark good looks.

'Hello, Tina,' he said, and I watched her flinch.

I stared at her. 'Tina?'

'I hate that name,' she said, not looking at me.

'Can we talk?' the younger man said, almost pleading. 'Just talk. That's all.'

She wrapped her arms around herself, as if suddenly freezing.

'You don't have to *do* anything,' he said, and it could have meant anything.

The younger man held out his hand.

He was not tall but thick with hard flesh, dark and handsome in an old-fashioned matinee idol way, and you could understand why a woman would give him her heart.

But Clementine – she was never Tina to me – made no move.

The man stepped forward and grabbed her wrist in his right hand and sharply pulled it down in some kind of restraining technique and I saw the pain flash on her face.

Then I was moving toward him and suddenly the old cop had my arms pinned behind my back.

He pressed the sole of his foot against the back of one of my knees and my legs collapsed as he held my arms in place.

They were very professional. They knew how to impose their will on the world.

I felt the searing pain somewhere in my shoulder blades.

'Go on, Steve,' the old cop told the younger man. 'School him, will you?'

Not letting go of Clementine, the man called Steve punched me in the face with his left hand. It seemed almost casual. There was nothing wasted in his effort, but he seemed to hit right through me, as if he was aiming for a point somewhere beyond the back of my head.

He's done that before, I thought, as the unbelievable pain tore through my brain.

He caught me just under the right eye, and I felt the skin split somewhere high on the cheekbone, and the bone fracture then sink into my face.

Then I was on my knees, undone by the shock of it, gasping with disbelief, none of them saying another word, black stars swarming in my vision as car doors slammed and two engines fired up, with the warm blood already sliding down my forehead from where I had been cut by his thick gold wedding ring.

Hands were helping me up. Voices I knew, faces I loved. Creased with concern. I doubled up, gagging. I suddenly felt so sick.

'You puke if you want to, boy,' Will Farthing advised. 'Better out than in.'

I sank back to my knees, looked up at the Farthings, all three of them, Will and Bet and Charlie, and saw Bet was holding a takeaway bag from the Lobster Pot.

She must have gone in to help Lisa because we were short-staffed tonight, because of my date. And Will and Charlie must have drifted into the restaurant later, the pair of them lost without Bet at home.

While Bet and Will bent over me, Charlie stood shouting at the two cars slowly winding their way through the narrow streets up to the cream-and-blue cottage, tears of impotent rage streaming down his face as he screamed his threats into the night.

You hurt her — and I'll kill you!

I'll kill you!

I'll kill you!

And I know they heard him, and I know they did not take him seriously.

BET FARTHING: *She had that wildness in her, and that's what the men liked. Even though her wildness drove them to the loony bin, that's what they liked. All of them. My Charlie. Our Tom. And him that came looking for her. His name will come to me. Her husband. They all thought they hated her wildness, but it was what they loved most about her. And I do believe it was a real love, because they were all willing to do anything for her. But I am not sure if any of them, for all the love that they lavished on the maid, got much happiness out of it. And if all that feeling — all that love — only makes you miserable, then what's the bloody point?*

10

'My God,' Lisa said, 'what happened to you?'

Lisa and Ryan were closing up at the Lobster Pot when I staggered in. It weakens you, getting seriously hurt. You lose your legs.

Lisa took me out to the deck and sat me down at a table still strewn with the pink, bony debris of two grilled lobsters and an empty bottle of champagne, turned upside down in an ice bucket beaded with moisture. I gulped the fresh air and stared out at the night, the waves of sickness worse than the throbbing pain under my right eye where the fist of the younger man – Steve – had struck me, where his wedding ring had cut me.

There were voices swirling around me, my vision full of black stars.

Lisa was talking, swabbing at my eye with something that stung. The black stars churned and swirled. Her voice ebbed and flowed. I couldn't think straight. Lisa was gripping my shoulders.

'Tom, who did this to you?'

The past did this to me, I thought, my brain somewhat scrambled. *Clementine's past. Who she was before she came here. Who she was before she met me. Who she was in real life. And it's not even the past, is it? Not really. It is who she was and who she still is.*

'Tina?' I said. 'Tina? Who the fuck is Tina?'

'Listen to me, Tom,' Lisa said. 'I think you've got concussion. You need a doctor. You need hospital.'

Despite my dazed condition, I was embarrassed.

'He only hit me once.'

'Who is he?' Charlie said. He was standing on the edge of the restaurant, bathed in light, and he had fallen to pieces. 'I mean – who *is* he?'

'Pull yourself together, boy,' his father snapped.

'He's her husband, my lovely,' Bet said, as gently as she could.

We let that fill the silence.

'But I thought her husband – Alex – was *dead*,' Lisa said. 'I thought Alex died on that crossing. I thought he was killed by some drunken policeman. Isn't that what she told us?'

'Well,' Bet said. 'He's not dead.'

'He's not even Alex,' Will said. 'He's Steve.'

I felt a surge of anger and humiliation.

'Whoever he is,' I said, 'she left him and she doesn't want him.'

'Stay still,' Lisa said, leaning close. It felt good, having her face so close, having someone to care for me. '*She doesn't need you, Tom,*' Lisa whispered. Or I thought she whispered.

I reeled back, stunned, staring at her.

'What?'

'I didn't say anything,' she said, concentrating on my cut. My right eye was closing now, and I stared out across the estuary with the torn, swelling flesh already shutting down my vision.

'He can't do this,' Charlie said. 'He can't take her away. Take her back. We should call the police!'

'Son,' Will Farthing said. 'They are the police.'

I awoke with a sore head at first light.

The sickness had passed but the pain was kicking in – a throbbing, insistent pain, like a tumour busy growing behind my eye. I stumbled to the bathroom and inspected myself in the mirror. My right eye was the colour of rotting fruit, deep yellow and brown and a purple that shaded into black. My face was a curdled white.

Again, that stab of embarrassment.

One punch did this. And he wasn't even trying!

I went to the deck and stared up at the cream-and-blue cottage. He was standing outside the front door.

Steve – isn't that what the old cop had called him? Not Alex then. So who was Alex when he was at home? Maybe there was no Alex.

Go on, Steve. School him.

Steve had schooled me all right.

He was taking in the early morning air, taking in the reality of our life here. He looked like a tourist on the first day of his holiday outside his B & B, lost in the wonder of this special place.

He was looking at how the rivers ran into the sea. How Polmouth, on the other side of the estuary, mirrored St Jude's, but how only our side of the water was still a working fishing village, where men plied that hard, unforgiving trade much as they had done for the last thousand years.

Steve smiled down at the males of the Winter family – father and son, Oliver and Harry – tentatively rowing away from St Jude's small beach on their hired paddleboards.

And he – Steve – turned his head as a baby seal barked up at the cloudless blue on the black rocks that marked the very start of the sea.

St Jude's was glorious that morning.

I could almost hear Steve sigh as he stood there basking in the sunlight, taking in all that beauty, all that nature, all that limitless possibility of pleasure and contentment, and I looked at the door of the cottage wide open behind him, and I waited for her to appear.

But she did not appear.

Steve raised his chin, as if listening to the soundtrack of the brand-new day. The seal's long mournful bark and the breaking waves. The laughter of the fishermen doing their chores down on the quay. The gulls following a fishing boat out to sea.

Then he closed the door behind him, and started down the narrow winding street that led down to the quay.

And when he got there, I was waiting for him.

He stared straight through me, and in those few seconds I took him in. I had only seen him briefly last night before he rammed his fist in my face, but now I saw him clearly.

He was not tall but he had a fierce presence and that was because he was built like a weightlifter – a strong man who would never enjoy being somewhere south of average height. He was good-looking, very dark, with thick black hair and skin that would tan easily. Short, dark and handsome, that was Steve. The big police sergeant had treated him like a son, I thought. But they looked nothing like each other.

He saw me staring at him.

His eyes were insultingly blank for what felt like an eternity, and then there was the slow dawn of recognition, and finally – infuriatingly – a flicker of amusement.

'Last night,' he said. 'You're the bloke from last night. Sorry about that, mate.'

My flesh crawled at the unearned intimacy of his hideous *mate*.

'I thought you were going for me.' He grinned, as if the idea was absurd and we both knew it. 'It was self-defence. No hard feelings, I hope?' He showed me his knuckles, the skin torn and bruised. 'See – you hurt me too.'

'Who the fuck are you?'

He thought about it, and clearly found his conclusions to be satisfactory.

'I'm the love of her life,' he told me. 'I'm the one who pulled Tina out of the gutter when she was a very bad girl indeed. I bet she didn't tell you any of that, did she? No, I didn't think so! Ask her about it some time. Do you know how we met? I *arrested* her. For soliciting in a bar when she was sixteen years old and on the run from her care home.' He raised his eyebrows in mock surprise. 'Do you know what that makes her?'

'I don't believe you. I don't believe one word of it.'

He laughed, indifferent to me believing him or not.

'Who the fuck am I?' he said. 'I'm Tina's husband and I've come to take her home.'

All this said without raising his voice. All this relayed without a change of expression or an adjustment to his body language. He was not remotely frightened of me. As if we had established with total clarity last night that he could beat the shit out of me any time he fancied without breaking sweat.

'Look,' he said. 'I'm a police officer, and basically we're the biggest gang in the country, so I have eyes everywhere, which made her easy to find, er . . . Sorry, I didn't get your name?'

'Tom Cooper,' I said, loathing the weakness in my voice.

He had turned almost conversational.

I was afraid he was going to shake my hand but instead he chuckled, indicating the cream-and-blue cottage high above us.

'Do you think I had to lock her in last night? Do you think I will have to drag her home?'

I didn't know what to think. But I knew I hated this bastard with all my heart.

'What did she tell you?' He smiled. 'Let me guess — that I fell off my perch and she's a merry widow!'

He saw the reaction on my face.

'Bullseye,' he said. 'This is what you have to understand about my wife. Tina lies and she lies and then she lies a bit more. It's second nature to her. It's pathological. She's been doing it all her life. There's something wrong with her in the head. Listen to me, Toby — *she pretended to be dead.*'

I was finding it difficult to breathe.

'Have you ever heard of Black Moss Pot?' he said. 'No? It's the most famous place for wild swimming in the Lake District. That's where our home is, me and Tina's home — Cumbria. Beautiful part of the world. It's where my family have been for generations. Tina, of course, she's lived all over. She's a citizen of nowhere. Bouncing from care home to foster home and back again when it all fell apart. And it looks prehistoric, Black Moss Pot. Sheer cliffs and this deep water, more green than blue. It's *remote*. You can't get to it by car. You walk for an hour from a village called Stonewaithe. And Black Moss Pot — there's a waterfall at one end. And it's *cold*, Toby — and when she didn't come home, when all they found were her clothes two days later, they thought it was the cold that did for her. That she jumped in, maybe hurt herself, banged her head, and the freezing cold water of Black Moss Pot did her in. That's what my colleagues thought. And that's what she *wanted* us to think. Because people die there every year. It's a beautiful spot — but you shouldn't swim there alone. Because when it goes wrong, it goes really wrong. And the body doesn't always turn up.'

He cackled at the memory.

'A tragic accident! But although Tina left behind her pile of clothes, and her watch, and her credit cards, it turned out that the little minx had taken all the money from our bank account – drained it dry! She couldn't help herself! Must have been getting out the daily maximum for months! Tina – oh, she's cunning, but she's not smart. Neatly left her clothes on this big round stone six feet high and disappeared – this woman who can swim like a fucking dolphin, this woman who is happier in the water than she ever is on dry land. Let us think she was gone for good. *Wanted* me to think it so I didn't come looking for her.'

He shook his head, chuckling to himself, still not quite believing it.

'Now I ask you, Toby – *why would the sick bitch do that?*'

Because she's afraid of you, I thought.

Because she's terrified.

Because you're so good at violence.

Because she's good. Too good for you, whatever she has been through in her life. And I thought, remembering the rolls of notes in the Cleto Reyes kitbag, *Because she needed to start again.*

'Tina will be all right,' Steve said, and even then it took me a delayed, stunned moment to realise that he was talking about my Clementine. 'She'll be all right once we teach her a lesson that she never forgets and take her back to where she belongs.'

I went to my secret place in the afternoon.

Maggie's Cove. She found me there. She sat beside me on the beach and we watched the breaking waves.

I didn't know what to say to her.

I was afraid my silence seemed like sulking. But I just had no words for her. I didn't know who I had slept with. I didn't know who she was. God help me, I didn't know who I loved.

'Maggie's Cove,' she said. 'That's what they call this place, isn't it?'

I nodded. 'Not on the maps,' I said. 'But that's what the locals call it.'

'Who do you think Maggie was?'

I indicated the cottage that sat at the end the beach and the start of the meadow beyond.

'A writer lived there. A famous writer. But she wasn't called Maggie. I think that Maggie was maybe just a character in one of her books. Somebody that didn't really exist.'

We were silent for a while.

'Is your eye all right?'

I stared at her with my one good eye, humiliated and embarrassed that just one punch had me on my knees, had me unable to protect her, had her whisked away with that barrel-chested ape called Steve.

'It's fine.'

'I owe you an explanation.'

Your husband is meant to be dead, I thought. *What else is a lie?*

But I looked at her perfect face, and the long, lean body I ached for even now, especially now, and that is not what I said.

'Stay,' is what I said. 'Please stay.'

She stared out at Maggie's Cove, as if she had not heard, or as if she was thinking about it.

'Leave him, Clementine, leave him for good,' I said. 'I don't care what your real name is! I don't care what happened before. Just stay here. Stay with me. You know you want to. I can tell you want to.'

She sighed. 'I can't. There are things that have to be sorted. This story – this nonsense – that I pretended to be dead. It's all rubbish. And the money I am supposed to have stolen. I just left him, that's all. And took what was mine. That's *my* money.'

I thought of the kitbag I had seen the night I carried her home from the Rabbit Hole.

And for the first time, a worm of doubt crept in.

'I ran away because I was scared,' she said. 'You see what he's like – you see how quick he is to get violent. He had told me that he would kill me before he saw me with another man. *And he said he would get away with it.* He said he would get away with it because he knows how to hide a body so that nobody would ever find it. No dog walkers, not the police, nobody. He told me that most murderers are scared and stupid and that's why they get caught. He said he wouldn't put my body in a skip or a river or a basement where someone would find it. He said he knew places – lots of places! – where I would never be found. He liked to talk about it! Steve is one of those men – one of those husbands – who will kill you for just *thinking* about someone else. If he knew what we did . . .' Silence. 'I don't know what he would do, Tom. He would go crazy.'

'I'm not scared of him.'

'I am,' she said, and she shivered. 'And you should be too. And be scared of that fat bastard. That's his stepfather. *Monk.*'

She spat the name out. She meant the massive police sergeant.

'That fat bastard was famous because he raped a young policewoman early on in his career. They were going for the same job. And they met to talk about it. And he raped her in the front of his squad car. In a police car park. Policemen saw them. They all laughed. They all thought it was funny. There are photographs, a film. And what happened? The fat bastard got promoted and she – the woman he raped, his fellow police officer – got told to shut up. She was told to get over it. That's what you need to know about that fat bastard.'

'And who is Steve? He told me he was a police officer, too. He told me he had friends everywhere.'

She laughed and shook her head. 'He's such a liar! *He's* the liar. Steve's not a cop. Not anymore. He *was* a cop. They kicked him out. Two years ago. He's been sitting around the house ever since. He beat some boy – some kid – so badly that the kid lost an eye. That's what he's like. He told me there was life with him or death in a ditch. He told me that nobody would ever find my body, Tom.'

And that's what gave you the idea, I thought.

The clothes left by Black Moss Pot. The body that will never be found.

But I didn't care what she had done before she knew me. I loved her for who she was now. In the end, what else is there?

'Stay, Clementine,' I said again.

'My husband is waiting,' she said, standing up, the words ripping at me, crushing all hope of her staying. 'So I can't, can I?'

I reached for her but she shook her head.

She swept back a long veil of red hair from her face.

'You will probably hear some things about me,' she said. 'They will not be pleasant things. They will not be anything that anyone wants to hear about . . . someone they care about.'

'I don't care what they say about you.'

'You might care. But don't believe it – please, Tom,' she said, and hearing my name in her mouth, I had the feeling that this was the woman I was born to be with, and no other would do. And even if I could not have her, that fact would still be true. I loved her with all my heart. Whoever she was.

She looked out to sea and I followed her gaze.

At the edge of the bay, the deep blue of the waves broke white and there seemed to be a sliver of black, the smoothest thing in the world, and it quickly sunk back beneath the waves.

It could have been dolphins or it could have just been the longing to see dolphins.

In my experience, you can't tell them apart.

11

I thought they would be gone in the morning.

Consumed by the self-pity that comes so easily when we love without reward or reason, I shifted sleeplessly in my bed all night long, listening to the sea, and the unflagging chorus of the gulls.

I stuck it out until dawn and then padded barefoot down to the restaurant, just in boxer shorts, for the day was noticeably warmer now, near the start of the new season, and I went out on the deck and looked back at St Jude's rising steep and jumbled and familiar behind me, expecting to see the cream-and-blue cottage abandoned, his car gone and Clementine with him.

But his car was still there.

And it was there all morning, as Lisa and I prepared for lunch – the phone ringing for bookings non-stop, like an overture to the coming busy period – and finally at noon, Steve appeared.

He stood shirtless in the doorway of the little cottage, scratching his ribs, staring down on the quay, his strong, stocky, muscled body covered with hair so wiry, you could have used it to clean pots and pans. My throat tightened with disgust at the thought of that body pressing down on Clementine. I pushed the thought from my mind but it kept bouncing back, mocking me and my jealous heart.

'We can't just leave her up there with him,' Lisa said, crossing the restaurant to answer the phone. 'We have to make sure she's all right.'

But the way Steve stood there, just another chilled tourist blissed out by the sight of the spring sunshine on St Jude's, listening to the gulls and the seals calling to their kind, the air so sweet and fresh and salty it could make you half drunk – it made another thought come unbidden.

She has done this before.

She has run away from him before.

And he has gone to claim her.

And then they go home.

Steve stood there taking in the sights, as though none of this was a big deal, as though he did not need to take Clementine kicking and screaming back to her old life, back to her real life.

How many times has he gone after her?

How many men have there been just like me?

A wave of something passed through me, and I could not tell if it was hurt or resentment.

Then Steve gently closed the door behind him, as if Clementine – Tina, he had called her – was still sleeping and he did not want to wake her, and he wandered down to the quay, staring at the two figures on their paddleboards pottering about on the water close by the harbour wall. Steve sat down on a bench and leaned forward, grinning. He liked the look of the old paddleboard, did Steve. He watched the Winters, father and son, Oliver and Harry, with a kind of amused envy.

That looks like fun!

'I'm going up there,' Lisa said, 'He might have hurt her.'

'Yes,' I said, but Lisa did not move, and together we gazed up at the cottage, as if it was a high tower in a fairy tale, expecting to see the captive princess waving desperately for rescue from an upstairs window.

But then Clementine was in the doorway of the cottage, in a maroon wetsuit, skin-tight and futuristic, like an intern on the starship *Enterprise*.

I never saw her look more beautiful than she looked at that moment.

And I never felt more betrayed.

Because she started down the steep streets towards the quay and her hairy, hard-bodied husband.

Lisa glanced at me. We said nothing but I knew she felt it too.

Clementine didn't look like she needed our help. She looked like she was on holiday.

This wasn't a kidnap.

It was a mini-break.

They rented paddleboards from the dive shop. Steve's was a garish purple, the shade of purple you see on children's backpacks. Clementine's was black. His and her paddleboards. And as Lisa and I welcomed the first guests for lunch, and Ryan rushed in late, pulling out his AirPods, muttering apologies, his long hair damp and flying, Clementine and Steve paddled out to join the Winters, who had summoned up the courage to paddle further out.

Always at home on the water, Clementine was good at paddleboarding, although for all I knew she had never done it before in her life. She was standing ramrod straight on her night-black board, long and lean in her maroon wetsuit, languidly moving through the water with her oar towards the Winters.

Steve was noticeably less adept. He was in his swimming trunks, lying on his belly and paddling on his purple board with his hairy hands, like a monkey who had been trained to master water sports in some cruel theme park. They did not look like a couple in crisis. They looked like they were on a second honeymoon.

And I thought – *Did they have sex last night? Did she like it? Was he better than me?*

How could I think anything else?

Around three in the afternoon – too late for lunch, too early for dinner – they came to the Lobster Pot.

Of course they did. If you stayed in St Jude's, then sooner rather than later, you rocked up at the Lobster Pot.

My stomach twisted with despair as Steve and Clementine suddenly appeared in the entrance of the restaurant, gazing around for a table. The lunch trade was almost over, just one couple left lingering over their coffees, and I saw that all of the Winter family were with them. The mother and daughter, Tamara and Saskia, as well as Oliver and Harry, the paddleboarding father and son.

Steve was still bare-chested, even in the Lobster Pot, as though he was going for a full English break-fast in the Balearics. Tamara Winter looked at him askance, her smile so frozen she could have had hypothermia. I suspected that Steve was not really the Winters' type. But Clementine's beauty trumped all. Then and always – the way she looked, the way she moved, the way she was – it changed everything for everyone.

'Sorry, you're too late for lunch,' Lisa was telling them.

'It's OK,' I said, intervening, and Clementine smiled with gratitude as if I was a special friend, doing her this kind favour. 'I'll put you on the deck,' I said, my voice strange. 'Just give me a chance to clean the table.'

I risked a glance at her, then looked away, but not before I saw the raw quality in her eyes, as if she had spent too long in the sun and water, or as if she had been crying all night long.

And there was no mistaking the livid red mark high on her cheekbone where a hand had slapped her face.

I cleaned the table in a daze, my stomach heaving, and I returned to the kitchen while Lisa seated them, trembling with rage. I placed my hands on the marble of the big kitchen island but they would not stop shaking. Lisa came into the kitchen, her face white with shock.

'Did you see it?' she said. Then, grabbing my arm: *'Did you see that mark on her face, Tom?'*

In our brief relationship, Steve had already frightened me, hurt me and made me almost insane with jealousy. But it was not until I saw the mark on Clementine's face that I wanted to kill him.

ANTON: *I was misled. I was misinformed. A friend I had once worked with in London saw something online and called me immediately. 'You remember that woman, Anton?' he said. 'The one who fought with her lover in the restaurant? She drowned. It's a tragedy.' But — no. He was wrong. Someone was — how do you say? — barking up the wrong tree. That woman — that beautiful woman — she did not die. It was her. It was them. I knew it! The couple I saw at the restaurant in London. The lovers who fought. The woman who was meant to have died. And I remembered them so vividly because they were such a striking couple. And I remembered them because of the way they fought.* Avec une telle férocité! *Glasses thrown, bloody scratches. We threatened to call the police and they both laughed at us. So I had seen that side of Clementine that nobody in St Jude's had ever seen. The untamed side. The feral side. Men — women too — they look at the face of a woman like Clementine and they think that they know her. But they had not seen what I had seen, and they did not know her at all. Only one man ever really knew Clementine. And it was never Tom Cooper.*

12

The Winters bailed out early.

Clementine and Steve now sat at the table alone, plates full of fish bones and an empty bottle of Cloudy Bay between them. Their faces were poker-faced and blank, the kind of married silence that can mean anything, but usually means – *we will settle this later*.

Ryan moved languidly around them, clearing the table. They gave no sign that they knew he existed.

'This isn't right,' Lisa said, hefting a plastic box full of cooked lobsters onto the kitchen island. She shook her head, taking out her tools for shucking. The wooden mallet, the stainless steel lobster cracker, the long thin metal lobster picks. 'Did you *see* her face?' she demanded again.

I watched them from the kitchen. Clementine had turned her head away from her husband to look at the view. Out on the estuary, the *Bonnie Bet* was returning. I could see the familiar figure of Will

Farthing in the bridge house in his yellow oilskins and red beanie. Clementine got up from the table and went to the edge of the deck to watch Will coming home.

Steve stared at her for a moment and then got up and came into the kitchen. The way he swayed made me guess that he had drunk most of the Cloudy Bay. He waved to me and made the little signing hand gesture.

'Settle up,' he slurred.

'I can bring the bill to your table,' I said.

Steve ignored me. He was watching Lisa shucking lobster with mute fascination. A neat pile of pink and white knuckles, claws and tails were already lined up before her. There was a violence and precision to lobster shucking that he seemed to enjoy.

I went to tot up his bill at the till in reception.

Clementine had turned her head and she smiled at me, and it could have meant anything, or nothing at all. One casual smile from her, and it tied me in knots.

When I went back to the kitchen Steve was still watching Lisa with frowning interest. She deftly twisted off the tail and claws, separated the head, pried off the tail shell. Then she turned to the sink, rinsed the lobster meat in cold water. Then returned to the kitchen island and separated claws and knuckles, using a silver lobster pick to remove the sweet, juicy flesh inside the claws. She briefly looked up at her audience, Steve and me, as she used a wooden mallet on the claws – one firm smack to destroy the hard shell. Then she pulled the knuckles apart and again used the thin silver lobster pick to pry out the knuckle meat.

I cleared my throat and Steve looked at me.

I gave him his bill.

'Service included?' he said.

'Don't worry about it.'

'No, I want to give you a tip.'

Silence.

'No need. I'll leave the bill on your table.'

Clementine smiled at me as I placed the bill on the table. I could not manage a smile.

'What happened to your face?' I said.

'Believe it or not, I really did walk into a door,' she said.

I stared out at the estuary. The *Bonnie Bet* had reached the quay. Will Farthing was holding up a plastic icebox to show Bet. A good day. The lobsters had been waiting for him.

'You told me your husband was dead,' I said.

'Wishful thinking,' she said.

I wanted to make her happy, I wanted to save her, I wanted her to stay. And I knew that none of these things were going to happen.

'You're going back with him.'

'Because there's nowhere else to go.'

'You know that's not true,' I said, and I returned to the kitchen where Lisa was still shucking oysters and Steve was still watching her with his mouth open.

Steve grinned at me. 'I've still got that big tip for you,' he said.

'I don't want your fucking tip.'

'Ooooh, get you! I'm going to give it to you anyway, little man. Here's my tip – *She's not for you*. And that's the best tip you are ever going to get.'

We stared at each other and the only sound in the kitchen was Lisa at her work. The cracking of the knuckles, the hammer coming down on the claws, the shells coming part.

Steve chuckled as if he had seen this all before, some lovesick random man making a fool of himself over his wife. And maybe he had. Maybe he had seen it many times.

He looked over my shoulder and I knew she was standing there.

'When a woman looks like Tina, men fall in love with her,' he said, his eyes never leaving her. 'Because she looks at you as if you are the last person left alive. That's how they get you – the beautiful ones. But you don't know her,' he laughed. Then he lost his sense of humour. 'And you don't know the

mess she leaves behind when she's finished with you.'
He swayed on his feet, finally feeling the heat of the
day and the big lunch and the bottle of Cloudy Bay.
'She said I couldn't give her the life she wanted. That
it wasn't enough. A working man's honest wages were
not enough for Lady Muck from Cow Shit Farm.'

Lisa looked up from her lobsters.

'You hit her,' she said. 'You bastard.'

'It's not true!' he said. 'I would never do something
like that. My father was a violent drunk and I saw
what he did to my mother. I would *never* treat a
woman like that.' He stared at her, wiping his eyes
with the back of his hand. 'I never even raised my
voice to her—'

'Liar,' Clementine said, pushing back her long red
hair, the red mark high on her cheekbone suddenly
unmissable.

'That?' he said with disbelief.

She let the hair fall over her face.

He went to her and pushed it back.

'You know how she got that mark?' he demanded
of us, as if Lisa and I were the court of public opinion. '*She likes it rough.*' The nasty smirk made a
sudden comeback. 'Oh, didn't she tell you, Toby?
Clearly not.'

Then his face darkened. And now he was only
looking at me.

'Oh God, Tina – you didn't actually *fuck* this old man, did you? I thought he just had a crush on you. Like all the rest of them.'

He swayed and grinned, although it did not come so easily now, as he narrowed his eyes at me, appalled and seeing it all.

'*Stop talking now,*' Lisa said, picking up her wooden mallet, bringing it down on some lobster claws.

'You whore,' he said to his wife, almost conversationally. 'Oh, you dirty little whore, Tina.'

'Some nerve,' Clementine said, rising to him, her familiar and detested sparring partner. 'You think I don't know about you and your squalid blow jobs in the back of your squad car? You and your police pussy wagon? You and the other worthless boys in blue laughing about it, all those filthy cops, sharing messages on your little Whats-App group? You think I never looked at your phone? You think I don't know the *real* reason they tossed you out?'

'Ladies man, are you?' Lisa said, smiling mildly, making small talk with the tourists. 'Put it about a bit, do you, Steve?'

Steve snorted with disgust and scratched the black fur on his bare chest.

'It's all right, darling, don't worry,' he told Lisa. 'You're safe from my attentions, all right?'

'I had a husband like you, funnily enough,' Lisa said, as if they were having a pleasant chat on the esplanade, then turning her back to us, letting none of this interfere with her work, again rinsing lobster meat in the big restaurant sink. 'My husband, yes – he died with his pants around his ankles and some teenager in denim shorts between his legs.'

She turned back to the lobsters, inserting a lobster pick deep inside a claw.

'Sounds sweet,' Steve said. 'Dying with a teenager in denim shorts between your legs. What a way to go! And to tell you the truth, sweetheart, I can't say I blame him. Because if I was married to you—'

'Please. Stop talking, please,' Lisa said, and then she stepped around the kitchen island and pushed the lobster pick deep into his neck.

Steve's eyes widened with shock and the blood was already pulsing through his grip as his hands clasped at his throat, the blood suddenly everywhere, and I heard a loud crash as something hit the floor behind me and I turned and there was Will Farthing standing in the kitchen door, and I saw that Will had dropped his plastic icebox full of live lobsters, and the lobsters had stirred and escaped and now slowly moved across the kitchen floor on their spilled bed of ice, clicking their claws at nothing at all, and clinging to what was left of life.

13

We were not murderers.

It was not in us. And thinking back on it all now, I see how different it could have been if we had followed our instincts.

And all our instincts were to save him.

For Steve did not die. Not then. Not there.

For a long moment we were all paralysed with shock. Lisa was standing there with the long sliver of stainless steel still in her hand, a single bead of blood hanging from the lobster pick's point like a teardrop, and Steve was dropping to the ground, more collapsing than falling, all the strength leaching out of him as if he had been punctured.

A long moment, as I say. But it was only a moment.

Will Farthing fell to his knees and at first, I thought he was trying to capture the lobsters who had escaped from the dropped icebox. But Will had sunk to his knees for Steve, and there was a fistful of paper napkins in his hand, and he pushed Steve's bloody hands aside and used the napkins to staunch the wound in his neck as the lobsters swaggered in slow motion across the kitchen floor, dumbfounded by this last-minute reprieve.

'Am I dying?' Steve gasped.

The blood was everywhere.

'No, old son,' Will said, and he even smiled. 'I've seen worse at sea.'

And I felt the truth of it.

I saw the endless wounds that Will had witnessed, and treated, and perhaps suffered, far from land, far from any help. All those long-gone fishermen with hooks in their flesh, the blood pouring as the *Bonnie Bet* bobbed and moved and rose and fell beneath their feet, and not a soul in sight.

'Keep your hands on that, Tom,' Will told me, and then I was kneeling by Steve, the blood-soaked stack of napkins under my palm, wet and warm and disgustingly soggy. 'Hard as you can, boy!'

Steve stared up at me goggle-eyed with disbelief as I pressed down against his neck.

The blood seemed to pulse with his heartbeat.

Already he was pale and clammy. He stared up at me without recognition. 'Am I . . .' he said, but that was all he could manage. Will came back with a glass of water, lifting his head, pouring in a sip, gentle as a mother with her newborn babe.

'Give him more,' Will told Clementine. 'Slow, mind.' And she immediately did as he instructed, wetting Steve's lips with the water, while Will elevated his feet, propping them on the overturned icebox as the lobsters clicked and crawled around us in bewildered circles.

'He's cold,' I said, and Will nodded.

'It's OK, it's OK, it's OK,' Will said to nobody in particular, or perhaps to all of us, although I suspected it was never going to be OK again.

Lisa stood paralysed with shock, the bloody lobster pick still in her right hand, and I wished she would put it out of sight, and then she suddenly looked around her as if she had awakened from some nightmare. Clementine and I knelt either side of Steve – my hands pressed against his throat, the blood already through the wadded-up napkins, Clementine lifting the glass of water higher to his lips. She savagely kicked away a lobster that had begun an exploratory crawl up her leg. She looked at me over her husband's body and I could not read her emotions. She stared up at Will as he pulled out his phone and punched three numbers. Will was calling 999. We heard the immediate response.

'*What service do you require?*'

And then there was Clementine's voice.

'Wait,' she said. 'Please wait a second, Will.'

Will stared at her, ignoring the voice on the phone as Clementine stood up, carefully putting the half-drunk glass of water on the kitchen island. She placed one hand lightly on Will's arm, gently lowering his phone.

Clementine pointed at Lisa. 'They'll take her son,' she told Will. 'You know that, don't you? If the police come now, right now, then they will lock Lisa up and take her son – *Paolo*. Is that what you want to happen?'

'Well, we can't just leave him!' Will cried, a blast of Cornish common sense, if not the bloody obvious.

I tossed aside the sodden stack of napkins, found another in a kitchen drawer, and got back on the floor and pressed them against Steve's ruined neck.

'*They'll take her son,*' Clementine repeated. She took the phone from Will's hand. Will did not try to stop her.

'*Hello? Which service—*'

Clementine turned it off.

Will shook his head, as if he didn't understand, although of course we all understood.

'Call the emergency services now and Lisa will go to jail,' Clementine said. She nodded at her husband on the floor, the hole in his throat leaking like a burst pipe. There was a clinical detachment about her and she spoke with what felt like a professional's pragmatic wisdom.

'What Lisa has done – it's assault with a sharp object, Will. It's GBH. It is maybe even attempted murder. And if he dies—'

'*If he dies!*' Lisa said.

'They will say it's manslaughter,' Clementine continued. 'Best-case scenario. Or they'll call it murder.'

'The lad is not going to die,' Will said, getting back on his knees.

But he made no attempt to call for help.

I was gathering up the bloody tissues. I began to stuff them in the rubbish bin and Will's face twisted with fury.

'Don't put them in there, you bloody idiot!'

I stared at them for a moment. Then stuffed them in a takeaway bag – the lobster in the top hat grinning below a speech bubble – *Take me home with you!* – and left it on the kitchen island.

Time to clean up later, I thought. *Surely plenty of time to clean up later?*

'And they will put Paolo in care,' Clementine said, still addressing Will as he turned his back to her.

'And when you are in care – take it from me, Will –
it damages the rest of your life.'

Steve's feet had fallen off the icebox. A curious
lobster was examining his knee. Will elevated Steve's
feet on the upturned icebox, shooed away the lobster.
Then he looked at Lisa, and something anguished
passed between them.

'Is the blood slowing, Tom?' Will asked me.

'I don't know,' I said.

Steve's eyes had closed. His face was the colour of
forgotten milk.

'Listen – we just need to think for a moment, OK?'
Clementine said. 'To work out what we are going to
say about' – a nod to her husband bleeding on the
kitchen floor – '*what Lisa has done*. And exactly what
we're going to tell them. All of them. The emergency
services. The police. A court of law.'

'What *can* we tell them?' Will said. 'Apart from
the truth?'

'The truth,' Clementine said thoughtfully. 'I don't
know, Will. I really don't. The truth might not be
good enough.'

Steve was trying to say something. I couldn't make
it out. He looked as though he was talking in his
sleep.

Lisa was staring at me, and something in her eyes
had changed.

'I can't lose my boy,' she said, her voice choked with emotion. 'I can't have Paolo taken away from me, Tom. I can't let them take me away from my boy. You know that, right?'

I nodded. Of course, of course. Will had one hand pressed against his mouth, as if what he decided now, right now, would never be undone.

'It's slowing down,' I said. 'The bleeding. I really think it's slowing down, Will.'

'Thank God,' Lisa said, and mumbled something in Italian. It sounded like a prayer.

The restaurant's telephone began to ring.

'You should open tonight,' Clementine said, so calm it shocked me to my core, and I looked down at the blood on my hands, and the floor, and the way the blood was in Steve's hair, his clothes. A lobster pecked at my arm. I brushed it away. The lobster was covered in blood.

'How can we open?' I said.

'You should behave as normal as possible until we work out what we're going to say,' Clementine said. 'Put him somewhere.'

'Put him somewhere?' Will said, flinching with disbelief. 'The lad needs a hospital!'

'Of course,' Clementine said. 'But just put him somewhere for now. Until we know what we are going to say about what Lisa has done.'

'We can't keep him here!' I said.

'Please, Tom,' Clementine said. 'Let's just put him somewhere so we can have a chance to think.'

'This is madness,' Will said. 'Not calling 999! Not getting him to a hospital! It's madness!'

Silence in the kitchen.

The sea and the gulls called to each other.

The telephone began to ring again.

'I might know a place,' I said.

14

'Service,' Lisa shouted from the kitchen.

I had just taken some orders for dessert and I was standing out on the deck, watching a kestrel hovering high over the water. In the fading light the kestrel looked like a gold crucifix, nailed to the darkening sky. For the longest time he was motionless, the great span of his wings not moving, and then they began to quiver and suddenly he swooped at a speed that took your breath away, disappearing from view by the rocks by our little beach, then emerging with what looked like a snake writhing in his maw. An adder, maybe. Or a grass snake or sand lizard.

'*Service!*'

I turned back to the restaurant. Everyone was looking at me. We were not quite full, but it was still a busy night, and I realised that Lisa had been calling me for some time. Her face was flushed red, but it was only when I went to the service station that I saw how drunk she was. There was a freezer-chilled bottle of Aval Dor, good local vodka, open by her side.

'Take it easy,' I told her.

'This is me,' she said, 'taking it as easy as I can, all right?'

Hours earlier we had watched Will guide Steve down the stone steps at the rear of the restaurant. Supporting him like a stag party drunk. If you saw them from a distance, from the esplanade or even the other side of the water, from Polmouth, that's what you would have taken them for – a pair of worse-for-wear townies who had overdone the local craft beer and organic vodka, off for their Cornish siesta. But if someone had met them on the steps, then they would have seen the blood seeping through the bandage that Will had wrapped around Steve's neck, and it would have all been over.

But nobody did, they saw no one on the steps, and no one saw them, and Will helped Steve into his van with a care that looked touchingly tender.

Clementine was not with them. She had disappeared. Will dealt with it alone.

Now Lisa brushed her black hair from her forehead. Her tongue touched her dry lips.

'Where is he?' she said. 'Where's Steve?'

Behind me I could hear someone calling for the bill. Lisa and I stared at each other, and the sounds of the restaurant merged into a white noise where we heard nothing, not even a repeatedly screamed request for the bill.

'Did he get taken to the hospital?' she said.

'Maybe not the hospital,' I said.

The lights were on at the cream-and-blue cottage.

Clementine smiled when she opened the door, not a care in the world.

'Lisa is in pieces,' I said.

She put her arms around my neck. 'I know. But listen to me, darling – they won't get her, and they won't take Paolo away – and that's the important thing.'

And I thought – *darling?*

She shuddered, as if at the thought of the lobster pick disappearing into her husband's neck, and as if at the thought of Lisa being led away by the law. As if she, Clementine, was merely a compassionate observer.

I slipped out of her embrace, although it felt as ridiculously good as it had done the first time, and I went to the window at the front of the cottage, staring down at St Jude's. It was near midnight now and our little fishing village had turned in for the night. I stared at the lights of Polmouth across the water. I could not look at her.

'What really happened? In your old life.'

'I don't know what you mean.'

'Why didn't you just leave him?'

She shrugged.

'That's what I don't understand,' I said. 'Why you let them think you were dead. Why you tried to make him *think* you were dead. All that pretence. All those lies.'

She was very calm. 'Because just leaving him – nothing more than that – would have been the end of me.'

She lifted her arm and rolled up the long sleeve of her Rag & Bone T-shirt. There were marks on her forearm, like black coins, from the crook in her elbow to her wrist. Marks I had never seen before. How had I missed them?

'Do you know what those are, Tom?'

I felt sick to my stomach.

'Cigarette burns,' she said. 'Because I *laughed* with one of his friends. I *laughed*. I didn't have sex with the guy, Tom. I laughed at a party. When we got home, Steve said I wanted to do things to his friend. With my mouth. OK? You following me, Tom? Do you get the gist? Steve said I needed to be taught to behave properly.' She rolled down her sleeve. 'And this was his way of schooling me. That's the kind of sick bastard I was dealing with. I am dealing with.'

She turned away but I took her arms.

I held her to me.

'Why not just go somewhere he would never find you?'

'Because Steve said he would *always* find me – and he did, didn't he? He was right about that. Him and that fat Sergeant Monk and all the other dirty cops they had looking for me. Steve always said his gang would find me and he would come and get me and if I didn't come back willingly then he would get rid of me and nobody would ever find the body.'

I slumped in an old armchair, the upholstery sagging after half a century of Grandma Jo sitting watching the harbour lights, and I looked up at the walls with their faded floral wallpaper, empty of any reminder of her old life.

I held my head in my hands.

She kept talking.

'It's not easy to get rid of a dead body, Steve said. But he told me the police knew how. He said the police do it all the time! Some innocent girl that one of them has and then doesn't know enough to keep her mouth shut so he has to get rid of her. Why didn't I just leave him, Tom? Because I was afraid that one day he would find me, and I was afraid of what he would do if he found me with someone else. Him and his stinking stepfather. I left the way I did because nobody looks for the dead. At least, that was the theory. Crap theory, right?'

'I don't understand how you thought you could leave a life behind.'

'There wasn't a life. Don't you get it? Leaving my old life behind was the general idea. A fresh start. A clean slate. *A chance to get life right*. Isn't that what everyone wants?'

This I could understand. This any incomer that starts a new life in Cornwall could understand. That's why we come here. A clean slate that smells of the sea, a new life that is limitless and free.

'I left a life behind too,' I said. 'Ten years ago.'

'It's *different!*' she said. 'You didn't have anyone threatening to cut your throat, did you?'

'Lisa wants to go to the police. She wants to tell them what happened. She thinks that if we explain—'

'I strongly advise against it. You don't know the police. Not like I do. And you don't know *him*. Not like I do. He hit me once and knocked me out.'

The thought came unbidden – *Is that true?*

And I felt a flush of shame.

Of course it was true.

I got up and headed for the door, but then she was pulling at my arm, not wanting me to go.

'Listen to me, Tom. If I had stayed, he was going to kill me, all right? Men say it, I know – they say it all the time! – but he *meant* it. It wasn't in any doubt. Steve promised that he would put me in my grave if I left him, if I looked at another man, if I wanted a life of my own. *I faked my death to save my life.* Is that a good enough reason for you?'

'I don't know how you thought you would get away with it.'

Suddenly she was all business. 'You can't have an Internet presence. Forget about all those adorable selfies. And you need a bit of money.'

My eyes drifted to where I had found the kitbag stashed with cash. It was no longer there. Maybe that was Steve's first clue that she still lived and breathed somewhere. The fact she took all their money.

'Leave your passport, ID and front-door keys at home,' she advised. 'Make it *believable*. And obviously you can't put in an insurance claim.' She put her arms around my neck again and I flinched. I loved her, and I wanted her – I could feel myself responding to her instantly, the heat flooding me, nothing else on my mind. I never wanted a woman the way I wanted her.

Is that how you know it's love?

Or is that how you know you have taken leave of your senses?

'When you saw me on that beach on the first night,' she said, 'a weight had been lifted from me.'

She felt me pull away. She wouldn't let me.

'Look at me, Tom. You see me. You know me.'

It wasn't true. I loved her. But I didn't know her at all.

'This is madness!' I said. 'There's no real choice, is there? *We have to let him go*. We can *explain* what happened. It was an *accident*. It was a provocation. It was self-defence.'

'Lisa will be in police custody before breakfast. Paolo will be in social care by the end of the day. And then he – Paolo – will be ruined for life. OK? Do you know what happens to a kid like that in care? A gentle kid? A soft kid? A pretty kid? Do you know what they do to you? Do you know what he would have to look forward to? Because I do, Tom. Remind me to tell you all about it one day.'

'I'll look after Paolo.'

'A single guy? They won't *let* you look after Paolo.'

'Bet and Will can look after Paolo.'

'They're too old! That's what the social services will say!'

'But we can't just leave Steve somewhere.'

'Fine,' she said, heading for the door. 'Then let's go.'

'What? Where?'

Her mouth twisted in what was not quite a smile. 'We both know where he is, don't we?' she said.

15

He was at the icehouse. Down by the harbour.

Clementine lifted a ruined lobster pot that stood at the entrance and retrieved a key. She opened the door. A blast of freezing air, conspicuously colder than the night. She turned on the electric light inside. Her breath steamed in the yellow light. I followed her inside.

Steve sat at the far end of the icehouse, tied to a chair.

The bandages around his neck had been changed.

His eyes glittered with menace and fear at the sight of us.

But he didn't seem too bad, I thought with relief.

He wasn't going to die.

But he was gagged. Some kind of material was tied over his mouth and sealed to his face with brown duct tape. As I got closer, I saw his eyes were wild with panic. He was squirming on his chair, rocking

144

his stocky body back and forth, frantically indicating the water bottle on the floor.

'It's OK,' Clementine told me calmly, looking at him. 'He can scream all he wants. Nobody's going to hear him.'

I listened to the night.

The village was sleeping. I could only hear the restless sea, a lonely seal. The gulls mourning for their empty nests. I shuddered. It was below freezing in here.

I pulled the tape and the gag from his mouth, and lifted the bottle to his lips. He greedily guzzled the water.

Clementine chuckled at his desperation.

'Listen,' he said to me. 'Please listen to me.'

'Better put his muzzle back on, Tom,' Clementine said. 'Think of Lisa and Paolo.'

But I shook my head. This madness had to end.

'I don't want your friend to go down,' Steve gasped. 'I don't want her to lose her son. Oh yeah – you think I didn't hear? I heard everything! Listen to me! *Tom.*'

So now he knew my name. No more getting called *Toby!* I felt strangely triumphant.

'Please – it's too cold in here to leave me all night long. Just let me go and – I promise – I'm just going to walk away. Pretend this never happened.

Let you get on with your life. And I'll get on with mine.' He indicated Clementine, and me, taking us both in with the nod of his head, as if we were undeniably a couple and absurdly, and in spite of everything, my heart lifted. 'I'll wish you well,' he said, hanging his head and beginning to weep silent, bitter tears.

Clementine laughed. 'Liar.'

'Listen to me,' he said, raising his head, immediately changing tack. 'You're in big trouble, *Tom*. You're smart enough to know it. But it's not too late. What happened? An argument that got out of hand. That's all! Listen – Tom, right? Tom.' He indicated Clementine again, looking her in the eyes this time. 'She's not what you think she is.' He laughed without humour. 'When I found her – I thought I would be enough for her. Stupid, stupid, stupid!' He furiously rocked the chair that held him. '*You don't know her!*' he screamed.

She slipped her arm through mine. She placed a chaste kiss on the side of my face.

And it was enough. It was enough to inflame him. To enrage him. A black cloud seemed to pass across his face.

'Let me go,' he said, his face a sick yellow under the bare electric bulb of the icehouse, almost too tired to speak. 'And I'll let you walk into the sunset holding hands. I'll forget all this ever happened – honest I will! I'll let you feed him the same stinking lies you fed me, Tina. Let you tell him you never felt like this before. Let you tell him that it's the best sex you ever had in your life.'

They stared at each other. He shook his head.

'I don't even have to ask, do I? If he's had you tonight, I mean. I can smell him on you, Tina, you slut.'

Clementine sighed. She smiled at me, raising her eyebrows.

'Sexual jealousy was always a bit of an issue, as you can see.'

He addressed me. 'Does she still scream – *I love your cock?* Or was that just for me?'

I lifted my fist, all sympathy gone. 'Stop talking now.'

He laughed at me.

'Go ahead. Knock my teeth out. Crack my skull. You can share a cell with that foreign bitch who stabbed me. And that old yokel who helped you.'

'Will Farthing saved your life, moron,' Clementine said.

'You're all going down,' he said. 'You know that, right? The lot of you!' He rocked and raved. 'And you,' he said to Clementine. 'You are today what you were when I found you. And we both know what that was, don't we? There's a name for what you were, Tina. A cheap, dirty little whore.'

'Shut his mouth,' she told me, finally angry.

And I did.

With pleasure. With fury.

I stuffed the oily rag halfway down his throat, making him gag. And then I wound the roll of brown duct tape over his filthy mouth, over his nose and his mocking eyes, this man who knew her before she knew me, one more thing I could never forgive him for.

Outside the gulls were screaming and screaming and screaming.

'Tighter,' Clementine said.

16

Even in my old life, that world left behind long ago, I wanted to sleep alone. Even when there was someone I loved in my bed and a pushchair in the hallway. Even back in the bad old days, given the choice – which I wasn't in a one-bedroom flat – I would have slept alone, as much for my loved one's benefit as my own. For I am not an easy sleeper. Sleep does not come quickly to me and it does not stick for eight hours when it does.

But it was different with Clementine.

I slept so well and so deeply with her. In fact, I slept better than I ever have in my life – God help me, even with her husband tied to a chair in a refrigerated shack with an oily rag stuffed in his mouth and an entire roll of duct tape holding it all in place.

Sleep with her was different, because it came so easily and because it was deep and restful. After leaving Steve in the icehouse we had returned to my flat above the Lobster Pot and we made love.

And sex was different with her too – everything was different – because it felt like those heady, feverish couplings of these first nights would echo down all the days and through all the years ahead, it felt as though the hunger would never wear off, the way it had worn off with everyone else I had ever known. And the sex was getting better because tonight we no longer had the shy desperation of when we were still finding our way around each other, mapping the contours of our love. I held her in my arms, and I looked at the length of her, and I wondered – could I ever get tired of this?

Everything was new with her.

I was young again. I was happy again.

I drifted off to sleep, nothing in my head and my heart full, and she slept in my arms, her conscience clear, as always, and the waves out in the night broke foaming white against the black craggy cliffs of the estuary, black and white the colour of our Cornish flag, black and white the colour of our hearts, as the sea whispered its song all night long.

I choose you.

I choose you.

I choose you.

Then I woke up in a cold sweat.

And I jumped out of our bed, our warm and loving bed, full of a sick dread, suddenly weighed down with a burden too heavy to bear, wondering what the hell we had done.

I dressed quickly, not turning on the bedroom lights, the night still pitch-black outside, the enormity of what we had done hitting me hard, my senses reeling.

Clementine stirred in her sleep.

'We have to let him go,' I said to her, to the darkness. 'Now.'

I didn't say the rest of it – *whatever it means, whatever happens next, whatever they do to Lisa, whatever they do to the rest of us*. We have to let him go because anything else was madness.

She did not argue with me.

As far as I am aware, she did not even wake. She slept on and she slept well, as if it was all the same to her, as if she could have her sweet blissful rest with me, or without me.

There was nobody down on the quay.

Nobody out on the water.

The last frosty bite of closed season was in the air as I walked quickly down the stone steps to the esplanade, then down to the quay. The ruined lobster pot was still outside the icehouse. I felt underneath, finding nothing, my fingers scrabbling in the dirt.

The key was gone.

I felt my heart fly with panic, desperately patting my palm against the ground. And then I touched the cold metal. I must have missed it in the darkness. Or someone had moved it.

I opened the icehouse door, and the freezing cold hit me immediately, far colder than before, my breath already steaming as I stepped inside and turned on the light.

Steve was gone.

The old broken chair still stood exactly where we had left it, but it was empty now and the duct tape and the rag and the fishing line that had held him was nowhere to be seen, as if it had been taken away with him as evidence.

I stood there smelling the ancient stink of fish in the wood of the icehouse as much as in the freezing air. And then I stepped outside, closing the door behind me.

And what I felt was a profound sense of relief.

Steve had released himself.

He had got away.

Of course he had. And whatever happened next, we would deal with it. Everything was going to be OK.

In the far distance, the air was alive with tiny yellow lights, like a host of fireflies descending on our village, and all the fishing villages just like it. It took me a moment to realise that they were cars, dozens of them, trying to get ahead of the rush.

The summer season was about to begin.

I looked up at the village, St Jude's rising steep and still and sleeping above me. All was darkness as I took the first step to home.

A quiet voice from the shadows stopped me.

'Put the key back where you found it, Tom,' he said. A pause. 'Best give it a little wipe first.'

I did as I was instructed.

I put the key under the lobster pot.

Then I turned to face Charlie Farthing.

'Did he get away?' I said.

Charlie seized my throat in his right hand.

'Get away? How the fuck was he going to get away? My old man tied him to a chair! And some other idiot gagged his mouth and blocked his nose! You try getting away from that, Tom.'

'But we have to let him go.'

Charlie's eyes were shining with rage in the darkness. He did not loosen his grip on my throat.

I thought – *Charlie wants to kill me.*

He released me with a snort of disbelief.

'Don't worry about it,' he said.

'Don't worry about it?'

I could still feel the heat of his fingers on my throat.

'You stupid bastard,' he said. 'Come and see what you have done.'

17

They are bringing the body down.

Will and Charlie. Father and son. They have finally stopped shouting at each other. Screaming at each other. I thought they were going to come to blows. The blame, excuses, disbelief and rage. It has all stopped now, while they bend to the task of bringing the body down.

They had Steve in what the Farthings call the box room. More of a telephone booth than a bedroom. At the back of the house, a place for storage and things that were destined to be dumped.

Like Steve.

He had been dead when Will went back to the ice-house. To give him water, Will had said, to make sure he was breathing so that we could work out what to do. So we had time.

So we could do it right.

And now there was no more time, and no more chances to undo what we had done, and I had seen

Steve on the unmade single bed of the box room, looking like a poor carbon copy of himself, all the life gone, just drained away.

They are shuffling around upstairs, talking to each other again, their voices low murmurs, but it is the practicalities they are discussing now. I bring the cup of steaming hot tea to my lips and I find that my hand is shaking so badly that I cannot drink it. I place it carefully on the kitchen table.

Bet reaches across the table and pats my arm.

It is a kind gesture that says — *it's nobody's fault*.

Not Lisa's for sticking the lobster pick in his neck.

Not Will's for taking him to the icehouse and tying him to the chair.

And not me for shutting his dirty trap with the oily rag and the roll of duct tape over his mouth, his nose, his eyes, when he would not stop talking, when he would just not stop saying those awful things about her.

Nobody's fault, then. But everybody's fault.

It is too late for explanations now and forever, too late to explain, too late for the police. Especially now that Will has taken charge of the body.

'The police are not the only ones who know how to hide a body,' the old fisherman had said, when it was clear that there were no more options, that we had to continue down the road we had chosen.

'Is that the plan now?' Charlie had asked his father, close to tears, close to fury but genuinely wanting to know.

And the sea roared its response.

'How's *ow meider?*' Bet asks me.

It is an old Cornish term of endearment. *Ow meider* means – *my honey*. And I know she can only be talking about one person.

'She's all right,' I say, reluctant to say her name for some reason. But we both feel it. Clementine should be here right now.

Bet exhales and lifts her eyes to the ceiling.

Here they come.

It's not going to be easy. These old fishermen's cottages are not built for this work.

I sit in the darkness of the kitchen, staring at hot sweet tea I can't even bring to my lips – *Good for shock, my lovely,* Bet tells me – hearing them shuffling around upstairs, working out how they are going to do it, then testing the weight of the body, negotiating the bedroom door, their voices inaudible whispers, subdued in deference to the lateness of the hour and the nature of the bleak task at hand.

And I think to myself – *How can it still be dark outside?*

This night has gone on too long. This night has lasted forever.

And I also think — *We never learn, do we?*

We should know by now — you can't get too close to outsiders. It always ends in tears. And things that are far worse than tears. The locals and the emmets — outsiders, tourists, derived from the Old English word for ants — can respect each other, be civil, be polite. Be nice. It is hugely underrated virtue — niceness.

And why on earth not be nice to the emmets?

They buy our day-caught fish and sprawl on our beaches and gawp at our postcard-pretty views on the coastal paths, dreaming of Poldark and pasties. And we take their money. We can smile at each other, concur on the glory of the brand-new day, chuckle wryly about the ever-changing weather. But don't get involved. There can be no happy ending or meaningful relationship when you get involved. Our worlds are too far apart. Never love an emmet. It's fatal.

And I also think — *This happened because I loved her.*

And here they come now, bumping clumsily down the ridiculously narrow staircase. Here comes the dead body, this sorry excuse for Steve, being carted to its fate in old bedding. I realise that I have stopped breathing.

Will and Charlie pause at the foot of the stairs, taking a rest. Their eyes glance my way.

I know I have work to do soon. Don't worry – I know.

Then the front door opens, releasing a blast of this place, the cry of the gulls and the smell of the seaweed and the salt that seasons everything.

Then the door slams shut behind them – too loud! – and they are gone, lugging the body towards the harbour, towards the *Bonnie Bet*, wrapped in its box-room duvet. They should get a move on. The first milky light of dawn is, I think, already streaking the horizon. Or perhaps I am just imagining it.

There is a part of me that believes – that truly believes – this night will never have an end.

And I shiver as I sit in the darkness in what passes for the sound of silence – even the gulls are at peace now – in our blessed, beautiful corner of the world.

Because there is never absolute silence around here.

There is always the sea.

After a handful of minutes, no more, I hear the *Bonnie Bet*'s engine start up and pull away from the harbour. The throaty sound has not died away when Charlie is back in the doorway, alone.

I drink my tea and stand up.

'Ready, my lovely?' Bet asks me.

*

I sit at the bow of the *Pleasure Dome*, the wind whipping back my hair, Charlie up on the bridge, taking us out of the estuary and into open sea. He turns the sleek white boat starboard, as he always does, out to the rocks where the seals sunbathe and where the dolphins play, towards Maggie's Cove.

It is really getting lighter now, it is not my imagination, and I swallow down the fear.

What if someone sees?

The fear will live with me now, there will never be a time when the fear is gone, or very far away.

And then there is Maggie's Cove, the little beach house shuttered and dark, the cliffs above it steep and craggy and black, the waves foaming white against them, white on black, the colour of our Cornish flag.

Charlie keeps going. I stare out to sea.

'This is a good place,' Charlie says eventually, as if we have come here to see the seals or the dolphins.

By my feet I have Steve's childishly purple paddleboard and oar, sitting in a puddle of salt water on the polished wood of the *Pleasure Dome*'s gleaming deck.

This is a wild and lonely place, not a place for tourists, the sea rough, the cliffs almost vertical, the coast path far too close to the edge, a place where hikers and swimmers can – and often do – get into more trouble than they can handle.

And high above that desolate spot, I see a sight that I think at first is only my boiling imagination.

A bus stop.

An old-fashioned bus stop in that place where no buses have ever stopped, or will ever stop, a ramshackle hut with a bench and a sloping roof that would do little to protect those who sit waiting from the elements – a bus stop staring out to the sea.

The bus stop is attached to a pint-sized cottage with a black door and black, boarded-up windows, and on the other side of the hut there is the bus stop's twin, another bus stop that stares out across the other half of the sea.

This is the Baulking House, a lookout spot where for generations the *huer* – the watcher – sat on the bench outside that cottage – the *huer*'s hut – and waited for the sea to turn black with the arrival of pilchards, the pilchards that would be the bulwark against starvation, the pilchards that meant the people of the village would live.

And when the sea turned black with the billions of pilchards, every man, woman and child on St Jude's and Polmouth would take to the sea. But now, today, the pilchards are a hundred years gone, and only the ghosts at the Baulking House watch us moving slowly closer to the shore.

Charlie cuts the engine, lets the tide take him nearer to the rocks. Their sharp points sticking above the waves like the rotten teeth of some great submerged beast.

'I can't get any closer,' he shouts above the gusty wind, but more to himself than me. 'It's too dangerous.'

I stand up and immediately almost fall, the boat rocking and falling away beneath me.

Then I carefully steady myself, pick up the oar and toss it over the side. A heavy wave hits it with such force that it snaps like a twig and is gone. Next, I throw the purple paddleboard into the sea, but a wave catches it and takes it to the rocks and leaves it stuck there. Charlie and I stare at it. It does not look as though it has been lost there. It looks like it has been thrown there. He glances up at the sky. I feel the sickness rising in me. Then a wave comes and recedes, and takes the board with it, sucking it under, dragging it away, and I see it no more.

On a big blue morning, washed with sunshine so bright that it felt like an overture for summer, Clementine was out on the water with the Winters. She was perched on the back of their hired speedboat, and they were trying to get her to stay with them, but as the boat idled between Polmouth and St Jude's she executed a perfect dive off the stern and swam for home.

The harbour was full of tourists and they all watched her, as if she was as much a part of the experience as meat pasties and organic ice cream and dreams of learning to surf.

I walked down to the quay to meet her. She came out of the water like the Mermaid of Zennor, the most famous of Cornish folk tales, the beautiful woman who everybody loved and nobody knew.

She stared at me in silence, her smile fading.

She was never lovelier, and she was never more distant from me.

'What have you done?' Clementine said.

PART TWO

The Baulking House

18

WILL FARTHING: *We were miners for a thousand years and then nobody wanted to pay a fair price for our copper and tin, no matter how many men had died to dig it up, and the mines were all closed. And we watched for the pilchards for centuries, but we used up all the little buggers over a hundred years ago. And now some of us nutters still go out on our boats every day to steal what we can from the sea. And what I am saying to you, sir, is — this is a hard, hard place. Don't be fooled by the sandcastles and surfers and jammy scones. This is a hard part of the world and a stranger can get into all kinds of trouble here. So as I told the other officer, I don't know what happened to that young man and I care even less. But he shouldn't have come down here throwing his weight about as if the people who live here mean nothing. If you ask for trouble in this part of the world, it will not be long before it knocks on your door and walks right in.*

OLIVER WINTER: *He was not really — how can I put it? — one of us. Stephen, I mean — Steve. We were friends with Clementine. Totally charming, absolutely delightful. Steve arrived later. The last time I saw him was the day we were out on the water, on the paddle-boards. Great fun, and Steve was pleasant enough company. But then we went for lunch at the Lobster Pot and Tamara — my wife, I think you spoke to her — was concerned when Steve did not change. He stayed in his shorts for lunch! I am of course aware that even the best places in Cornwall never ask for more than smart-casual — and the Lobster Pot is no Rick Stein's, let's face it! — but even so. It was embarrassing seeing Steve sit there in his soaking wet swimming trunks, with his big biceps on display, knocking back the Cloudy Bay and sucking on lobster claw. Frankly, it was disgusting. He was dripping everywhere.*

LISA: *Every love story is a lie. Because those love stories all pretend that we love equally. And this just in — we never do. Couples never love equally. We never do! Someone always holds the power — because they love a little bit less. Even in the greatest love story, someone loves with the passion dialled down, or they don't love at all. And the one who loves more, that one will do anything — bloody anything! — to stop the one who loves less from walking away. That's why it ended the way it did. That's why the hairy fucker died. Because someone always loves more.*

19

Clementine got a job.

She was Anton's new hostess at Le Poisson Imaginaire. Having a hostess greeting diners at the reception desk was not a Cornish thing, or even a British thing. The role was more Manhattan than Mevagissey. But Anton always had big city aspirations, and charged big city prices.

And it worked. For him. For her. Having her there, this flame-haired vision with a surfer's sea and that golden beach behind her, ravishing in some high-necked, tight green shiny frock that I had never seen before, her big smile disarming the couples and families that formed an orderly queue to take their tables at Anton's restaurant.

I felt the aching gap between the Lobster Pot and Le Poisson Imaginaire. My place was everything that I had dreamed of in my old life. Good fresh food in a great location overlooking the sea. Wasn't that enough? But the Lobster Pot had bare floorboards and scant protection from the volatile weather. And if the lobsters were hiding, calling our place the Lobster Pot was a bit of a stretch. And we didn't have the rave reviews in posh papers that Le Poisson Imaginaire had. We didn't have a fancy wine list. And we did not have floor-to-ceiling glass walls that meant you could see all the way through to the big waves beyond.

And we didn't have her.

I joined the queue snaking outside Le Poisson Imaginaire, feeling absurd, feeling the shame of being there, and how desperately I needed to hold on to her, to discuss what had happened, to stop her slipping away. And just to talk to her. Only that.

There was a bit of a wait.

She either didn't notice me or she did a good job of pretending she didn't notice me. And when the fashionable young couple ahead of me were escorted to their table by one of Anton's politely hot young waiters, she looked up and I saw her smile freeze.

She hadn't noticed me then.

It was some kind of Asian dress she was wearing. Chinese, I guessed. A *cheongsam*. It clung to her long, lean frame. That dress really loved her.

She looked stunning. Even with the frozen smile.

'Wait for me outside, will you?' she said, moving me to one side with a small lift of her eyebrows.

168

And then Anton was there, all solicitous, only slightly embarrassed by my unannounced presence.

'My friend,' he said, touching my arm, and somehow I knew that he loved her too. 'I will find you a place at the bar. Come.'

But I would have been imposing on Anton's hospitality for Le Poisson Imaginaire's small bar was already full of diners waiting for their tables. Michelle, Anton's effortlessly elegant wife, was standing at the far end of the bar, sipping a glass of champagne. Michelle had been Le Poisson Imaginaire's original hostess. She looked at me with something like bleak amusement, as if there was no place in these changing times for either of us. And I could see the kitchen, smell the kitchen, see how busy they were tonight. But Anton would have found me a space, and brought me a glass of something sparkling. He was my friend.

But it was not what she wanted.

'I'll see you on the beach, Tom.'

I nodded mutely, not moving.

'I may be some time,' Clementine said.

I wanted to hold her and she didn't even want to see me. These things were excruciatingly plain. But the look in her eyes was not unreasonable. *I'm working,* that look said.

Anton was smiling by my side, ready to escort me to the bar.

'I'll wait for you,' I said.

Forever, I wanted to say.

But I held my stupid tongue, and I said nothing, and I went down to the beach to wait for her.

There are no beaches like these in the world.

Not in the Caribbean, or in Australia, or in Asia.

The beaches on that particular stretch of north Cornish coast look like the beaches you see in dreams, or commercials – soft, golden sand that goes on forever, beaches so big that even the height of the season would not fill them. And always, in this part of the county, the big waves with their pluming whitecaps, rolling in forever.

We could live here, I thought. Truly, we could build a life here together. The north coast was more her speed, I saw now – the endless beaches, the wine lists, the restaurants with stars by their names and chefs imported from London and Paris and New York. Location, location. Maybe I should have thought about all that when I rocked up in St Jude's all those years ago. But the Lobster Pot had been more than enough for me. The little fishing village where I had built a life had been enough. And it was only now, standing on the beach and watching the surfers, the fairy lights that decorated Le Poisson Imaginaire twinkling like jewels behind me, that I saw with awful clarity that my life in St Jude's would never be enough for her.

'I can't stay long,' she said.

She seemed shorter than when I stood before her, dumbfounded, in the restaurant. Ah, her shoes — those fancy ones with the red soles and the high heels — were in her right hand. She could not wear those shoes on the beach.

'How are you?' I tried a smile that didn't quite make it.

She brushed a rogue lock of copper-red hair from her pale face. There was a dusting of freckles across her nose from where she had spent too long in the sun.

'Busy,' she said.

'We need to talk,' I said, and she waited for me to say what to me was painfully obvious. 'About Steve. About what happened.'

A flash of panic in those green, green eyes. She held up her hands. 'You know what? I really *don't* need to talk about Steve. I *left* Steve. Why would I need to talk about Steve?' She looked back at the restaurant as if she should be there now.

'Please listen to me,' I said. 'Lisa is talking about going to the police.'

She licked her lips. Breathing was suddenly a problem for her.

She composed herself quickly.

'Lisa must do what she thinks is right and proper,' she said. 'And I don't know quite what you mean. And – you have to understand – I don't know what you have done – what you have all done. And please listen to me, Tom – *I don't want to know*.'

She went to walk away. She was actually walking away. I could not believe it.

'*We did this for you*,' I said.

'For me? No, Tom. You did it for yourself. Lisa stuck that . . . thing . . .'

'Lobster pick.'

'That *lobster pick* in Steve's neck because he was taunting her, he was abusing her in that special Steve way he has of beating a woman up with words.'

Steve was still in her present tense, I noted.

'That's why Lisa did what she did – I saw it, Tom! She didn't do it for me. Lisa – I like her! – but she did me no favours by assaulting my ex-husband with a sharp object. *It is not what I wanted*. It was not what I ever wanted. And Will did not cart him down to the icehouse for me. And you didn't tie him up for me, Tom – you did it because you wanted to shut his mouth, you wanted to punish him.' She shrugged. 'Because – let's be frank – you wanted me for yourself.'

'They will come looking for him,' I said. 'Sooner or later. The law. You know they will. Someone is going to report him missing. That big ugly sergeant. His stepfather. Sergeant Monk. He's not going to let it go, is he?'

'Missing,' she said, as if someone going missing was her specialist subject on *Mastermind*. 'You know how many people go missing every year in this country? Almost two hundred thousand! That's an entire town of the missing, Tom. People who are dead and never found. People who walk away from their lives. If Steve didn't go home – and personally I have no reason to believe he didn't go home – then he is just another one of the missing.'

I shook my head. 'They're coming for him. Because I don't think he's ever going to make it back home.'

'I don't want to know!'

'And when they do, they'll be coming for all of us.'

'*Not me.*'

I stared out at sea.

There was one lone surfer far out, catching the last wave of the gathering evening. I watched him rise, and I saw him fall.

And I almost believed her. I almost believed that we did it for ourselves.

But not quite.

'And what about Bet Farthing? You know what Bet calls you?'

Clementine smiled fondly. 'Bet calls me *my lovely.*'

I shook my head. 'No, Bet calls everyone *my lovely.* She calls you *ow meider.* It's old Cornish. It means *my honey.* It's—'

Something choked up inside me and I could not tell her how much *ow meider* meant. It was special. Bet did not say it to everyone. Only her.

'And what about Charlie?' I said.

'Come on,' she said. 'Charlie Farthing had a crush on me. You know he did.'

She acted as if it happened all the time. And of course it did! It had been happening for years, men giving her hearts she never asked them for.

'The Farthings didn't do it for themselves,' I said. 'They did it for *you.* They're good people. They are the best people I ever met.'

She looked at the fairy lights in Le Poisson Imaginaire. She glanced out at sea. Everywhere but at me.

A wind was up now. She brushed some sand from her hands. I waited for her to show – not gratitude, no, but just some acknowledgement that we did what we did because we wanted to protect her. That was part of her power. Beyond the rare beauty there was a fragility that needed protecting, there was something precious – priceless – that was easily smashed to bits. And there was more – it's true I wanted more. I wanted her to see how much I loved her, and to hear her say it meant something. But she looked at me directly and I had seen that look in a previous lifetime.

It is the goodbye look.

'I've met someone,' Clementine said.

20

Sergeant Monk was the first to come looking. He came before all of them. Steve's massive stepfather came before the real police, the police who were involved in the investigation, and he came before the cameras, and he came before the ghouls who love to have a mini-break in someone else's misery.

He was looking for someone he was never going to find.

And perhaps he sensed it.

I did not recognise him at first. Partly this was because of the crowds. The season proper had started now, and the quay and the beach and the downalongs were crowded with outsiders. But mostly I did not recognise him because he was no longer wearing his pristine police sergeant's uniform. He wore shorts and a T-shirt and trainers, every inch the middle-aged emmet on his holidays, holding his ice cream like a microphone as he stared out to sea, ready to report some breaking news to the seagulls.

Standing up on the deck of the Lobster Pot, I could have missed that one man among the crowds, if he had not turned his head and looked up at me, his meaty features set in impassive loathing.

And my face began to throb in that instant; high on the cheekbone where Steve had smashed his fist, the bone pulsed with a memory of pain and humiliation that was indistinguishable from the real thing.

'*I know what you did!*'

I started with shock, my heart leaping. The voice – raised, angry, shaking with emotion – came from behind me, inside the restaurant. I turned towards it as Ryan carried on laying the tables out on the deck, oblivious behind his Apple AirPods, and as Lisa tore up fresh lobsters in the kitchen. Only I had heard the voice.

'I said – I know what you did.'

A man in the shadows came forward. And I half-expected it to be Sergeant Monk, even though I knew that was impossible, that the fat old cop was down on the quay with his Cornetto.

It was Oliver Winter. He had lost that smooth London sheen, and his accent had a trace of Essex menace in it now, and he was trembling with rage.

'*I know what you fucking did, you little bastard!*'

I shook my head, pleading ignorance. But he had brushed straight past me as if I was not there.

He had been talking to Ryan. The boy looked up from his table-laying chores, and I saw the guilt and fear in his dreamy eyes.

'Stay away from my daughter, you little shit!'

I had a memory of the Winter girl. I had not seen as much of her as I had of the boy, but I remembered a long-haired, Bambi-limbed girl, staring at her phone, either bored out of her brains or doing a good impersonation of it.

Ryan was now backing away from her enraged father. He had a dazed, slightly surprised look on his face – although to be fair to Ryan he always looked that way, as if he was surprised to find himself on dry land when he would have preferred to be on a surfboard on the north coast.

Lisa had looked up now and was watching with mild curiosity, as if the appearance of an angry dad confronting our boy waiter was not quite enough to shake her from her own thoughts.

'We're in love,' Ryan said, as if that explained everything.

And perhaps it did!

I stepped out on to the deck where Winter had cornered Ryan, telling myself I would only get involved if it turned violent. But Ryan's talk of love seemed to take some of the steam out of Winter's anger.

'Love?' he chuckled. 'Saskia is going to *Cambridge*. Do you honestly think she is going to give all that up for a misjudged summer romance with some ignorant yokel?'

'Enough,' I said. Because his words, his snobbery, his middle-class arrogance, it all felt like a kind of violence.

Winter turned to look at me. 'The money I've spent in this shithole,' he said.

'That bought you dinner,' I said. 'It didn't buy us. You've said your piece. Please – leave now, Mr Winter.'

'Just keep him away from my daughter,' he said, jerking a contemptuous thumb at Ryan. 'If you don't want the police on you.'

He left us alone. I looked at Ryan, then down to the quay.

Monk was nowhere to be seen.

'Sit down,' I told Ryan.

We sat at a table for two with a sea view.

'How old is this girl?'

'Saskia. She's great, Tom. Her eyes, her mouth. I've never met anyone like her.'

'I'm sure she's great. How old is she?'

'Eighteen. Nearly.' He paused. 'Same as me.'

I didn't know what to say to him. Perhaps if I had had a son, I would have been full of paternal wisdom. But I never had a son.

'Look,' I said. 'I don't think it's going to work out with you and Saskia.'

Ryan held up his hands. 'I know we come from different worlds,' he said. 'You don't have to tell me about it.' His West Country accent had never seemed broader to me. 'And I know that she's going off to university.' He brightened a little, finding a reason for hope. 'But I could visit, right? Visit her at uni, like. And they get long holidays, those students. Saskia is going to come down here in the holidays. Help me when – you know – I open my surf shop.'

'She's eighteen years old,' I said. 'She's going to meet lots of people. And you're going to meet lots of people too. And many of those people – the ones she meets at university, and the women you meet down here – will be great people. This is what you don't get, Ryan, until you're older – *there's lots of people who you could love.*'

He smiled as if he pitied me.

'But we both know that's not true, don't we?' He leaned forward and fixed me with his stoned surfer's gaze. 'There's *not* lots of people you can love, is there? In the end, really, there's only one.'

We sat in silence out on the deck of the Lobster Pot. St Jude's sounded different now the season had begun. The soundtrack of sea and birdsong had been joined by car engines inching along the esplanade, music coming from multiple places, and the laughter and cries of the children.

'I don't know how you did it,' I said.

He looked hurt. 'Saskia's lovely.'

'No, I get the raging hormones bit. I mean – I don't know how you got away with it. I can't understand how it got this far. You live at home with your mum and dad in the old town. Saskia's with her folks at some self-catering cottage miles away.' I shook my head, amazed that young love had found a way. 'Where did the pair of you go?'

Ryan glanced towards the kitchen and then lowered his voice.

'The Baulking House,' he said. 'We've been going up there ever since that first night they came to the Lobster Pot. She sneaks away from her parents, and I go up when I'm not working – every chance I get. And sometimes she can't get away because her mum wants her to look at some paintings or sculpture or something. But often she does. And there's nobody around, up at the Baulking House. You know, where they watched for the sea to turn black with pilchards in the olden days? I would wait for her hours sometimes. Just staring out to sea.'

We stared at each other for a long time. His dazed surfer's gaze looking straight through me.

'It's up on the coastal path beyond Maggie's Cove,' he said. 'The Baulking House, I mean.'

'I know where the Baulking House is,' I said.

'I'm sorry, Tom. I really am.'

I had stopped breathing.

'Why are you sorry?' I said, although I already knew.

'Because I saw what you did,' Ryan said.

21

When the lunch trade was done – and it was like the peak of the season already, all the tables taken with more punters at the door, smacking their lips at the thought of lobster Thermidor, Newburg or grilled – I walked the coastal path up to Maggie's Cove and beyond, where the sounds of St Jude's faded away and there was only the high winds that always blew here, sounding as though they were whipping through the sails of ghost ships.

She met someone.

The road grew ever wilder. Dipping down to black cliffs, then climbing steeply to the winding coastal path, the bends and turns in this part of the coast soon leaving all that was behind me long gone.

She met someone.

Well, of course! How could she not meet someone? Standing under the fairy lights at Le Poisson Imaginaire with her big smile and her tight dress – she was always going to meet lots of someones. And how stupid I was, I thought as my legs ached with the effort of the rising road, how stupid I was to think for a second that I would ever be enough for her. What did I think? That we would live out our days in my poky little flat with the wheezing boiler and watch the sunrise – ten thousand sunrises – from the deck of the Lobster Pot?

Yes, that was exactly what I thought, and planned, and pinned my pathetic dreams to. Those ten thousand sunrises.

But Clementine had met someone.

And either he lived on the north coast, or he was staying there, because as the days and nights went by, her cottage in St Jude's was left empty, as deserted as it had been before she came, as if she had never been there at all, as if we had never shared a bed, as if I had never watched her face as she slept.

I reached the top of the rise, and paused to find my breath, and there it was before me.

The Baulking House.

I walked towards it, and the coastal path edged perilously close to the cliff edge, and the drop to the rocks below would have been like stepping off the roof of a skyscraper, a vertiginous and very swift drop to oblivion.

I reached the Baulking House, a medium-sized cottage – whitewashed brick walls, three windows boarded with black wood – two above, one below – like a child's drawing of a surprised face. And on either side, the bus stops with their wooden benches that were not bus stops at all, but the place where a hundred years ago the *huer* – the watcher – had kept lookout for the day the sea turned alive with a billion pilchards, and he lit his bonfires to call every single man, woman and child in St Jude's and Polmouth to the boats, with the happy knowledge that they would eat this winter.

Now the pilchards were long fished into oblivion, and the sea was empty of boats, and the wind whipped through the rafters of the Baulking House as I opened the door and went inside. A sleeping bag and a few empty Bad Apple cider bottles were the only evidence of Ryan and Saskia's presence.

I came out of the Baulking House and took a seat in the *huer*'s lookout and stared out to sea.

And that was when I saw it.

Trapped between the teeth of two black rocks, much closer to the shore than where I had thrown it. The purple paddleboard. Or at least a broken fragment of it, pinned tight between two jagged rocks as the wind and the sea whipped it but could not dislodge it. Even from up here, the garish man-made colour stood out against the black of the rocks, the deep blue of the sea and the foaming whitecaps of the breaking waves.

I walked to the edge of the cliff, the panic in my veins, staring at it – and I saw it more clearly now – the broken shard of Steve's paddleboard, perhaps half of it, maybe a bit less, wedged with stubborn determination between the rocks.

Someone called my name, and the sound was almost lost in the wind.

'I came to check everything is all right,' Charlie Farthing said.

'It's not,' I said, and he followed my gaze to the rocks below. I watched him stare at the broken paddleboard, and my heart sank. You could not miss it.

Charlie smiled coldly.

'This is good for us,' he said.

'How the fuck is it good for us, Charlie?'

'Don't you see? It's a tragic accident. Some dumb emmet took out a paddleboard further than a paddleboard should ever go and didn't even have the wit to wear a life jacket. He never wore a life jacket this guy, did he? Steve?'

I shook my head. 'No life jacket for Steve.'

'No life jacket,' Charlie said with some satisfaction. 'No training. Probably half pissed – or a bit more than half pissed. Then he decides it's a good time to go out into waters where he knows less than nothing about the currents and the tides and the rocks.' We looked down at the broken purple board. 'Came off his board. Smacked his stupid head. Happens all the time,' Charlie said. 'Especially this time of year. The crowds have come but the sea is still choppy. And even when it is dead calm, it can still kill you with no trouble.' Charlie punched my arm with some force. 'Don't you see? This is *good* for us.'

'Not if somebody saw.'

'What?'

'It's not good news if somebody saw us. It's not good news if someone saw your boat and watched me throwing Steve's kit into the sea. Then it's not good news, is it? Then it's not an obvious accident, is it, Charlie?'

He stared at me silently, squinting and wincing as the wind whipped his face.

'Who saw us?' he said.

'Ryan,' I said.

'The surfer?'

'Yes.'

'How did Ryan—' His eyes drifted to the Baulking House behind us. 'Ah – Ryan was probably up here with some maid, was he?' Charlie stared at the ancient cottage. 'I used to come up here with girls myself. There's nowhere else to go in St Jude's. Who's the girl?'

'Saskia. The Winters' daughter. The London family.'

'And did *she* see?'

I felt sick. The thought had not crossed my mind.

'I don't know. I don't think so. Ryan didn't say.'

'What does it prove?' Charlie demanded. 'Even if they saw us. Even if they took pictures with their phones. It proves bugger all.'

'That's right,' I said weakly, wanting it to be true, not believing it for a second.

We stared at the rocks far below.

'They're never going to find the body, are they?' I said.

'No. And Ryan's not going to say anything, is he?'

'Of course not.'

'That's good,' Charlie said. 'Because the police are here.'

22

DCI GRAVES: *It is not illegal to go missing. Going missing is not a criminal offence. Going missing is a choice that many, many people make. And you have every right to go missing unless you have been detained under the Mental Health Act, or you are in the care of another person. And if you go missing and we locate you, then you have the right to stay missing once we have determined that you are safe and sound. So – go missing if you must. But – you knew there was a but, didn't you? – if you go missing, then there's one thing you always have to remember.*

I am obliged to come looking for you.

Lisa and I were out on the deck of the Lobster Pot, watching the crowds gather down on the quay. There were all sorts, and every sort. Tourists, as if this drama was an unexpected part of the holiday. Locals, responding with that unthinking and unconditional community spirit that held St Jude's together. And on the fringe of the crowd, already pulling on their white spaceman suits, the police search team.

A small, older woman was addressing the crowd. She was standing on some kind of box so they could see her at the back. She had the amiable authority of a well-loved headmistress. She had to be nearly sixty and she was tiny, smiley, knocking on a bit — but when she spoke, everyone listened. And that was my first sight of Detective Chief Inspector Gillian Graves. She had come to St Jude's because a man had been reported missing.

'We should join them,' I said. 'Join the search.'

Lisa shot me a look. 'Are you out of your mind?'

'It will look strange if we don't help.'

'I don't care how it looks!'

Ryan came out on the deck.

'Are we opening up today? Everywhere else in town is closing. Because of all this caper.' He jerked his chin, indicating the crowds down on the quay, receiving their final instructions from DCI Graves. 'Because of the search party.'

'We're closing,' I told him. 'But let me pay you for today.'

Leaving Lisa out on the deck, Ryan and I went back into the quiet of the restaurant. He watched me open the till at the reception desk and take out some cash. He cleared his throat.

'Can I get an advance on next week?' he said.

I looked at him.

He stared boldly back at me with his dazed surfer's stare. There was a long moment's silence when both of us reflected on what he had seen – and all he had not seen – when he was waiting for his girl up on the windy cliffs outside the Baulking House.

I smiled at him. It was not the easiest thing I ever did. Ryan licked his sun-cracked lips and grinned at me.

'No problem,' I said, counting out the extra notes.

I headed down the steep stone steps to the esplanade, as the search party set off in all directions.

Some were heading inland, to the meadows and woods above St Jude's, others were climbing up to the coastal path. And some were going out to sea, for the boats of St Jude's were searching too. There was a small flotilla heading for the mouth of the estuary, fishing boats and pleasure boats and a couple of larger yachts from the other side, Polmouth, the big bluewater sailboats that you only ever saw during the season.

I joined the search party that was heading down the coastal path towards Maggie's Cove.

Ahead of me, among the crowds, their mood strangely excited, I could see Anton, and although I would have preferred to walk alone, I found myself hurrying to catch up with my friend after he waved to me. Unlike the majority of the search party, Anton's mood was subdued and sad.

'This beautiful place,' he said. 'And every year it claims so many. They're not going to find him alive, are they?' He paused. 'I knew he would come to a bad end. The night I saw him for the first time. At the restaurant in London. Arguing with her. I saw the violence in him.'

He waited for me to say something – a confession?

But I was staring at the tourists ahead, giddy with excitement, and high up on that coastal path, the wind punished my face until my eyes were streaming. Anton and I trudged on in silence. The police search team in their white suits moved ahead, setting the pace. The crowd followed, festive and laughing.

And then there she was, coming over the crest of the meadow that rose beyond the coastal path, holding the arm of a man I had never seen – gripping him so tightly she seemed to fear she may blow away in that high, gusty place.

The man Clementine held onto had the aura of a well-heeled bohemian about him. Cornwall was full of them. He was perhaps ten years older than her, at the far end of his thirties perhaps, my generation, and a good-looking man, studiedly casual in his Hunter boots and Barbour jacket. A scarf was tied loosely around his neck – an affectation that made me hate him even more, if that was possible, and it wasn't.

The sight of them together filled me with the all-consuming sickness of jealousy.

They joined the search team towards the front, and if Clementine noticed me, she gave no sign.

'He's a painter,' Anton said. 'They come down here for the summer. The artists, I mean. It has always been a big part of the county's charm. They have been coming for nearly two hundred years. Since they built the first railway. The Newlyn School. The St Ives school. Barbara Hepworth, Patrick Heron. They come for the light. That heavenly light we take for granted. He met her at Le Poisson Imaginaire . . .' He paused, perhaps considering an apology or expression of regret, as if he had been some kind of accidental matchmaker. He spared me that humiliation.

'What does he paint?' I asked, as if it mattered.

'The sea. The coast. All of this. His paintings are good – at least, he makes a living, apparently. Clementine showed me some of them on her phone.

Seascapes. Paintings that look like this place but seen in a dream.'

And I knew then that she was gone from me forever.

Then we heard the screaming up ahead and my heart fell away because it meant that they had found Steve, or at least found evidence that he was not going to be found alive.

But it was Sergeant Monk, and he must have been near the front of the search party, somewhere between the police and the tourists. And he had seen Clementine.

The police were already pulling him away from her.

'You bitch! Your murdering bitch! *She* killed him! My boy! My beautiful boy! My son!'

Then we saw him no more, and we walked on to Maggie's Cove and beyond, and to the lonely part of the coastal path where the wind never stopped.

A young woman fell into step beside us.

'Who was *that* guy?' she laughed. 'The screamer?'

She's a tourist, I thought, enjoying the fun. You could tell from her shoes – some kind of funky trainers, totally inappropriate for walking the coastal path. She was full of the brittle bonhomie of the big city. But Anton fell into the usual conversation with her – where are you from? How long are you staying? – and it turned out she was not here for entertainment.

'I'm a journalist,' she said, and a distant alarm bell rang. 'Scarlet Bush. Like the porn star.'

I looked at her properly. She was young, early twenties, fresh-faced and friendly, wrapped up in a thin coat that was not fit for this weather on this high and windy path, and there was something in her eyes that made me wary of her, a hungry, knowing look that reminded me of the people I knew in another time.

'It's a hard industry to make a name for yourself in these days,' she said. 'It's even hard to make a living. But everybody loves a scoop.' She nodded at the search party. 'Land your scoop and the doors still open up. Podcasts, panel show, book deals, reviewing the papers on breakfast TV. I thought there might be something here – the missing policeman.'

'There's nothing here,' I said, when I should have said nothing.

'Tom was a journalist,' Anton said.

She looked at me with interest. 'Oh? Who for?'

'All over.'

'What was your beat?'

'I was on the back bench.'

'It must have been great. Back in the day.' Did I look that old? 'Four-hour lunches at El Vino's. Papers selling millions a week. No Internet!'

I forced a smile. 'It was great and then it wasn't so great.'

'And then you moved down here.'

Anton patted my back. 'Tom has a good restaurant – the Lobster Pot in St Jude's.'

Stop talking, Anton.

The journalist – she had told us her name but I had forgotten it immediately – chattered on but then we turned a sharp bend on a rising part of the coastal path, and I did not hear her words anymore, because there was the Baulking House.

I stared down at the sea, expecting to see the paddleboard far down in the rocks below, flapping in the wind like a plastic purple tombstone. But it was almost totally gone, carried away by the whim of the sea.

Almost but not quite.

One thin shard of it remained, inexplicably refusing to be carried out to sea, grotesque against the black rocks but no longer recognisable as part of the thing it had been. Nobody noticed, nobody saw. The great incriminating mass of Steve's purple paddleboard was gone forever.

So that was the good news.

The bad news was that they had found the body.

23

DCI GRAVES: *People get hurt in paradise. That's just a fact. Happens all the time. Happens every season. They take risks that they would never take back in their real life. Out on the water, three sheets to the wind, dicking about in a kayak or a sailing boat when they shouldn't be skipper of a rubber ducky. Driving too fast on roads they don't know. Taking a bloody selfie on some part of the coastal path that is just about to drop into the sea. And then they don't turn up at their rented fisherman's cottage for their pasty-of-the-day because they are lying at the bottom of a cliff with two broken legs, or perhaps one broken neck. So muggins here, or someone just like her, has to go looking for them – the missing. But there is another reason why outsiders get hurt in this beautiful place. Because people in this county are a bit different to everyone everywhere else. And they always have been. Read* Jamaica Inn. *Read* Frenchman's Creek. *Read* Rebecca, *for God's sake. Daphne du Maurier will explain it to you better than I ever could.*

These people were smugglers, wreckers, outlaws. Not all of them. Of course not. Some went to sea. Some dug for tin. Hard, honest lives. But somewhere deep down inside all of them — and I do mean all of them — the rebel gene is still in the blood and bones. The locals think the rules don't apply to them.

We stood on the quayside of St Jude's and we watched the big Spanish trawler entering the mouth of the estuary. It came to port slowly, as if observing some ancient funeral rite for those lost at sea, and the fishing fleet of our village were its guard, the 25-foot boats tiny next to the Spanish trawler, four times their size, the mouth of its trawl net big enough to scoop up everything on the bottom of the sea or mid-water as it passed.

Even the remains of what had once been a man.

As the Spanish vessel approached St Jude's the skipper must have given a signal, because the net was slowly hoisted and we saw him clear now, Steve's body covered in smaller creatures, adorning him like jewellery, glittering and shining in the spring sunshine as he lay on the net's bed of larger fish.

For the first time that day, the crowds who had flocked to St Jude's were totally silent. In front of me, a father turned his child's face away. Behind me a woman began to weep. The trawler edged closer to the quay, as tenderly as it could, and the crew of the Spanish trawler hauled their net on board.

Through the front of the crowd the police began to move forward. Ready to take charge.

And we all watched, as if we were part of some eternal ritual we were bound to attend, even if we could not discern its true meaning. But there was a solemnity on the faces of the crew who lined the deck – mostly Spanish, they looked, with men from Africa and the Philippines among their number – and they watched us watching them. And we all watched. Charlie from the deck of the *Pleasure Dome*. Will on the bridge of the *Bonnie Bet*, one of the ships that had accompanied the trawler into port. Lisa by my side, gripping my hand. Ryan moved through the crowd, his ponytail bobbing, unsettled by it all.

'Old Steve always loved being on the water,' someone said, a London accent, close to tears.

We watched the net being opened, and the body being lifted from the net and carried back to land. We all stood and watched and paid our respects for those in peril on the sea.

Apart from Clementine.

She was already with the police.

24

DCI GRAVES: *When the next of kin identifies a body, you see all sorts of reactions. Some people unravel, just come apart, and you know they will never put themselves back together again.*

Not in that room.

And then — rarer, but it happens — you see the other end of the spectrum. Not a single tear. Not even surprise.

Call it shock but it is more like someone is trying to comprehend what is quite literally unimaginable. A different world. A life suddenly taken. The brain refuses to process the new reality. It denies the evidence. And that was what she was like. Dry-eyed. Calm. Totally in control.

I shivered as Mrs Clementine Monk looked at the body of her late husband, and that was only partly because the temperature is kept just above zero in a morgue. I shivered because there should have been more of an emotional reaction when the morgue technician

pulled back the sheet and showed her the husband who
had been in the water for a week. I shivered because
she should have cared more.
And I shivered because her words shocked me.
'That's not him,' she said.

We gathered in the kitchen of the Farthings' cottage.

Will and Bet and Lisa and me at the kitchen table.

And Charlie pacing the tiny space, his blood boiling, endlessly pacing, like a creature in a cage too small for it, tormented and maddened by its captivity. Night came and nobody turned on the lights. It was as if we could speak more honestly in the twilight, our faces in darkness.

'You said that the body would never be found,' Charlie told his father, his words slow and deliberate. 'You said – and I quote – *the police are not the only people who know how to hide a dead body*. I thought you were the expert, Dad.'

'There are no experts, son,' Will said calmly. 'You never know with a body in water. In cold water it takes longer for a body to decompose. It takes longer for the crabs and fish to get nibbling. And you never know what those big Spanish nets are going to catch.' Will shrugged. 'Big net, bad luck. And a bit of bloating will get them floating.'

Lisa lowered her head. 'Oh God,' she said. 'What have we done?'

'Nobody's going to suspect foul play,' Bet said cheerfully, getting up to put the kettle on again.

'Suspect foul play?' Charlie exploded. 'My God, Mum, you sound like we're in an Agatha Christie story. Don't you get it? Any of you? *They have found him*. And now they are going to find out exactly how he died.'

'Don't bet good money on that,' Will said. 'Not after a week in the water. Whatever the temperature.' He stirred his tea. 'The sea hides its secrets.'

Lisa was staring at me. 'And what about Ryan?' she said.

I shot her a look. How did she know about Ryan?

'He showed me,' she said, answering the unspoken question. 'On his phone. Because he did what every eighteen-year-old does, Tom. *He took a photograph*. Because if he doesn't take a photograph, he can't be sure of what he really saw, and he can't be certain it actually happened. But he's sure of this all right.'

'Don't worry about Ryan,' I said quickly. 'Ryan's fine.'

Will Farthing looked dumbfounded.

'Wait a minute – *what about Ryan?*'

'Ryan's been taking the Winter girl up to the Baulking House beyond Maggie's Cove,' I said. 'He may have seen us throw away the paddleboard.'

'He *may* have seen it?' Will said.

I felt a tremor of irritation. 'All right – he *did* see it.'

Will shook his head with disbelief. 'And why didn't you tell me, Tom? You've got to keep the skipper informed of all developments, lad.'

'Because Ryan's nothing to worry about,' I said. 'Because you didn't need to know. And because I already told Charlie up at the Baulking House and I wish I hadn't. Because look at the state of him. I'm worried about you, Charlie. You're wound too tight.'

Charlie took a breath, tried to calm himself.

'Topping a tourist then dumping his body in the briny,' he said. 'Bound to be a bit of stress involved, wouldn't you say, Tom?'

'Is he keeping his mouth shut?' Will said. 'Young Ryan?'

'He asked me for money. Next week's earnings.'

'Blackmail?' Charlie said.

'It's not blackmail, all right? He's a good kid, but he knows what he saw and he has a picture. So he asked me for money. He needs money. He always needs money. We don't need to worry about Ryan. He's not going to post it on Instagram.'

Charlie thought about it. 'Well, young Ryan wants to watch his step,' he said. 'Or he'll be next.'

I felt my blood spike with anger.

'He'll be next? What are you – a hit man now, Charlie?'

He was suddenly calm.

'If Ryan tries to tap you up for money again, Tom, then let me know.'

Charlie had been my closest friend in St Jude's when I first arrived. The amiable young local had acted as my guide. To Charlie I had been – I don't know – some kind of ambassador from a fantasy city that existed only in his head.

But Charlie and I were not friends tonight. We didn't even like each other.

'We did it for *her*,' Lisa said, close to tears. 'Why isn't *she* here?'

'It's not her fault,' I said, remembering Clementine's words outside Le Poisson Imaginaire. 'She never wanted this, she never asked for this. She just wanted to be free and safe and to start again.'

Lisa turned on me. 'Of course it's her fault! None of this would have happened if she hadn't come to St Jude's. Why do you stick up for her, Tom? Even now? She should *be* here. She should at least take her share of the blame, of the weight. She should be part of this – not having her arse shagged off in some second home by her fancy man.'

Bet placed fresh tea in front of all of us. She eased her large frame into a kitchen chair.

'That lad – Steve – got what was coming to him,' Will said philosophically. 'You come down here, you should respect this place. Respect the locals.'

Lisa laughed bitterly. 'Locals? Clementine – *Tina* – whatever her name really is – had only been here for half an hour when he showed up.' She shook her head at me and Charlie. 'So stupid, the pair of you. Letting someone see you.'

'Be kind to each other,' Bet scolded us. 'We have to be kind to each other now.'

'We're all going to jail!' Lisa said. 'How much kindness is there going to be in jail, Bet?'

'Stop it, my lovely,' Bet said. 'Nobody's going to jail, you hear me?'

'It's going to ruin our lives,' Lisa said.

Bet took her hands.

'It's *not* going to ruin our lives. Is that what you think, you silly thing? It all ends – our lives in St Jude's because of him? One violent husband? One bad copper? We didn't ask him to come down here. He came anyway. And – look at me, Lisa – *we have not done anything wrong.*'

But the pulsing blue lights of the police car came slowly down the esplanade and edged through the narrow winding streets of the old town, and we sat there saying nothing at all as the lights finally filled the tiny kitchen of the fisherman's cottage as it stopped right outside the front door of the Farthing home, first bathing our faces in the harsh blue light, and then plunging us back into the shadows.

25

The following morning, DCI Graves came slowly up the stone steps from the esplanade.

She was not a young woman, and she could have been one of the gentle, bookish visitors who come to our part of the world carrying a battered paperback copy of something by John Betjeman or Winston Graham or Daphne du Maurier, more at home hiking the coastal path in sensible footwear and seeking out the real-life locations for the Poldark novels than chomping on a pasty with the milling crowds beside the sea. I stood on the deck of the Lobster Pot, and my mouth was dry. She smiled when she saw me waiting. A warm, genuine smile. She looked too old to be investigating murder.

A nice lady, I thought.

Who had it within her power to ruin all of our lives.

'Mr Cooper? DCI Graves. We didn't meet. But I think I saw you on the search party.'

We shook hands. Her handshake was gentle and there were generations of the West Country in her voice.

They had taken Charlie away late last night – blameless Charlie, the only one of us who could lay some claim to innocence. They had been scrupulously polite. We had watched him being taken away in stunned silence. He had not come home.

I didn't like to ask. But she told me anyway.

'Your friend – Mr Farthing – is helping us with our enquiries,' she said as we took a seat on the deck, squinting against the bright morning sunshine. 'He's been very helpful. There have been some initial problems with our investigation.' A beat. 'Mrs Monk failed to identify the body of her late husband.'

It took me a long moment to realise that she was talking about Clementine.

Mrs Monk. Yet another name for her I have to learn and remember.

The kind, birdlike detective was all sympathy.

'It can be an impossible task for the next of kin. Identifying a body. The mind is in shock. Denial. And there is the real problem that she could simply not recognise him. But we could. Dental records. A skull tattoo on his left buttock. And Stephen Monk was a former police officer. We know it is Stephen

Monk, whatever difficulties Mrs Monk may have recognising him. There's no question – it's him. What we don't know is how he died.'

'There are over three hundred miles of coastline in Cornwall,' I said, as casual as I could manage. 'A lot can go wrong out there. And it does. Every year. As you know.'

She nodded, and that was when I misjudged her, that was when I thought she would be easy to fool. That was when I kept talking, filling in the silence with my stupid mouth.

'People get drunk,' I said. 'People get cocky.' I thought of dear, departed Steve. 'They take chances they should never take.' She stared out at the estuary, the spring sunshine turning the water to molten gold, and I was not sure if she had heard me. 'Is that what you think happened to Mr Monk?' I asked.

She chuckled. 'That's what we hope to find out. That's the subject of our investigation. That's what Mr Farthing is helping us with.'

'But – why would you think that Charlie had anything to do with it?'

She looked genuinely surprised.

'Because Mr Farthing threatened to kill Stephen Monk,' she said.

I felt my heart drop to my stomach.

TONY PARSONS

I felt my cheekbone throb with the memory of pain and humiliation.

I remembered the night the Monks had taken Clementine away – no, the night she had gone with them.

And his brute of a stepfather had held me while Steve drove his fist deep into my face, one punch enough to end all debate and doubt.

I remembered Sergeant Monk's big paws holding me while Steve punched my lights out.

'Threats were made on a man's life,' DCI Graves said, almost regretful. 'And then that man lost his life.'

And I remembered Charlie with tears streaming down his face, screaming after them as they drove up to the cream-and-blue cottage.

I'll kill you.

I'll kill you.

I'll kill you.

'Somebody heard,' Graves told me. 'They heard Mr Farthing threaten to kill Mr Monk.'

I shook my head. 'No,' I said. 'Oh, no. That's not true.'

She shook her head, and if she was not such a nice lady, I may have thought that she was mocking me.

'He didn't say it? But we had multiple reports that Mr Farthing threatened to kill Mr Monk.'

'What does multiple reports mean?'

'It means – more than one,' she said drily.

'But that doesn't mean he did it. People say it – they say it all the time. Don't they?'

'But then Mr Monk actually died. I agree that it is unlikely Mr Farthing acted alone. If Mr Monk was murdered, then someone managed to get an 85 kilogram body out to sea. And I don't believe anyone can do that alone. But you can see my problem, Mr Cooper. A death threat that was followed by death.' She sighed. 'Mr Farthing hasn't been charged with anything. Nobody has been charged with anything. Our enquiries are ongoing.' She smiled wryly. 'Let's hope they don't go on too long and everyone can go back to enjoying their holiday.'

I could not let it go. 'There was some violence,' I said. 'Not by Charlie. Never by Charlie – who is the sweetest, kindest man. When Mr Monk came looking for Mrs Monk.' I was babbling now. 'Charlie – he had nothing to do with it.'

'Yes, Mrs Monk,' Graves nodded. 'Yes, we understand there was some unpleasantness. And then some more unpleasantness during the search. And we know that Mrs Monk has had multiple partners since arriving in St Jude's.'

'What does multiple partners mean?' I said, unable to keep the annoyance out of my voice.

'It means more than one,' Graves said. 'That's what multiple always means, Mr Cooper. More than one.'

We stared at each other.

'You,' she said. 'And Charles Farthing. Multiple lovers.'

I thought of the day Clementine swam across the water and Charlie picked her up on the other side. I remembered the sleepless night I had spent wondering what had happened when he walked her home to the cream-and-blue cottage. The night of the lock-in at the Rabbit Hole. It was all seared into my memory forever. But what I remembered most of all was the pathetic gratitude I had felt when Lisa said that Clementine and Charlie did not look like two people who had just had sex.

'She didn't – I don't think . . .'

But how do you know, Tom? I thought. How can you ever really know?

'Charles – Mr Farthing – seems quite keen on Mrs Monk,' DCI Graves said with a twinkle.

'They were just friends,' I stammered. 'I think they were just good friends.'

Two uniformed officers were standing at the reception desk. Lisa and Ryan hovered behind them, uncertain what to do.

'Your car's outside, ma'am,' one of them said to the elderly detective.

Graves held up her right hand, the fingers splayed.

And it could have meant anything.

It could have meant – *not now*.

It could have meant – *five minutes*.

It could have meant – *go away, we are just getting started here*.

'Now,' DCI Graves said, leaning forward. 'Is there anything you want to tell me?'

26

BET FARTHING: *We saw her in St Jude's and then we didn't. She just wasn't around much anymore. She was on the other coast. She had a man there. That first night on the beach — I was the one who went to get her. I was the one who brought her home. I was the one who put the kettle on and buttered the toast. And of course she is beautiful. And of course that makes men do crazy things. I didn't talk to her about her personal life. Never. None of it. None of my business. But I knew there had been trouble. Why? Because she was helping me wash up one time — she was like that, a lovely girl despite all the cruel things you heard about her — and I saw them. The cigarette burns he gave her. And — I'm sorry — but I think any man who does that to a woman deserves whatever he gets.*

'You can't keep coming here, Tom.'

It was a busy night at Le Poisson Imaginaire. They were all going to be busy nights now. The queue for tables snaked out from the big glass doors of the restaurant to the boardwalk. Clementine greeted the diners with her smile, her fabulous smile, and she gave no indication that she had seen me standing outside until she left her post and walked briskly out, her smile disappearing now, as if she had a smile for everyone but me. Michelle, Anton's wife, the restaurant's former hostess, sat at the bar – radiant, chic and totally dumbfounded, staring after Clementine with wonder. Who was this woman?

'We have to talk,' I told Clementine, and the words choked in my throat at the sight of her.

'No, we really don't have to talk. Look – *did you really think it could be the same?* After – *what happened?* Whatever happened. And I don't want to know!'

'The police have got Charlie,' I said, and I saw the fear in her. 'That old detective, DCI Graves, I know she thinks Charlie—' What did she think? 'She thinks Charlie has blood on his hands.'

Clementine shot a look at the queue for Anton's restaurant. Anton himself was watching us through the glass and I felt our friendship creak under the strain of my unscheduled visits. Beyond him, alone at the bar, his wife Michelle watched all of us, a flute of champagne in her hand and a world-weary expression on her beautiful, fifty-year-old face.

'It's got nothing to do with me,' Clementine said, too quickly, and did the thing she did with her hair when she was uncomfortable, sweeping it back from her face and then giving a small shrug, as if to hold it in place.

'It's got everything to do with you.'

'But what do you expect me to do?'

She had me there. I just wanted some acknowledgement of what we had done for her. All of us. And I wanted some brief sign that she saw how scared we all were, and how much it mattered.

And there was something else. I needed to know who she was.

'Is it true?' I said.

'Is *what* true?'

'The things he said? Steve. He said he met you when he arrested you. That's how you met. Is that true?'

I felt her entire body stiffen.

'Look, I had just turned seventeen, all right? I was on the run from my last foster home. I will spare you the gruesome details of what that place was like. And you know what, Tom? It's *past*. All of it. Including Steve. And let me tell you something about Steve — he always twisted the truth until it bore no resemblance to anything that actually happened.'

And then he was coming down the boardwalk. The new guy. We watched him coming, and I cursed his good looks. And now she was all smiles.

'It's over,' she said, and I didn't know quite what she meant apart from the cruel fact that everything was over. Her unknowable teenage years. Her marriage.

Us.

That felt over more than anything.

She took his arm, and she made no attempt at introductions, and he did not even look at me – *he did not even look at me!* – as they went back inside the restaurant.

And then came the voice behind me.

'She's been fucking him for a year.'

Sergeant Monk, in his holiday clothes, bared his teeth in an approximation of charm.

'You don't think she met him down here – this painter guy. You don't buy that story, do you? What? He strolls into – what's it called? – the Imaginary Fish and their eyes meet across a crowded room? Give me a break! He's not just the plat du jour. He's her special dish. Tina's been banging his brains out for a year. Steve found out – the usual way. Little love messages on her phone. Photographs. Of a sexual nature, if you get my drift, and I believe you do. Man of the world like yourself.

That's why she left in a hurry. The plan was always that the painter man would follow her. Steve found out,' Monk said, and I saw his eyes shining with tears of murderous rage. 'My Steve. And he was going to kill the pair of them. Hunt them down and kill the pair of them in their filthy bed sheets.'

'And how did that work out?'

Monk stared at me as if he wanted to rip my face off. Then he smiled.

'And you are too stupid to see that you were always part of her plan.'

'What plan?'

'Tina's master plan. She had it all figured out. Go missing in the back of beyond – but not *too* missing, not so missing that she couldn't be tracked down. But park her tight little arse somewhere off the beaten tracks and then start wagging her lovely tail and smiling that big fake smile. *Get a bunch of local yokels eating out of her hand.* No offence.'

'None taken,' I said.

'And when Steve finally found her – and she knew it wouldn't take long – she fucking *knew* she could get the local yokels to do her dirty work.' He nodded encouragement. 'Is that about what happened? Did she get a bunch of pussy-whipped village idiots to kill my stepson? You see, I worked it out. Powers of deduction, from the old job. Maybe they came up

with the plan together — Tina and the painter man —
maybe she came up with it alone. But it worked,
didn't it?'

I turned away and he gripped my arm in one fist.
'Didn't it?' he said.

Then he let me go, chuckling as I rubbed my arm
and turned to walk away, heading down the boardwalk,
the last of the day's surfers still out on the deeper blue
of the water.

And he fell in step beside me, and I could not escape him, and part of me wanted to hear what he had
to say, and the other part listened with naked dread.

'That lad — the artist! — was up in our neck of the
woods last summer.' He smirked. 'Painting nature
in all its rugged beauty. And shagging her peachy
tush off. God knows how they met. But a woman
like Tina — there's always, *always* a herd of men following her scent. It's been like that since the
start — when Steve nicked her in that bar when she
was just a kid. And it will always be that way for a
tart like her.'

I swallowed hard. I stopped and turned to face
him, wanting the whole bitter truth now, welcoming
it, wanting a reason to stop caring about her, to stop
loving her.

I looked at the lights of Le Poisson Imaginaire
shining like jewels in the gathering dusk. *There are*

people having happy lives in there tonight, I thought. Simple, uncomplicated lives.

I watched her through the glass. It was too far to see faces but I could make out the figures standing at the bar. The man – her man – chatting to Anton and Michelle, and Clementine – she was still Clementine to me, she would always be Clementine to me, no matter what the rest of the world called her – was holding his arm with a proprietorial tenderness that cut me deeper than I could have believed possible.

I turned to face this cruel ex-cop and he saw it all over me. The hurt she had done.

'I am not the bad guy here,' Monk said, and his voice had a tone that I had not heard before. 'I am the bereaved. I am a grieving father. I am in mourning. He was not my son, it is true, Steve was never my son, but when his mother died when he was four years old, I raised him as my son and I loved him as much as any father ever loved their son.'

The gulls were screaming above my head and I could taste the salt of the sea on my lips.

'She uses people,' he said, shaking his head. 'You know it's true. I *told* Steve – I told him from the start. *I warned him*. And he said – She's *had* to use people, Dad. He called me Dad. *She's had to use people, Dad, because her life has been so hard.* So you see – even Steve was eating out of her hand.'

Why did I stand there listening to him?

Because I wanted to hear it all.

Because I wanted to stop loving her, because no good would ever come of loving her.

'I want exactly what you want, Tom,' he said. 'That's all.'

'And what do I want?'

He looked surprised and I stared at him, waiting for him to tell me the secrets of my heart.

He turned to look at the fairy lights shining in the darkness.

'You want justice,' he said. 'You want to bury the wicked bitch.'

27

CHARLIE FARTHING: *I blew it from the start with Clementine. Blew it before we even had a chance to begin.*

I should have been old school when I took my boat to Polmouth, picking her up when she swam across the water. I should have been cool. I should have been Cornwall's Vanilla Ice. But I could not help myself. She was more than I had ever seen. She was more than any of us had ever seen. It's as simple and as brutal as that. She overloaded our circuits. But the beautiful ones don't want you drooling over them. They don't want your rapture. They don't want your compliments. They don't want your love! It sickens them. They have heard it all before. She will turn away the moment you start to babble because she has heard nothing else since she was, oh, twelve years old. When you fall at the feet of beauty, you turn yourself into a cliché they have seen too many times before. Or was that just Clementine? And she had all the power, not because she was the beautiful one, but because she cared the least.

Always, the one with the power is the one who cares the least. Clementine taught me that. She taught me so much.

And now the police want me for murder. I believe that DCI Graves — this nice little old lady — has me in her sights. I am currently helping with enquiries, as the saying goes. A scary place to be, a place where you watch the rest of your life unravelling before your eyes. DCI Graves knows so much. As if she watched it all play out from some secret cliff. The same questions, gently asked, but again and again and again, waiting for the stumble, the fall, the moment you give yourself away. Or give others away. And you feel dirty in here, under the airless yellow light of the police station, you feel soiled, you feel worn out. It sticks to you — the way they look at you, the questions they ask, the doubt in their eyes. The guilt. And I think of Clementine. Because someone wants to bury her.

And they want me to dig her grave.

They released Charlie.

As Lisa and Ryan prepared for the lunch trade, I watched him moving through the early-morning crowds down on the waterfront with a steady, upright gait, almost too self-consciously upright, like a drunk desperately trying to seem sober. There was a milling queue of young families and couples by the *Pleasure Dome*, hoping for a trip to see the seals and the dolphins. Charlie walked past them without a glance, as if the seals and the dolphins and this glossy boat had nothing to do with him. The sightseeing trips were cancelled today. He walked past the police search team in their white suits who had cordoned off the icehouse and were poking around inside, turning my stomach. Charlie headed down the esplanade in that strange self-conscious walk and came up the steep stone steps that led to the deck of the Lobster Pot.

He looked like a man who had been awake all night long.

'Where is the little shit?' he said.

'What little shit?' I said, as Ryan came out of the kitchen with a tray of cutlery. Charlie flew at him. The cutlery went flying, and Charlie had Ryan over a table, forcing his head down.

'Been spying on us, have you?'

'I haven't been spying!'

I was trying to pull them apart when Charlie broke away with Ryan's phone in his hands. Ryan made a half-hearted attempt to retrieve it and Charlie shoved him away. He began scrolling. He began to shake his head.

Then he looked at me and laughed.

He held out Ryan's phone. I took it from him and I saw that it was full of photographs of Clementine. So many images. At the doorway of the cream-and-blue cottage. Walking down to the quayside on the day she swam across the water. In the sea at Maggie's Cove, and seen from the cliffs above, towelling herself dry on the sand. On and on the images went. Looking at her phone at a table for one in the Lobster Pot, her face sunburned and bored.

It was like a timeline of my dreams.

'You too?' Charlie said to Ryan, starting to laugh now. 'She even got to the only surfer boy in St Jude's, Tom.'

Ryan was trying hard not to cry.

'I haven't been spying on anyone,' he said. 'Not her. Not *you*. I was waiting for my girlfriend up at the Baulking House. That's how I saw you two on the boat, Charlie's boat, throwing things into the water. I deleted that image! I was waiting for Saskia, that's all.' He looked at me desperately. 'I haven't told them anything.'

'Someone's told them things,' Charlie said, tossing Ryan his phone back. He just about caught it. 'Because DCI Graves knows so much.'

'Like what?'

'She knows that Clementine — *Tina* — *Mrs Monk* — was going to go back to her husband after their recent

225

marital difficulties. She knows that I threatened to kill the bastard.' He raised his eyebrows, looked across at me. 'She knows about you and Clementine.' His mouth twisted. 'And worst of all, she knows my old man took his boat out two hours earlier than usual on the day that old Steve went AWOL. Now how does she know any of that, Tom?'

Sergeant Monk, I thought. *The stepfather*. But I said nothing.

Lisa appeared in the doorway of the deck. Charlie slumped into a chair, suddenly exhausted.

'What did you tell them?' she asked Charlie.

'Not what they wanted.'

'And what do they want?'

'They want a confession.'

Lisa stumbled half a step sideways into a chair, straightened it, stared at us through eyes glazed with vodka. Charlie raised his chin at her.

'Maybe sober up, Lisa,' he said. 'Maybe get a grip. Or are you going to be drunk when they take you in for questioning? When they keep you for twenty-four hours without charge? You going to be pissed then, Lisa? Are you going to be hungover? Because they *will* take you in, Lisa. And you, Tom. And little Ryan here, with his multiple images of the grieving widow. Better delete them fast, sonny, or there will be some tricky questions to answer.'

It was true Lisa was drinking too much. She began early on the bottle we kept in the restaurant's big industrial freezer. Aval Dor, Cornish vodka from the Colwith Farm Distillery. But it did not affect her job at the Lobster Pot, filleting fish with the sharpest of knives, shucking oysters and chopping lobsters at her usual blink-and-you-miss-it speed. And as always she was a loving and dedicated parent to Paolo.

'Lisa's holding it together,' I told Charlie.

His gaze skittered across me, Lisa, Ryan, and out to sea. He laughed shortly.

A speedboat full of whooping teenagers tore down the middle of the estuary.

'Why would they take me in for questioning?' Ryan said, his thumbs frantically deleting his collection of Clementine images.

Charlie glared at him.

'Because the last place the deceased was seen is your place of work, Ryan. Right here. The Lobster Pot. And because you have been locking yourself in the bathroom with Clementine's picture beating your meat while your old mum does the hoovering.'

I took a seat at the table.

I stared at Charlie. I waited. He shrugged.

'DCI Graves,' he said. 'That nice little old lady? Maybe she's not so nice after all. Because she wants me for murder, Tom. She's convinced I did it.' He glanced bitterly at Lisa. 'Alone.' He shook his head. 'I can see it in her eyes. Someone's leading her straight to me. Someone's stuck a bullseye on old Charlie's back.'

I nodded at Lisa and she led Ryan away, wiping his nose with the back of the hand that held his phone.

'Ryan's not going to rat us out,' I said. 'I promise you, Charlie.'

'He should get shot of that phone.'

'OK. I'll tell him.'

'Not good enough.'

'I'll get him to give me his phone and I will ditch it myself. All right?'

Charlie nodded, satisfied. 'Please do it.'

'Ryan saw us throwing a purple paddleboard into the sea. And that's all he saw.'

But he wasn't listening to me now. His eyes had a wild, faraway look in them.

'You ever see *Murder on the Orient Express*? It's one of my mum's favourites.'

He watched me nod blankly.

'Remember who did it? Who killed the bad man?'

I thought about it. 'They all did it.'

Charlie clapped his hands.

'They *all* did it! They all stabbed the bad man on the *Orient Express*. And some of their stabs were feeble and shallow, and some of them were strong and deep, and some of them were hurried, medium-sized stabs. But they all did it. And it is a comforting thought – the guilt is shared out so equally that it gets watered down, diluted until it hardly feels like guilt at all. *But it doesn't happen in real life*. Not when a man is murdered. Someone has to pay. Someone has to be blamed.' He nodded emphatically. 'She's smart, DCI Graves.' He shook his head. 'Whiplash smart. Seen it all. She's got this sense when someone's lying. She can smell it. That's what makes her so good, what makes her so dangerous. It is a lifetime of listening to people tell her lies. She is a very nice lady and she terrifies me, Tom.'

'You didn't do anything wrong, Charlie.' I was right. He was the only one among us who was innocent. 'You're not going down for something you didn't do.'

He covered his face with his hands and for the first time I saw the depth of his despair.

'DCI Graves has got me like a dog with a bone,' he said.

I thought of Sergeant Monk and my cheekbone began to throb where Steve had punched me in the face while his stepfather held me. And I thought of Clementine's boyfriend – Alex, the seascape artist – who had waited for her to escape from her marriage. And I wondered if what Sergeant Monk had told me was really true – the plan to programme some smitten yokels to kill her inconvenient, violent husband.

I felt the anger surge in me, that toxic cocktail of jealousy and hurt that was becoming so familiar to me now. I glugged it down every day, because I was overwhelmed by the feeling that good people had been treated like mugs.

If Ryan was a fool, then so was I, and so was Charlie, and so was Lisa, and so were Will and Bet Farthing, and so was anyone who tried to be kind to her – Tina, Clementine, whatever her name was. How stupid we had been to love her, to try to be her friend, to try to be kind, to give her our hearts to kick around.

'My parents can't be touched by this,' Charlie said. 'And I don't want you to lose the Lobster Pot.' He looked around, as if seeing it for the first time. 'Such a bloody good little restaurant.' He looked at me with wild eyes. 'And I don't want Lisa to lose her son. And I don't even want little Ryan to stop catching the wave or whatever the fuck he does in his spare time. But most of all – my mum and dad, Tom.' He lapsed into a terrible, tearful silence. 'They are decent people. They have good hearts. They can't be locked up because of this. They don't *deserve* it, Tom. It was all just a terrible accident.'

I stared at him in silence.

'Wasn't it?' he said.

28

LISA: *If I had looked like her, then Tom would have loved me. It's as banal as that. That's how pathetic men are — how shallow. Biologically programmed to be dickheads. If I had looked like her, then he would have been a father to my son, and a faithful partner and best friend to me, and we would have had a happy life. It is so cruel, so crass. But he didn't want me. He wanted her. She treated him like shit and he still wanted her. So everything that happened, all of it, Tom brought it on himself. I mean — Tom's my friend. I will always think of him as my best friend. But sometimes your best friend can be really, really stupid.*

I saw them out on the water.

There was a water sports place on the quay, Polmouth side, and now the season had started they were doing a brisk trade in kayaks, paddleboards and all kinds of sailing boats — training dinghies, single-handers, double-handers, cruising boats and multihull dinghies, which were a kind of baby catamaran.

They – Clementine and Alex – his name was Alex, and that name would always be a stab in the heart to me for the rest of my life – were out on a double-hander, a three-sail trapeze dinghy, considered far too tippy for the average landlubber tourist by the locals. She – inevitably – handled it with a grace that looked effortless, and I wondered where she had learned to sail, and who had taught her.

The sunlight turned the water a shimmering gold.

He – Alex – sat in the stern and she stood on one side of the sailing dinghy, leaning far out above the water, her red hair falling behind her as the wind caught the third sail, the bright red spinnaker, and it filled with energy and powered the little boat towards the open sea. Heads turned to look at them from the pottering kayaks, paddleboards and training dinghies. They looked like an advertisement for a better way of living. They looked like a couple in love.

'Thanks so much for doing this,' DCI Graves said, turning around in the passenger seat of the police car to smile at me. 'It should be about thirty minutes to Bodmin.'

I nodded at her and looked back at the sea, but we had already entered the climbing road for outbound traffic, the little fishermen's cottages crowding in on both sides, the tourists walking down to the water flattening their backs against the old stone walls to let the police car pass, and I knew that Clementine was already lost to me.

'Stephen Monk was a violent man,' DCI Graves said.

We had arrived in Bodmin and it seemed to me that she did not look quite so old within the confines of the police station, and her West Country burr seemed stronger in here, as if she expected to be understood under the sick yellow lights, as if she demanded to be respected. 'He was extremely violent in his marriage. He was extremely violent in his professional life. He was exactly the kind of policeman that gets the rest of us a bad name.'

I picked up my mug of tea for something to do. It was still boiling hot. I put it back down on the scarred Formica tabletop of the interview room.

'He always seemed perfectly pleasant to me,' I said. 'In fact, what I saw of him – I quite liked the guy.'

Graves glanced at the young woman sitting next to her. A young, tough-looking detective with cropped hair. Detective Constable Burns. The silence grew. Graves was a virtuoso of the silence, the grandmaster of letting you open your cakehole and filling the silence with truths better left unsaid.

I licked my lips.

'Even when he did that?' Graves said, nodding her head to indicate the mark on my face that had not quite faded, and perhaps never would. There was still discolouring of the skin high on my cheekbone where he had hit me, a stain of burst blood vessels that were never going to be quite the same.

'A misunderstanding,' I said, resisting the urge to touch my face where he had hit me, hurt me, humiliated me.

'Not a fight then? Because we heard it was a fight.' She glanced at DC Burns and then back at me, wanting to understand. 'What was the misunderstanding about?'

'I didn't realise that Mrs Monk had a husband back at home.'

'And you were having an affair with her,' she said.

'It was hardly an affair,' I said, and she widened her pale blue eyes, as if she did not believe me.

'Then what was it?'

'More like a holiday romance.'

'Do that very often, do you?' DC Burns snapped, as if she was on patrol for the sex police. 'Have a holiday romance?'

'I'm single,' I said. 'I own a restaurant. My working life is built around entertaining visitors who come to our charming little fishing village for a good time.' I shrugged. 'It happens.'

'Quite a bit?'

'Now and again,' I said. 'Here and there.'

'You were one of the men Tina Monk had an affair with after she arrived in St Jude's,' DCI Graves said. 'You were one of her lovers.'

Tina Monk.

One of the men.

One of her lovers.

All this expressed in the most gentle, softly spoken manner imaginable. But I thought I saw a light in her eyes when she saw that she had hit the mark. The room had suddenly started to feel very small.

I was aware of police officers braying at each other beyond the frosted glass of the interview room. Sickly yellow light, cop light, a parody of sunlight. An airless place, smelling of fast food and sweat and fear.

I picked up my tea. Still too hot.

'She – Mrs Monk – did not have multiple lovers in St Jude's,' I said.

'That's not what we heard,' said Graves' little helper, this rude DC Burns, her face twisting in a censorious snigger.

'Can I tell you something, Mr Cooper?' Graves said. 'This is my last job. I mean – ever! I am about to turn sixty, and that is what we call the CRA – the Compulsory Retirement Age. I was hoping to wind this up quickly. *Death by misadventure*. A fatality that occurs due to a risk that is taken voluntarily. Specifically – if I may use a technical term – a pissed peabrain on a paddleboard.'

I had never heard her use profanity before. I was paying attention. I wanted this to be over.

'And Steve Monk was an idiot,' she said. 'And a pig. All right? You don't need to pretend you were chums. He was violent towards his wife. He was violent towards persons in his custody during his time as a serving police officer. He was violent to *you*. But this is also true – threats were made on Monk's life by his wife's lover – Charles Farthing.'

'Charlie wasn't her lover,' I said, and she didn't believe me.

'Threats were made on Monk's life by his wife's lover,' she insisted. 'And then he died. And the specific suspect has no credible alibi for the night that Steve Monk died.'

DC Burns snorted with derision.

'He doesn't remember where he was,' she snickered.

I could not bear to look at her.

'And that is why this is a murder investigation,' DCI Graves said. She looked at the younger police officer and sighed. 'So smelling the roses in blissful retirement will have to wait until this is all wrapped up.'

The younger detective leered at her. 'You love it, boss. Locking up bad people.'

'Listen to me,' I said, desperate now, all my attempts to play it cool and play it smart stripped away. 'Charlie Farthing had nothing to do with the death of that rotten bastard.'

But DCI Graves did not believe that either.

29

Paolo was at the Farthings'.

The boy was in the little front parlour, homework spread before him on the coffee table, the old black Lab dozing at his feet. Will Farthing sat across from him, his eyes never leaving the boy even when he spoke to me.

'His mum's resting,' Will said with the forced jollity grown-ups use around children when the adult world is falling to bits. 'So old Paolo here is spending the evening with us. You stay as long as you like, mate. We'll make a fisherman of you yet, won't we, boy?'

Paolo nodded politely, accustomed to Will's hearty hospitality, not looking up from his schoolbooks.

'They're in the kitchen,' Will said to me.

Bet was making toast and putting the kettle on. Charlie paced the short length of the tiny kitchen, and then turned back.

He could not stop moving.

'Lisa was in the Rabbit Hole,' Charlie said. 'She could hardly stand, what with all the vodka. Sandy called Mum. Mum took Lisa home. And we've got Paolo until she sobers up.' His mouth twisted with despair. 'This is *killing* us!' he said.

His mother laughed shortly.

'This is not killing us,' she said. 'This will not kill us.'

I took my usual seat at the table. Charlie walked the short length of the modest kitchen, and then turned back. I did not know what to say to him.

'So – how was it for you?' he asked me.

'It feels like DCI Graves has already made her mind up.'

Bet was watching me from the sink.

'What do they know?' Charlie said.

'They know what Sergeant Monk wants them to know. That you threatened to kill Steve Monk. That – you liked Clementine. They think she had multiple lovers in St Jude's. Me, you and God knows who else.'

Charlie could not look at me. The blood was draining from Bet Farthing's face. Perhaps Bet was wrong, I thought. Perhaps this would kill us after all.

'You're going to have to tell them something, Charlie,' I said. 'About the night . . . he disappeared. Because they think it's you.'

'What do you want me to tell them, Tom? The truth?'

'I don't know. Something. Anything. But someone's going down for this. I get the impression the police want the guilty party. And if that's not possible – someone else.'

'The guilty party,' he smiled. 'And who might that be? You don't mean Lisa, do you? Or my folks? Or yourself? Listen to you! When you talk about the guilty party, you mean *Clementine*, don't you? You don't think any guilt attaches to you. You blame her for everything.'

I said nothing.

'How you must hate her!' he laughed, and I felt the blood rising in me.

'I don't hate her,' I said. 'I don't have it in me to hate her. But either you go down for this – or we all do.'

'Or she does,' Bet said, as the kettle boiled and Charlie paced the kitchen, as if he was already in a cell.

The lights were off at the Lobster Pot.

Another night when we did not open. I came wearily up the steep stone steps from the esplanade and it was only when I reached the deck of the restaurant that I saw he was waiting for me. He was sitting at a corner table, looking out across the water, the lights coming on all over Polmouth.

'Get me a beer, will you?' Sergeant Monk said.

I stared at him for a moment and then went into the kitchen and took two bottles of Korev from our big industrial fridge. I went back on the deck, handed one to him and went to sit down opposite him.

'Did I tell you that you could sit down?' he said quietly.

I remained standing.

He laughed, odious and obscene.

'I'm shitting you, Tom. Take a seat. It's your fucking restaurant, mate.'

I joined him at the table and watched him glug down half of his Korev in one go. He wiped his mouth with the back of his hand and belched.

'Pardon me,' he said. 'Look – I don't know what you have heard about me.'

'I heard you raped a young policewoman early on in your career,' I said. 'I heard that you were going for the same job, you and this young policewoman. I heard that you got the job and she was told to keep quiet. That's what I heard about you, Sergeant Monk.'

He grinned at the memory. 'Consensual sex,' he said.

We sat in silence. The sea ebbed and flowed, as if it was alive, as if it was breathing.

'They like your pal for it,' Monk said finally. 'The – what is he? – the tour guide. The dolphin botherer. The seal watcher. DCI Graves thinks he topped Steve.'

The idea seemed to amuse him.

'But you and I know better,' he said. 'That milksop – what's his name?'

'Charlie Farthing.'

'That seal-loving milksop Charlie would never get the drop on my Steve! A dozen Charlies wouldn't have managed it. But it doesn't look too good for him, does it?'

'So who do you think did it?' I said.

He shrugged.

'My guess – a few of the younger fishermen did him – for her. Maybe money changed hands. Maybe Tina just fluttered her eyelashes and wagged her tail. I would not rule out some form of sexual contact. Or some of the stag-do boys who come to town and fancy themselves as big city hard nuts. Whoever jumped my Steve, I think they did it because they wanted to jump Tina. And I think they're probably long gone.'

'What about her boyfriend?' I said. 'The artist? Alex?'

He chuckled. 'Him? With his silk scarf and his Hugh Grant fringe? An even bigger pussy. No, I think your mate Charlie is unlucky because he threatened to kill Steve when he was shagging Tina.'

I couldn't let it pass.

'But he wasn't,' I said, and his face lit up with sick delight at my discomfort.

'Are you sure about that?' He finished the rest of his beer and leaned across the table. 'I've known her for years, friend, and I can tell you this about Tina — *you never know what she's up to.*'

Clementine, I thought, Clementine. Still somehow holding on to the belief that I knew her better than anyone.

But it was all slipping away from me now.

'I think your mate Charlie is going to get done for accessory to murder. Secondary liability. Aiding and abetting. Maybe his mum and dad too.'

I didn't like to ask what that meant in jail years. He told me anyway.

'It's the same sentence as the principal offender. So for a murder case, you can work it out yourself — up to life in prison without parole.'

He let that settle between us.

'Why are you telling me all this?' I said.

He leaned forward and I could smell the beer on his breath.

'Because I saw it on your face that night you were watching her with her boyfriend through the glass wall of that restaurant,' he leered. 'I saw it clear as day. You want the same thing as me, Tom. You want to see the guilty punished, don't you? You don't think your yokel chums should go down for this, do you?'

'No,' I said, my voice sticking in my throat. 'No, I don't.'

'You want to see Tina in the dock. You want to see her take the rap for all this . . . chaos. All this sadness. All this misery. All this loss. You want to see her done for murder. Don't you?'

I could not breathe.

'Charlie,' I said. 'He never hurt anyone in his life. His parents – Will and Bet – they are the most decent people I ever met. They showed Clementine – Tina – nothing but kindness from the first night they took her into their home. And Lisa – she's a single mum who loves her son.'

'Who the fuck is Lisa when she's at home?'

'My friend – my colleague – she works at the restaurant. She tried to be Tina's friend.'

'How did that work out?'

The tears sprang to my eyes and I hated myself for looking weak in front of this man.

'I loved her, too,' I said. 'I tried to love her.'

'You can't love her, son. And you can't be her friend. And it's a waste of time trying to be kind to her. She is too damaged. I warned our Steve from the off – I *told* him – she will chew you up and spit you out.' He leaned back and looked at the lights of Polmouth. 'And she did.'

'What do you want from me?'

'I want you to help me. I want you to tell me what you know. If they had enough on your pal Charlie they would have arrested him by now. Not just had a little chat and made him sweat. We need to put that whore—' Here his voice cracked with emotion. 'That murdering whore in the frame. She can't get away with this.'

We were silent for a long time.

'I know what she did with Steve's paddleboard,' I said. 'To make it look like an accident. To make it look like he had drowned. I know where she dumped it because it got caught on the rocks.'

'Where?'

'It's called the Baulking House,' I said.

30

On this part of the coastal path, the wind never stopped.

Even on a mild spring afternoon, it came off the Atlantic in furious bursts, so loud that conversation was impossible, and so hard that it made you watch your steps on the thin muddy path, and made your gaze drift to the sea crashing against the rocks far below. To our right there was only the gently rising meadows, and to our left there was only the drop to the sea. The wind felt as if it was everywhere.

The winding coastal path reached a steep peak and below us there was Maggie's Cove while ahead of us the coast seemed to go on forever, a jagged black border full of tiny coves, secret golden beaches and places that no one knew and no one could ever go.

Sergeant Monk cursed behind me.

'This the place?' he said. I turned to look at him. He was a hard man, but he was not in good shape.

'A bit further,' I said, and I turned my face to the wind, and we took the coastal path that wound beyond Maggie's Cove, the little beach deserted now, the cottage behind it looking as though it had been shuttered and locked for a hundred years. We walked on, and on, the wind battering us without mercy as the coastal path dipped and rose again, and I paused to get my bearings, for we were looking for a place I had only seen twice, and one of those times from the water, a place that had no name on any map that I had ever seen.

With his cop radar, he saw me floundering, suddenly unsure of myself.

'Dumb arse – do you even know where you are?' he shouted above the wind.

And then I saw it. It stood on a distant clifftop, half a mile away, like a place that had been forgotten by the ages. The Baulking House.

My gaze traced the cliffs that fell sharply below and I could see no rocks sticking from the sea. For a moment I wondered if I had found a different Baulking House, because they still dotted the coast of our county. But then the waves sighed and retreated and there they were, more clearly than I had ever seen them. The rocks where Charlie edged the *Pleasure Dome*, fearful of going aground, and I had felt the deck heave and move below my unsteady feet as we did what had to be done.

Sergeant Monk stood by my side, his face ruddy with the wind, staring at the Baulking House. It did not look like much. An old-fashioned bus stop perched on a clifftop, a homely little hut with a bench and a sloping roof staring out to the sea. The bus stop attached to a pint-sized cottage with a black door and black, boarded-up windows, and on the other side of the house there was its twin, another improbable bus stop that looked out towards the horizon.

'What is this place?'

'It's the Baulking House,' I said. I had to shout in his face, for the wind never stopped. 'It's where they watched for the pilchards in the old days. The *huers* – the watchers – would sit on the bench and wait for the sea to turn black with a billion pilchards. And then, when the sea was churning with pilchards, the *huer* would light a bonfire and every man and woman and child would get in their boats and fish. And it would be the best day of the year, better than Christmas Day, because they would know they were not going to starve that year.'

He was silent for a moment.

And then he laughed, his voice thick with contempt.

'Fucking *pilchards*,' he said. 'And do they still wait for the pilchards to show up?'

'No,' I said. 'This was a long time ago. Come on. We're nearly there.'

We walked on to the Baulking House, and it took us far longer than I expected because the road in that lonely place fell and rose and twisted and seemed to turn back on itself, as the coastal path does when it is attempting to drive you mad, and by the time we reached the dead black cottage, we were both fighting for breath.

I felt his hand grip my arm.

'What you got for me, boy?' he said.

I nodded towards the clifftop.

We walked slowly to the edge, for the wind was very fierce up here, and I pointed towards the black rocks below.

It was still there.

And it was far more visible than it had been on the day of the search. The broken tip of the purple paddleboard, about the size of a snowboard, wedged between a large black rock and a smaller rock that seemed to fix it in place, although it shuddered as the waves covered it and crashed into the shore and then rolled away.

But the broken purple fragment remained.

'I can't see anything,' he said.

'Then you're not looking in the right place.'

I pointed and he followed my finger down to the jagged rocks far below.

'See?' I said. 'That flash of purple. See it?'

And he started to weep quietly.

'Oh, that bitch,' he said. 'That fucking bitch.'

'You see it now,' I said, nodding, taking a step back, for the wind was high and unpredictable and the drop would kill you, it would kill you any way it could, if you hit the rocks or if you hit the sea.

He had his phone out and was taking pictures.

He said something but I was behind him now and his words were lost in the wind.

'What?'

He half-turned. 'I said — *can we get down there?*'

'You can only get to those rocks from the sea. And even then you need someone who knows their way around a boat. We can't do it by ourselves. Don't even think about it.'

He turned to look at me.

'Then how did she do it?'

We were facing each other now. The wind had done something to my hearing. I felt off balance, half deaf, as if placing one foot in front of the other would take an enormous effort, and as if I could get it wrong. I felt on the edge of exhaustion, for it had been a long hard walk. And yet I had never felt more alive.

'Who?' I said.

He snorted with the contempt that came so naturally to him.

'Tina,' he said. 'The whore.'

'Call her by her name,' I said. 'Her name is Clementine.'

He stared at me, frowning, amused but measuring me. He had no physical fear of me. He had seen how easily I was undone with one casual punch from his stepson.

'I'll call her what I choose,' he said. 'That slag. That slut. That little whore who could make a dead man come. That piece of trash who just wants to get her legs around as many men as possible.'

'I did it,' I said, and I saw the look on his wind-blasted face turn from disbelief to dumbfounded to understanding. It took a single heartbeat. 'Me and Charlie Farthing,' I said. 'We took his boat out here and threw your stepson's paddleboard away to make it look like an accident. But it wasn't an accident.'

I wanted to tell him everything.

I wanted to tell him that Steve came into the kitchen at the Lobster Pot and tormented Lisa until she was forced to teach him a lesson he would remember. And I wanted to tell him how Will Farthing had carted Steve off to the icehouse until we could work out what we were going to do. And I wanted to tell him that I listened to his stepson's filthy mouth until I could listen to it no more and so I shut it good.

Tighter. Tighter, she said.

Most of all, I wanted to tell him that I knew her and she was worthy of love. That's what I longed to tell him most of all.

She deserved to be loved.

But there was no time.

Because he flew at me.

And he had me in some vicious police headlock, twisting my neck sideways so that my mouth was pressed hard against my shoulder and I was suffocating myself, no longer breathing and in sudden, incredible pain as he kicked my legs behind the knees and I felt myself collapsing. All these well-earned tricks he knew to dominate, to enforce immediate submission, to make you bend to the full force of the law. And he had no fear of me, because I was just another milksop, another pussy, another local yokel. And I broke away from him easily, that unfit old man. I just dropped my centre of gravity and then burst up, breaking his grip, and to the gulls who tried to make themselves heard above the wind, it must have then seemed like we were locked in some strange dance, for a few moments passed when we both wrestled for a grip on the other, and I only broke free of him again when he attempted to force his thumbs into my eyes.

But finally he felt the strength in me.

And the rage.

And the love.

And now he feared me.

We stared at each other.

'Don't,' he said, already begging. 'She's not worth it.'

But I stepped forward two paces – there were to be no more words – and I shoved him hard in the chest, and he took two stumbling steps backwards, and the first step took him off the coastal path and the second off the clifftop and into the gusty thin air, where he paused for a moment in time, the Baulking House watching him with those blind eyes.

Then he disappeared from my sight and fell backwards to the rocks below, with no time left to scream.

PART THREE

The Sleeper Train

31

WILL FARTHING: *The police from Truro said he was lying there for a week. Sergeant Monk. Retired, as it turned out. Still liked wearing the kit, apparently. Still enjoyed the fear it provoked among the great unwashed. But — retired for a while, they said. Left under a cloud. There was this thing he liked doing — nicking women he fancied. So they had kicked him out with full pension. And he just lay there on those rocks for seven days before they found him. For it was a lonely place, where they watched for the pilchards all those generations ago. Folk never hung about up there by the Baulking House. Too bloody windy! Too far to fall! They don't care that if you want to understand Cornwall — to really understand Cornwall — then you need to understand the Baulking House. How hard lives were here. How hard they had to fight to feed their children. Outsiders don't care. They don't know about the pilchards. Pilchards? What pilchards? They just hurry past.*

They don't linger by the Baulking House. That's why he was down there for so long. Those cliffs are not sheer, they're serried. Police told us he was stuck in a crevice close to the water. The gulls found him in the end. Maybe the body shifted. Gets right gusty out by the Baulking House. Some of those waves could overturn a horse. Anyway, a mob of gulls were down there, squawking and feeding. That's what alerted a pair of walkers on the coastal path. They had a peek over the edge, see what all the commotion was about. And they saw him down there, near the bottom. Sergeant Monk, retired. Eyes long gone, young copper told us down on the quay. Pecked out by the gulls. Not the prettiest sight in Cornwall. Quite a business winching him out of there. Needed special lifting kit and some clever chaps from Truro.

And they came for our Charlie in the morning.

32

CHARLIE FARTHING: *You should never feed wild seals. Not good for you and not good for them. Two reasons. A full-grown seal – be it grey, common or harbour – will take your hand off for some nosh, and also it trains them to think that human beings are their friend. And that's not true.*

But once I had established the ground rules with my punters, we had a good day out at Seal Island. The boat was completely full and more than a hundred seals had hauled – that's when they leave the water, we call it hauling out – and were sunbathing on the rocks. It looks like they are posing for the cameras, but they are digesting their food, and resting their bodies after long, exhausting swims. A kind of hush falls over a boat full of people looking at a hundred seals. It is a reverence in the presence of nature, and there is a silent joy and stillness about it. For as long as I can remember, I dreamed of getting out of my family home, getting out of St Jude's, getting out of Cornwall. But when a boat full of people gazed upon a hundred bathing seals with big, gleaming bodies sprawled all over the rocks, and the only sound was the sea, staying home did not seem so crazy after all.

And this was a good day, one of the best days. And as I brought the Pleasure Dome *through the gap in the rocks that led to the estuary, as we headed for home with Polmouth on one side and St Jude's on the other and I saw the police waiting on the harbour, I thought that this was a good day to end it on, with a hundred seals and a boat full of men, women, and children who would never forget that moment for the rest of their lives. It was a good day to end it on, I thought. A good day to be the last day, as we came into harbour and I saw DCI Graves and her officers were waiting for me.*

From the deck of the Lobster Pot, Lisa and I watched them take Charlie away.

'They're charging him with double murder,' she said, not looking at me, still staring down at the tiny white-haired figure of DCI Graves standing before Charlie in all his placid bulk. 'One of the cops told one of the fishermen and he told Sandy. *Double murder,* Tom.'

She did not say – *he's an innocent man.* She did not need to.

And then a woman's voice from inside the restaurant.

'Hello?'

'We're closed,' Lisa called.

It was the journalist. Her name escaped me, if I had ever known it. But I remembered her on the coastal path, on the day of the search, and something twisted in my gut at the sight of her. She came out on the deck with an ingratiating smile.

'Mr Cooper? Tom? I don't know if you remember me? Scarlet Bush. Like the porn star? And I don't know if you heard. They arrested your friend for double murder.'

'We know,' Lisa said, furious at the sight of her. 'Anything else, Scarlet Bush, like the porn star?'

'And I just wondered if I could have a few words.' She turned from Lisa and stared at me with her young, polite, pitiless gaze. 'With you.'

She was all calm and politesse and endless persistence. She may have missed the glory days of the newspaper industry, but she understood the principles of doorstepping.

'It's OK, Lisa,' I said, because ignoring Scarlet Bush was not going to be a good idea.

We took a table out on the deck. It was a glorious day, but Scarlet Bush was once again overdressed, wearing a coat over a fancy frock, as though she had some kind of condition that needed protection from the sun.

'I struggled to find a room,' she said, as if this was a pleasant chat between old friends. 'There's nothing in St Jude's.' She raised her chin to the estuary below, gleaming molten gold in the blazing sunshine. 'I found a little Airbnb on the Polmouth side.'

'It's high season now,' I said.

She shook her head. 'It's more than that. The media have started arriving. True crime podcasters. Freelance hacks like me. Traditional media. This is going to be a big story.' She almost smacked her lips. 'Two policemen murdered in the same sleepy little fishing village! This is going to be *huge*.'

I attempted a smile that did not quite come off. 'Murdered?'

She played it straight. 'Well, that's what the police think.'

'The police are stupid.'

She shrugged, all non-committal. She was a good interviewer. If she had been born fifty years earlier, she would have had a high-flying career at a red-top tabloid on a healthy six-figure salary, knocking on the doors of people who did not want their doors knocked on. And perhaps she would still have a good career. Perhaps she would build it on the bodies of everyone I loved.

'That sweet old lady – DCI Graves? – seems like a wise owl. And she clearly believes that your friend Charlie is responsible for the deaths of the two men – both disgraced police officers – who came looking for his new girlfriend. That's the theory. What's your theory, Tom?'

I took a breath. I could hear Lisa furiously shucking oysters in the kitchen and I felt I was being lured into a trap that I would never get out of.

'I don't have any theories,' I said. 'But my hunch is that the first death – Stephen Monk – will turn out to be an accident. Death by misadventure. What we call in these parts a pisshead on a paddleboard. A drunk who didn't have the wit to wear a life jacket in waters that he knew bugger all about. Currents, tides, rocks, weather. He didn't even think about this stuff. And the second death—'

Scarlet Bush smiled. 'Sergeant Monk, retired,' she said.

'Suicide,' I said.

She raised her overplucked eyebrows. 'I thought you were going to say death by misadventure.'

'That would be a lot of misadventure.'

'Indeed. But I haven't heard anyone suggest that the body they found below the Baulking House was suicide.'

'Just a theory.'

'I thought you didn't have any theories.'

'Just a hunch.'

'You met him, right? Sergeant Monk.'

'Briefly.'

'I remember him ranting and raving out on that coastal path on the day of the search party. He was – volatile.'

'That's a nice way of putting it. Yes, he was a very volatile man.'

'But did he strike you as the type to kill himself?'

'I'm not sure suicide has a type.' I stared out at the estuary, alive with pleasure boats today. 'Unless it is someone who has run out of all other options. But – what I saw of him – Sergeant Monk was devoted to his stepson. They were more like a real father and son.' I shrugged as casually and realistically as I could manage. 'It was too much.'

'And what about the woman?'

I listened to the gulls driven mad by the food being consumed down in the narrow streets of St Jude's.

'They – the two policemen – thought she was dead, right?' Scarlet Bush continued. 'I mean, it *looked* like she was dead. There was stuff online saying she was dead. She clearly wanted her husband and his family to think she was dead. The clothes by the rocks at the bathing pool, the credit cards and phone left behind.

Mrs Tina Monk faked her death and did a runner — didn't she?'

This had gone on too long, I thought. I had said too much. Lisa was right — we should have shown Scarlet Bush the door from the off.

I stood up. Interview over.

'Look, Scarlet, I want to help you but I'm really busy. We need to get ready for the lunch trade.'

She stood up too, smiling apologetically.

'Sorry — I'm just trying to get Mrs Tina Monk clear in my mind.'

Good luck with that, I thought.

I began walking from the deck. Scarlet Bush had no choice but to fall in step beside me.

'As I understand it — she left,' I said. 'She left because her husband was violent. He came after her and they kissed and made up. End of story.'

Scarlet was struggling to keep up with me.

'Well — he died. Then his stepfather died. That's the end of story. Or the end of one story.'

We paused at the exit to the restaurant. I held out my hand in dismissal, and she shook it. A weak, limp handshake she had, the handshake of someone from a generation who didn't really go in for the old hand-shaking routine.

But she didn't let go.

'And what about you, Tom?'

'What about me?'

'You were a journalist too,' she said. 'In that old lost Fleet Street when people still bought physical newspapers. Four-hour lunches in El Vino's on expenses. Papers selling millions a week. No Internet!'

I felt like we had already had our good-old-days conversation.

'It was wonderful,' I said. 'But everything ends. Good luck with your story, Scarlet. And your career. Charlie Farthing is a decent man and I am sure that these lunatic charges are not going to stick.'

She nodded. 'But it's funny,' she said.

We stared at each other while I waited to hear what was funny.

'I asked around a few of those old Fleet Street faces,' she said. 'And none of them had ever heard of you.'

33

I knew she would call.

I knew that she would not turn her back when Charlie Farthing was in a cell in HMP Dartmoor, accused of killing her husband and her stepfather. I knew her heart, you see, and despite everything that was said about her – then and later – I knew she would call.

'Why do you keep looking at your phone every five minutes?' Lisa said, placing two lobster Thermidor on the hatch. She was dressed in her white kitchen scrubs, a blue-and-white stripy butcher's apron on top, and her chef's hat pushed far back on her lush black hair. 'Service!' she shouted.

She wiped the sweat from her brow. It was a warm night and the Lobster Pot was fully booked. But the vodka I could smell on her breath wasn't helping.

'Service!'

But Ryan was clearing a big table out on the deck for the new arrivals waiting at the reception desk so

I delivered the lobster Thermidor myself. My phone began vibrating as I went to escort some new arrivals to their table.

'Tom?'

That voice. Her voice. I don't know what it was about her, even now, but I knew that I wanted her and no one else and it would always be this way.

'How are you, Clementine?'

The new arrivals looked baffled as I held a finger up, asking them to pause while I took this call. They talked among themselves about the lobster in this restaurant, and how it was all day-caught by a local fisherman.

'I had to talk to you,' she said, and I wandered away from the new arrivals to a quiet corner of the deck, and I heard Lisa say, 'Jesus Christ, Tom!' and I vaguely saw Ryan out of the corner of my eye stop what he was doing to go and escort the new arrivals to their table.

'Charlie,' I said. 'You know they arrested Charlie, right? For two murders. And you know – you know they found Sergeant Monk's body, don't you?'

'Good riddance to that cruel bastard,' she said. 'I always thought he looked like a candidate for killing himself.'

'Charlie,' I repeated. 'They've charged Charlie with his murder.'

I don't know what I wanted. I wanted the same thing that I had wanted since her husband stood in the kitchen of the Lobster Pot, taunting Lisa. I wanted the same thing I had wanted since Will Farthing had half-carried, half-carted her husband – ex-husband? It was so hard to tell – to the icehouse. I wanted what I had wanted when she told me – *tighter, tighter.*

I wanted to know that we mattered to her, that we – all of us – counted in her life. I wanted her to acknowledge that we were on her side, and that – yes – it meant something to her.

But this wasn't the reason for her call.

'I'm leaving, Tom,' she said.

My head swam.

'Leaving where?'

'Leaving St Jude's, leaving Cornwall,' she said. 'I have a cabin on the midnight sleeper from Penzance.'

To London. The sleeper train from Penzance left late every night. And you woke up in Paddington at dawn.

She was going to London. And I knew – of course my jealous heart knew immediately – that she was going to be with him.

'Alex was going to stay in Cornwall for the summer,' she said, and I stared at the crowds in the

Lobster Pot without really seeing them. One man was making that little signing gesture in the air to tell me he wanted the bill. I turned my back on him and felt my hand tightening on the phone.

'But he had to go back to London,' she said. 'Some emergency at his gallery. I don't know what exactly. But – now he's gone back – I know I can't live without him. It's like when we are not together, there's a light that goes out in my life. Does that sound nuts?'

I shook my head. 'No,' I said. 'It doesn't sound nuts in the least. You thought he was going to be here all summer long. And now he's not. And you realise – you know – what he means to you.'

'So I'm going,' she said, 'I'm going tonight. We are such a long way from everywhere down here. But not when you have a cabin on the sleeper train from Penzance.' I could sense her smiling. 'You get on board and go to bed and then you wake up in London.'

'OK.'

I was aware that Lisa was standing by my side.

'And I wanted to thank you,' Clementine said. 'I just wanted to thank you for everything, Tom. And I hope that we will always be in each other's life, and we will always be friends. And don't worry too much about Charlie because I know he is a gentle soul who would never hurt a fly.' A pause. 'And I just called to say goodbye.'

She had to go – so much to do before she boarded the train – and in the light of everything that happened, I should have left it there. But I found myself looking at my watch – just after nine – as I headed towards the exit door. There were fifty miles between St Jude's and Penzance. I thought I could just about make it.

Lisa blocked my way.

'She's leaving,' I said. 'Clementine's leaving. Tonight. On the sleeper train. She is going to London to be with that guy. Alex.'

'I heard,' Lisa said, and she seemed totally sober now. 'What did she say about Charlie?'

'Charlie? Nothing. I mean – she said he would be all right. They'll release him. Because he wouldn't hurt a fly. But that's not why she called. She wanted to tell me that she's going to London. She's in love.'

But not with me.

'Please listen to me, Tom. As a friend. I know you like this . . . this girl, this woman. I know how much you like Clementine.'

I checked the time again. I could still see Clementine before she got on the train to London. I just needed to see her, to be in her presence for a few minutes because once she was on that train, I thought it was very likely that I would never see her face again in my life.

'But you'll get through this,' Lisa said. 'Believe me. Time heals all wounds, and all that. *You'll get over her.*'

I nodded. There was a long queue waiting to be admitted to the Lobster Pot. Business was booming.

'But I don't want to get over her,' I said as I turned away.

34

Penzance railway station is the end of the line. Or the start of the line, depending on which way you are pointing. Clementine was on platform one, where the sleeper train to London would depart from, and she was staring off towards the sea as it whispered and sighed in the night, looking as if she was committing the sounds to memory, in case she never heard them again.

There was this long moment when she did not know I was watching her. And I paused, wanting the moment to last – wanting it to last forever, in truth – as I took her in, looking so beautiful and brave and hopeful as she stood there with just one suitcase at her feet.

Then she saw me, and her face split into that smile of hers, that special smile and she came to me and held me and hugged me close and it was probably our most natural moment ever, that moment of goodbye as she went off to the man she loved in

London, who would be – I assumed – waiting at the station for her when the Great Western Railway train pulled in to Paddington at dawn.

'Don't worry about Charlie,' she said. 'They are not going to lock up a man who has done nothing wrong.'

And then she looked at me. And we looked at each other. And I calculated how long we had left before the train pulled into the station.

The platform was crowded with travellers, for the sleeper train to London is enormously popular and always oversubscribed. Mostly tourists who could not face the eternal drive, who wanted only to wake up in the morning and be in London, so that the sleeper always felt more like time travel than an ordinary railway journey.

So many people on that station. I saw only her.

'You can ask me anything,' she said.

I laughed. 'What?

'I'm not this mystery girl, Tom. There's actually nothing remotely complicated about me.' She smiled sweetly, with what I took to be real affection. She liked me. She liked me a little bit. 'This is the time for any questions,' she said. 'In the morning I'll be gone.'

'You don't owe me any answers,' I said.

She kept smiling at me, and I saw the sadness in that smile.

'Monk,' I said. 'Steve. Your husband. Ex. Whatever.'
She nodded, waiting.

'He said that the night he met you was when he arrested you.'

'Yes,' she said. 'Steve always liked to say that. And it was true. I had just turned seventeen. I was on the run from my last foster home. Which was – hell. It was just – hell.'

She stared off down the railway track.

'And I went into this bar in Manchester,' she said. 'I had read about it online. A very fashionable bar. It was definitely the place to be. And I remember that I was cold, and I was hungry. I was so hungry that I was eating the peanuts they had on the bar in little silver bowls. And the bartender – young, bearded, not quite as good-looking and irresistible as he thought he was – was very amused. He brought me more peanuts! And then he started hitting on me. The bar was in a hotel. He told me he could get a key to a room. And he didn't like it when he realised that I wasn't going to a hotel room with him for a handful of peanuts. He didn't like it at all. And we had a row, Tom. And I have a temper, which you have never seen. It was an ugly little scene. Everyone was watching. A disturbance in this trendy bar, a loud argument about peanuts, although peanuts isn't what the argument was really about. And he called the police. And Steve came.'

She glanced down the railway line. There were lights in the distance, coming out of the night. The sleeper train, coming to collect her.

'And PC Steve arrested me for breach of the peace. Although breach of the peace wasn't really the reason he arrested me. He arrested me because he fancied me. He fancied me quite a bit. And the thing is — those cops, those dirty cops, they can always find a reason to arrest you, especially if you are a pretty girl. A *maid*, as they say down here.'

I smiled weakly. What was this cruel world she came from?

'Steve and all his dirty cop friends used to laugh about the women they had arrested,' she said. 'They had a filthy little WhatsApp group, laughing about it all. And do you know who taught them that dating tip?'

'Sergeant Monk,' I said, and I saw the look of surprise on his wind-flushed face as he went backwards over the cliff by the Baulking House, a look of total surprise and the phone still clutched in his right fist.

'And we just talked, Steve and I,' she said. 'We sat in his police car and we talked for hours. It was warm. Hours went by. We may have kissed. He was nice.'

'Nice!' I exploded, knowing it was not a good look. 'He arrested you for no reason!'

'He was nicer to me than my foster parents had been. She – that old bitch – accused me of wanting to steal her fat husband. And *he* – the fat husband – was the one who kept coming into my room. What hell it is to have no lock on your bedroom door. Anyway – more water under another bridge.' Then she looked at me. 'So there you are – it was true Steve arrested me the night we met. But I wasn't on the game. And I wasn't a prostitute. And I wasn't sleeping with men for money. And I was not a bad person. I was a homeless kid stealing peanuts because I had not eaten for a long time.'

I didn't want to ask any more questions.

I didn't want to hear any more of the sadness in her life. The train was coming now, snaking slowly towards Penzance out of the night, white lights blazing.

'My mother,' she said. 'She was fifteen when she had me. A baby having a baby. She got "in trouble", as they say. We don't think of that happening these days, do we? Girls getting "in trouble". But my mum did. And she gave me up. And I saw her once when I was growing up. One of my foster parents – one of the good ones, one of the kind ones – arranged it somehow. And she was just this incredibly beautiful woman who looked so fragile you thought she could break at any moment. And she said – some people get all the luck, all the breaks, all the chances for happiness. And some get none. But I *have* had some good luck, some good breaks. And one of the best was you.'

The train was pulling into the station. I was overwhelmed with love for her.

'I hope it works out for you,' I said. 'The new life.'

She took my hands and I could not stand it.

She smiled at me.

'Maybe the next time we meet, I'll be a mum, and we will sit on the deck of the Lobster Pot and look back at our time together in St Jude's. As friends. The best of friends.'

'Yes,' I said, remembering when we lit a candle and let it burn while we were sleeping, and somehow I had the most peaceful sleep of my life with her in my arms, and nothing ever felt so easy or so right and natural. And when we woke in the morning with the sound of the sea beyond our window, the candle had burned itself out.

'I'm sorry, Tom. But I love him.'

The train pulled into the station and we looked up at it, the Great Western Railways Night Riviera Sleeper.

It was such a beautiful shade of green, that gorgeous deep racing green of the Great Western Railway line. She would sleep through the night in her cabin for one as it made its way across the country. St Erth, Redruth, Truro, St Austell. Par, Bodmin Parkway, Plymouth, Exeter, Taunton. Reading – set down only – and then Paddington at five in the morning, where he would be waiting for her to fly to his arms.

But for now she was with me.

'Clementine?'

She kissed me lightly on the mouth – more than friends, in all truth, but already something less than lovers – and I tasted the salt of our tears and the salt of the sea and they were impossible to tell apart.

35

The lights were still on at the Lobster Pot.

Lisa should have locked up and gone home by now but when I reached the top of the stone steps that led up from the esplanade, I saw why she had remained open.

DCI Graves was waiting for me. Ironically enough, she was sitting at the same chair at the same corner table out on the deck, looking out across the water at the same lights in Polmouth that Sergeant Monk had stared at, the night he also waited for me.

'Is everything OK?' Lisa said, and it could have meant anything or everything. She could have been talking about the sleeper train that was already winding its way through the night, or of our friend sitting in a cell in Dartmoor prison, or the nice little old lady who was waiting for me on the deck.

'Everything's fine,' I said, which was a bit of a stretch under the circumstances. I looked at Lisa's concerned face and I knew that she worried about me in a way that Clementine never did. I lightly touched her arm.

'Thanks for staying open, Lisa. I'll see you tomorrow.'

I joined DCI Graves out on the deck. Her face told me nothing. There was a plastic bag on the wooden table. Inside it was a phone with a smashed glass.

'When I was a child, people would say – we have the best police in the world in this country,' she said. 'Nobody ever says that these days. Did you notice? And that's because of *them*. The Monks. The cruel cops. The modern cops who are in it for themselves, who are drunk on their own power, acting like they can do what they like with anyone. Mocking the people we are sworn to protect, as well as the decent police who think they are doing a noble job for the greater good.' She smiled at me. 'Do you really think you are the only one who hates the police, Mr Cooper?'

'I never said I hated the police.'

She smiled her twinkling old lady smile.

'Ah, I see it in your eyes! But I will let you in on a secret – *me too*. I feel the same way. How do you think a decent copper feels when they hear about scumbags like the Monks using their warrant cards to pick up vulnerable women? We don't feel good! I will tell you something for nothing, Mr Cooper – *nobody hates a bad cop as much as a good cop.* So I will be glad to be out of it. Retirement can't come soon enough for me. Because nobody respects us anymore. Nobody cares. Why should they, with cops like the Monks in the world, arresting women so they can get them in the back of their squad car on some industrial estate at midnight. People fear us, at best, these days. They despise us, at worst. But – I want to get this job right. If this is murder, then I want to see the guilty party punished. Because if I don't, then the job I just gave a lifetime to is a joke, a waste, a travesty.'

She indicated the phone in the bag between us. 'Sergeant Monk's phone,' she said, and I felt my heart fall away. 'He was holding it when he fell.' She held up her small right hand, slowly clenched it into a fist. 'He didn't let go, even after that fall. And he didn't let go, even after he died. And he didn't let go, even when the gulls picked his eyes out.' She nodded at it. 'There are pictures on that phone. I would show you, but there's nothing to see. Rocks. The sea. I don't know what he was trying to photograph. You can't see anything.'

I tried to hide the relief I felt flooding through my veins.

'But here's the funny thing,' she said, picking up the phone in its plastic bag. 'There *is* an audio file.

Sergeant Monk was recording a conversation when he fell.'

We stared at each other. The gulls were laughing, laughing, laughing.

I felt my breathing stop. I wondered if there were police waiting for me down on the esplanade now, if there were more sitting outside the front door of the Lobster Pot, tired and bored, waiting to put me away so they could go home to their rest.

She pressed play.

I heard that loathed voice.

'Don't. She's not worth it.'

DCI Graves shook her head. 'That's actually where the recording ends. It starts a bit earlier.'

I watched her fumbling with the phone. An old lady flummoxed by modern technology.

But I could see him with total clarity, high above those black cliffs. He had his phone out and was taking pictures. He said something but I was behind him and his words were lost in the wind. I remembered him asking me how he could get down to the rocks where the paddleboard was wedged. I remembered telling him that he would only access that place from the sea. And I saw – clearly now, though it had hardly registered at the time with the blood pumping through my veins – I saw him press a button on the phone as we faced each other in those final moments of his life.

He had been recording our last little chat. What an efficient dirty cop he was, the dead sergeant. But the wind – the wind screamed and howled down the coastal path, and his voice was clear whereas the other voice in the audio file was lost in the wind.

'*Then how did she do it?*'

We faced each other again, me and Sergeant Monk The sea stretched to a misty horizon behind him.

'*Who?*' I heard myself say on the phone, feeling it again, wanting to hear him say her name, longing for him to say it, but my voice was very distant, very different, unrecognisable even to me, like a voice that has been imagined or heard in a dream.

DCI Graves and I leaned our heads closer to the phone inside the evidence bag, straining to hear every word the wind allowed.

Again Monk snorted with the contempt that came so naturally to him.

'*Tina. That* – [inaudible].'

'*Call her by her name. Her name is* – [inaudible].'

'*I'll call her what I choose. That slag. That slut. That little whore who could make a dead man come. That piece of trash who just wants to get her legs around as many men as possible.*'

'*I did it*. [Inaudible] – *boat out* – [inaudible]. *It wasn't an accident.*'

The wind, the wind, the furious wind.

'Don't. She's not worth it.'

And then a curious silence, as the wind seemed to diminish and there was only a sickening thud and then the sea, nothing but the endless sea, ebbing and flowing.

DCI Graves carefully pressed stop. She placed the plastic bag with the phone back on the deck.

'That's a confession by the murderer,' she said.

I stared at her.

'Do you know who that other man is?'

I waited.

'That's Mrs Tina Monk's lover,' she said. That's your friend. That's the man we have rotting on remand in HMP Dartmoor.'

'That's Charlie Farthing,' I said.

36

BET FARTHING: *They all wanted my son to take the blame. And it was just so wrong. Charlie was a good boy. Charlie never did anything bad. And all of this mess – whoever was to blame, it certainly wasn't my beautiful boy. I call him my boy! A grown man now, of course, but there is a part of your heart where they are still the baby you held in your arms, and always will be. A grown man now but still the skinny little boy who ran around St Jude's with the other little harbour rats. All grown up, yes, but still the teenage boy who cried in my arms when he was dumped by his first girlfriend. And they all said they loved him! And they said they cared! But it just wasn't true. Or maybe they cared – but not the way his mother did. They didn't love him enough to keep the police from his door, did they? They didn't care enough to keep him out of Dartmoor. And my husband, my Will, he told me – calm down, girl, it will all work out in the end. Charlie will not be done for these murders.*

But as time went on, I saw that my Will was kidding himself. They wanted Charlie to take the blame. All of them wanted it. It suited that old detective – my age, she must have been – who just wanted to retire and put her feet up, as far as I could tell. It suited Clementine. It suited Lisa. It suited Tom. And I can't help believing that it even suited my husband. They all said they cared about Charlie, but they did not care enough to swap places with him. They all wanted Charlie to pay for their sins. And I would never allow it. I would not let these lies stand. Because they all said they cared about my Charlie but none of them cared as much as me. And before Charlie went down for these murders, I was prepared to do anything. And I mean – anything. How stupid they all were to not take me seriously. How stupid they all were to mess with a mother's love.

I looked around the visits room. That's what they called this place in HMP Dartmoor – the *visits* room. Not the visiting room. There was a blank stupidity about prison life – the visits room! – and I knew that I would rather die than be in here.

The visits room was full of wives, partners, children – especially children – children of all ages, from tiny toddlers who squawked and fidgeted and wept, to surly teens who had taken a vow of silence and

whose mouths were set in lines of permanent dis-
satisfaction. The men they had come to see, the men
who sat opposite them on tables that were secured
to the floor, were not my idea of jailbirds. They were
all shapes and sizes, ages and races, but what they
shared was they all looked like ordinary men.

'In St Jude's, I was always my father's son,' Charlie
said. 'And that's all I ever was – no matter what age
I was, no matter what I did. When I was a little
harbour rat, hanging out with my mates down on
the quay. *That's Will Farthing's boy.* When I came
back at the end of term from university. *He's Will
Farthing's boy, that lad right there.* When I started my
business. *There's Will Farthing's boy – the fucking
tourist guide.* That's all changed in here. My dream
of being my own man finally came true. Isn't that
lovely?'

'We're going to get you out of here, Charlie,' I
said.

'Dartmoor is a Category C prison,' he said, not
listening to me and my big promises. 'Mostly
white-collar types. A few sex offenders. A lot of us
on remand, waiting for our trial date. Category C
is – *Those who cannot be trusted in open conditions but
are unlikely to try to escape.*'

'Escape seems unlikely,' I said, and Charlie
laughed. This monumental prison had been built

in the early nineteenth century to hold POWs during the Napoleonic wars. Its high granite walls dominated this part of Dartmoor. I had not breathed properly since passing through the huge steel gates.

'And – the one good thing, Tom – in here, I am finally more than Will Farthing's boy. I am a big man! A dangerous man!' He leaned forward conspiratorially. 'The man who topped two dirty cops.'

'Listen to me, Charlie,' I said.

'Do you think anyone pushes me around in here? They talk about what prison takes away from a man. His job, his family, his status on the outside. Prison is all about taking things away from you. Your freedom is just the start, Tom, believe me.' He looked around the visits room with something like affection. 'But it's given me something that I never had before.' He hung his head. 'Finally I am more than Will Farthing's boy.'

I wondered if he was going to weep. 'You didn't do anything,' I said. 'You're an innocent man.'

He lifted his head, and his handsome face split in a cheeky grin. 'We're all innocent in here,' he said. He gestured around the room. All those unhappy meetings, nobody allowed to leave the table – apart from the children in the sad little play area – not allowed to touch, all of us watched by the guards with their bored, mask-like faces. 'That's the first thing you learn in Dartmoor – they got the wrong man!'

'Please listen to me, Charlie,' I said.

But Charlie wasn't listening.

'Remember when you first came to St Jude's, Tom? You were desperate to be a part of our fishing village – and I was desperate to get out. I guess we both made it, didn't we?'

'Charlie, I spoke to my bank. I'm going to remortgage the Lobster Pot. We are going to get you the best legal representation in the country. You are going to get through this.'

A cloud passed across his face.

'Do you know what sea boils are?'

'Charlie—'

'Sea boils are what a fishermen gets. They are like these red welts that are caused by the bacteria in seawater interacting with the oilskins that fishermen wear. And it causes these horrible red welts on the skin that nobody wants to put on a postcard from Cornwall. And I came home from university one Christmas holiday with this girl I liked. And when we walked in, my dad was sitting in his pants in the living room while my mum bathed his sea boils in warm salt water. And *that's* when I decided I wasn't going to be a fisherman, Tom.'

'You can be what you like, Charlie. You are young enough to start again. Do what you like. But you are not going down for something you didn't do.'

He reached across the table and seized my arm just below the elbow.

'No touching!' a guard barked.

Charlie smiled at me, took his hand away. Neither of us looked at the guard, but we waited for him to pass.

'Tom,' Charlie said. 'Oh Tom! Did it ever occur to you that they got the right man?'

I said nothing. I shook my head. It was a form of madness that had touched him, I thought, just as it would touch me if they put me behind these walls within walls within walls, if they ever locked me up behind these high granite walls and endless steel doors in the middle of Dartmoor.

And I felt a flood of shame.

Because I knew that I would do anything within my power to free my friend from behind these walls, anything at all apart from the one thing that would guarantee his freedom.

I would never confess my crimes.

'You know nothing,' Charlie said, with a weariness that infuriated me.

'Charlie—'

'No, you listen to me,' he said, and he licked his lips, and quickly scanned the room. No guards nearby, our nearest neighbours lost in their own tearful little dramas.

'You think it should be you in here, Tom? Or Lisa? Or my old man?'

'I don't think it should be you, Charlie.'

He should have got out. Out of St Jude's, I mean. He should not have come back after university. If he dreamed of Australia and Thailand and California – and he did, and he always would – then that was the time. Leaving was never easy. But sometimes you have to leave just to survive.

'Maybe they got the right man,' Charlie said, almost casually. 'That old detective – DCI Graves – maybe she knows something that you don't. Did that ever cross your mind, Tom boy?'

'I think we shouldn't be talking about these things. Not here. Listen – we will get you out, Charlie. I told you, money is not going to be a problem.'

He smiled sweetly. 'But I went down to the ice-house,' he said. 'After you had been down there with Clementine. My parents were talking. I was alarmed, to say the least. Dear old Mum and Dad had a man tied to a chair in the icehouse. And my mum was afraid he was going to choke on his vomit.

And so I went down there. And when I took the gag off . . .'

He shook his head, and the sounds of the visits room filled his appalled silence. The tears of the wives and mothers. The laughter of the children. The orders of the guards to not touch, to never touch.

'He – her husband, although I can never quite get my head around that – Steve – he said such terrible things about her, Tom. He said such terrible things that I needed him to stop talking immediately. Do you know what I mean?'

I nodded.

Charlie's voice was not quite a whisper. 'I did not want to kill the guy. I just wanted to stop him talking. So I went outside and found the first thing I could to shut him up.'

'You put something in his mouth?'

'No, I beat his brains out with an oar. And later, when we went out to throw his kit away, that morning below the Baulking House, you were wound too tight to even notice that Steve's paddleboard oar had his blood and brains on it.'

I stared at him dumbfounded.

'I hit him so hard with that paddle it killed him,' Charlie said. 'What do you think, Tom? That Lisa killed him with that little stab? Or that you topped him with a bit of tape around his cakehole? Or my dad is to blame because he parked him in the ice-house?' Charlie shook his head. 'I killed him, Tom, and that little old detective can smell it on me.'

'Did you kill Sergeant Monk too?'

He stared at me for a while. Then he shook his head.

'That was a suicide, wasn't it? Looks like a suicide to me.'

'Clementine's husband would have died anyway,' I said. 'Perhaps your mum was right. He was going to choke. And maybe he had lost too much blood from that—' I glanced around the room, suddenly convinced that everyone was watching us, everyone was listening to us.

I leaned as far across the table as I could, and lowered my voice to the level of the Lord's Prayer. 'Steve had been stabbed in the neck, Charlie. And he was tied up too tight. Maybe we did all kill him. But what you're saying – it's not true.'

'What part of it isn't true, Tom?'

'All of it!'

'Are you sure? Are you *sure* that none of it is true? What if I did what you lacked the guts to do? What then? What if I am a more of a man than you are, Tom?'

'I think you did it in your dreams, Charlie. I think you wish you had beat his brains out.'

'You think you're the only one who cares?'

'I think you have your reasons for confessing to a crime you didn't do.'

'And what's that, Tommy boy? Explain my reasons to me.'

'Because you want to protect your parents. And you want to protect Lisa and Paolo.'

We stared at each other.

'And you want to protect me. Your old pal.'

A distant bell rang.

Visiting time was over.

And I saw in his eyes I was wrong.

Charlie's eyes slid away from me, and I saw there was something else. The reel of his brief fling with Clementine played in my mind. I would never know exactly what had happened in the night and day between Charlie picking her up Polmouth side the day she swam across the water and the moment they came into the Rabbit Hole on the night of the lock-in. And I did not want to know. But I was aware that, whatever it had meant to Clementine — not much, was my guess and my prayer — those hours alone with her in the cream-and-blue cottage had hooked Charlie for life.

And I saw that whatever he had or had not done in the icehouse, and whatever he said now, it had nothing to do with protecting his parents, or Lisa and Paolo, or me.

Because Charlie Farthing thought he was pro-tecting Clementine.

And I saw Clementine in his arms, and I saw her mouth on Charlie.

And I pushed it all away.

Because I have learned that the past only lives if you let it.

37

We had a table for four out on the deck of the Lobster Pot. Will and Bet Farthing, and Anton's wife, Michelle, and me. Anton was in the kitchen, cooking for Will and Bet at last, as he had always promised to cook for them on some special night at the Lobster Pot. It was not a celebration, of course, not with Charlie on remand for murder in HMP Dartmoor. But the night was an affirmation of friendship, and a distraction, and a way of Anton expressing something deeply felt to the Farthing family that he could never express in words.

At least that was the idea. But it wasn't working. It was one of those special meals that feels more like a punishment than a treat.

Will and Bet had eaten at the Lobster Pot a thousand times. But it was always after hours, or in the kitchen — not a crowded night at the height of the season with loud people from London with posh voices braying about the price of property. The Farthings had touchingly both dressed up for the evening. Will in an old dark suit that he may have been married in with a white shirt and tie – probably the only tie within a 25-mile radius of St Jude's – while Bet was in a cotton dress decorated with sunflowers, the black and yellow colours faded with years of washing. I always thought of them as fearless, but they were self-conscious to-night in a way that I had never seen them before, whispering to each other while Michelle and I exchanged anxious glances.

'I love your dress, Bet,' Michelle beamed. 'It's so pretty.'

'This old thing,' Bet said.

Will guffawed. 'Scrubs up well, my maid,' he said, reaching for his wine glass. Their plates were before them. Will had wolfed down the grilled lobster that he had caught at the other end of the day while Bet had hardly touched her Cornish plaice meunière. They had both had hefty starters – and I suspected that Bet was already full before the entrées arrived.

'You OK, Bet?' I asked, and she smiled uncomfortably, and I smiled at her to convey – *your son will be free and you do not have to eat your Cornish plaice meunière if you don't want to.*

'Oh this is all so lovely, so lovely.' And to Michelle. 'Anton shouldn't have gone to so much trouble.'

Michelle smiled, shook her head.

'It's his pleasure, Bet.'

Anton was in the exposed kitchen, helped by Ryan, who looked dazed and bemused to be treated like a sous-chef in some fancy Michelin-starred restaurant. As she wasn't cooking tonight, Lisa worked the room.

There was a party of journalists who were trying to engage her in conversation. I was concerned, fearing they were attempting some kind of sneaky interview. Scarlet Bush was with them – very much the junior partner among a table of smooth, hard middle-aged faces – and I vaguely recognised one of the men from some dusty corner of television – late middle-aged with a tan and teeth that were the toilet bowl white of minor celebrity. Handsome once, but not quite the Brad Pitt he took himself for. More than all of them, he was trying to talk to Lisa.

'OK?' I asked Lisa as she headed back to the kitchen. 'What does that guy want?'

'Lobster Thermidor and my phone number,' Lisa said.

Michelle clapped her hands. 'Bravo, Lisa!'

'Is he going to get it?' I asked, feeling a stab of something that could not possibly be jealously.

'Think so,' Lisa said. 'I think Anton's still got one lobster left.'

Will and Bet were whispering among themselves. Will's face was flushed from the bone-dry Chablis we were drinking, and Bet wanted him to slow down. Michelle turned to me and smiled. 'You know Anton loved her too?' she said.

'Who?' I said, although I already knew.

'The girl, of course! The one whose husband died. Our hostess at Le Poisson Imaginaire. Clementine! He thought he was in love! Anton denies it – he furiously denies it! – but I could tell. Staring at her with his mouth open in wonder, looking at her when she checked a booking as if she was painting the Sistine chapel.' She waved merrily to her husband in the kitchen. 'My husband – like most men – can't tell love from desire and they think that love has gone when it is just desire that has faded – as it always will. I think he actually dreamed that they might have a life together. And she saw nothing more than a bald old Frenchman who had given her a job. But still he dreamed! Can you believe it? Insane!'

I smiled weakly.

I could believe it.

And Michelle was right – it was insane.

'I liked her,' Michelle was saying, sipping her wine. 'Very beautiful. Very ambitious. But I am glad she has gone back to London. Perhaps once Charlie is

300

released, things will get back to normal. Such a sweet man, Charlie Farthing. Such a *good* man. I know he had nothing to do with these crimes. I know for a fact.'

We drank to that.

'When you say Anton loved her,' I said, because I could not let it go. 'When you say he *loved* her . . .'

'Sometimes we love because it is all we can do,' Michelle told me. 'We love without reason or hope – only with the dream of some other life that will never be. It's harmless. Until people start dying.'

I started. 'What?'

Michelle was watching Lisa with the journalists.

'Some people are loved too much. And some – most – are not loved as much as they deserve.'

'I'm not sure I can manage all this,' Bet said, frowning at her lovingly prepared fish, and my heart ached for her.

'Leave what you like, Bet,' I said.

'Good bit of fish that,' Will said, knocking back his Chablis. Bet was right. He had had enough.

'What's for afters?' Will said.

I watched Lisa return to the party of journalists with their drinks. The tanned man with the toilet bowl teeth reached out a hand to touch the base of her spine and Lisa gently pulled away. She was wearing a black dress and heels, her glossy black

301

hair piled on her head too quickly, because it kept falling down over her face.

Lisa saw me watching her and she smiled at me, and one hand came towards her face as she touched her glossy black hair.

38

When his school broke up for the summer half-term holiday, Paolo would go out on the ebb tide with Will Farthing on the *Bonnie Bet*. I always rose early enough to see them setting off – Will standing in the wheelhouse, staring out to open sea, in yellow oilskins and red beanie, and Paolo in the stern, baiting the lobster pots for shooting.

Lisa came out on the deck with two cups of coffee.

'He wants to be a fisherman,' she said. 'My crazy kid.'

'You don't mind him going out?'

'Are you kidding? When he's with the Farthings, it's the only time I feel he's safe. If something happened to me, I know that Will and Bet would look after him.'

'Nothing's going to happen to you.'

'You know what I mean. If they put me away.'

'Nobody's going to put you away!'

'Charlie can't pay for what we did, Tom.'

'Nobody expects him to. Listen to me, Lisa – *we didn't do it.*'

'What?'

'Charlie went to the icehouse to set Steve free. But you know what that bastard was like – he could not shut his filthy mouth. And – Charlie finished him off. He finished Steve. Don't ask me how. Charlie told me in Dartmoor. You didn't do it, Lisa. We didn't do it. Charlie did it. He did it for Clementine.'

'Is that true?'

I nodded, pushing down the thought. *I want it to be true*.

We were silent, watching the *Bonnie Bet* until it had passed through the mouth of the estuary to the open sea.

'So – it's all going to work out fine?' I could hear the scorn in her voice. 'Apart from – you know – Charlie being locked up for life.'

'Trust me.'

She sipped her coffee and then she leaned towards me and kissed me lightly on the mouth. A coffee-flavoured kiss.

'I do,' she said.

I looked at her. 'What happened with the guy last night?'

She laughed. 'He got my number and his lobster Thermidor. But that's all he got.'

I felt relief.

'What – do you think I'm going to go back to his hotel in Fowey? Or take him home with me? That would be lovely for Paolo in the morning, wouldn't it? Seeing some B-list breakfast TV presenter tucking into his Weetabix!'

We watched the esplanade. This deep into the season, there were already the first tourists wandering down to the quay. It was going to be another beautiful day.

'You make it sound as though the only thing stopping you was opportunity,' I said.

She shrugged. 'I still believe in love. But as you get older, you start to think – *what exactly am I saving it for?* When we're young, we sit around waiting for lightning to strike. And when it finally does – all you get is burned. Lightning strikes – true love! – and you get fried. Look at me and my old man. Look at you and Clementine.'

'You think I'm ridiculous.'

'I think you are no more ridiculous than every other man who looked at her and wondered how good it would feel to be loved by her. I understand – I really do – you get lonely.'

'What? No! Not at all. I'm not lonely, Lisa. I love my life.'

'You can love your life and still get lonely. Because life in St Jude's is so different from when you were a single guy in the city. A big shot journalist going to all the parties. Chatting up the maids.'

I laughed. 'That wasn't my life. Apart from the single bit. It was work I grew to hate and then a takeaway for one.'

'I get lonely too,' she said, and then she gave me another coffee-flavoured kiss, but harder this time, and I felt the power in her small frame, and I brushed back her glossy black hair from her tired, pretty, Italian face, and she smiled with some strange brew of shyness and amusement just before I put down my cup and kissed her back.

'Finally,' she said, and there were no more words as we went upstairs to my apartment with hours before the world would come to our door demanding to be fed.

We sat on the bed and we kissed like a couple of necking teenagers, consumed with passion but paralysed on the edge of something more.

We had been friends for so long that the shyness was real, and tangible, and something we would have to negotiate. I stood up and pulled off my T-shirt and she laughed and watched me and raised her eyebrows in amused appreciation at my hard-earned abdominal muscles and I was just about to return to the bed when my phone began to vibrate. I went to turn it off and then I saw her name on the screen.

'I have to take this,' I said. *Clementine*, it said.

Clementine should have been in tears. She should have been broken in bits and overwhelmed by what she had discovered in the city. But her tears had been shed already.

Like a wounded animal crawls somewhere secret to die, Clementine always believed that crying should be as private as prayer.

'I went to his home,' she said, calm and collected now. 'Unannounced. Unexpected. A lovely surprise!' She laughed bitterly. 'Unwise.' I heard her exhale and it was as if she was letting go of a life that was never going to be. 'He – Alex – answered the door. Small mercies, and all that. But I could hear his wife in the kitchen, asking him who it was. And I could hear these two beautiful little girls – maybe four and two years old? I don't really know anything about children – bumping about the place. Clapham, it was. A lovely little house in Clapham, very close to the common. Do you know Clapham, Tom?'

'What did Alex say?'

'He said – *you can't come here, Clementine*. That was it, really. No apologies, no explanation, no acknowledgement of everything he had been keeping from me. You know – his real life. I thought he was single. I thought he was mine. I thought he had never been married and he did not have any children knocking around. But he had this perfect little family back home in Clapham. So no – he didn't have anything to add to what he said when he opened the door and saw me standing there. But what else does he need to say? *You can't come here, Clementine.* That says it all.'

I was aware of the day waking up beyond my window. The voices down on the esplanade. The gulls wheeling and cawing. And in the room, I was aware of Lisa standing up slowly, smoothing her clothes.

'Come back,' I told Clementine. 'Come home. Come to me.'

'I can get the night train. The sleeper. It will get me into Penzance around this time tomorrow.'

'I'll be waiting at the station.'

'No – don't wait at the station. Meet me at the usual place. The place where we would always run into each other, accidentally on purpose.'

She laughed, and I smiled to hear her laughter. It meant the world to me to know she could go through all that – turn up at her lover's home and find he had a family – and still laugh out loud.

'Maggie's Cove,' I said.

I hung up and turned to look at Lisa, feeling my face burn with shame.

'Oh, you're fucking shitting me,' she said.

39

'What's wrong?' she said from the bed.

'Nothing's wrong,' I said from the window.

It should have been enough. These last mad, blissed-out twenty-four hours — truly, it should have been enough to still and calm and silence the part of my brain that kept asking questions. The drama alone should have been enough to ease my mind. Waiting for Clementine on the beach at Maggie's Cove, waiting for hours because I went as soon as we closed the Lobster Pot for the night, staying awake all night long, dozing then waking with a jolt — *she's coming!* — checking my watch to track her journey west through the night — Taunton, Exeter, Plymouth, Bodmin Parkway. Coming back to me, coming home to St Jude's, fleeing her great betrayer in the city. Par, St Austell, Truro, Redruth, St Erth. It was enough for me, wasn't it? It was everything I wanted. It should have been enough to know that she was on the train when it pulled into Penzance at dawn, and the thought of her face as she walked across the meadow to Maggie's Cove – the taxi from the station brought her as far as he could, but it was just the two of us when we met again.

Her face, her face. And then she was in my arms, her red hair flying everywhere – and not a single tear between us. Just laughter, and kisses that tasted of the sea air at dawn, and then the walk back to St Jude's along the coastal path, our fishing village not yet awake as we climbed the steep stone steps from the esplanade to the back of the restaurant. And then to bed, and it was everything I hoped for, and I will carry the memory of our lovemaking to my grave and beyond – fevered, desperate the first time, and then slow and gloriously unhurried the second time, as though we had years of this before us.

Yes.

To my grave and beyond.

And those twenty-four hours when we never left my apartment – I put the *Catch you later!* sign on the door and turned off my phone, for our romance, I had realised, was easier to sustain when we were alone.

It should have been enough to shut me up, and to keep me happy and turn off my mind.

But it was not. Even with my body still slick and wet from our most recent coupling, the questions nagged at me as I stood at the window twenty-four hours after I met her on the beach at Maggie's Cove and watched the day begin in St Jude's and Polmouth across the water.

'I told you,' she said again from the sheets, turning her long body over, stretching out and yawning. 'You can ask me anything, Tom.'

Does she still love him? I wondered. *Her handsome arty married man with the two adorable little girls and the undeniable wife in Clapham?* I knew that love was not turned off so quickly. *If he called – right now! – and said that he was leaving his wife, and his daughters would understand one day, would she run to him, still wet from our bed? Well – would she?*

And there was more. Of course there was much more.

Because how could we live – how could we ever be happy and at peace forever after – if Charlie paid for all our sins?

And there was more.

Did she guess what I had done to her father-in-law? 'Don't,' he had said, 'She's not worth it!' and one hard shove to the old man's chest and over he went to his death. Did Clementine suspect me? And if she knew the truth, would it make her like me more or less? Does she understand how much has been paid because we cared about her?

'Anything,' she said. 'Ask me whatever is on your mind, Tom.'

But it was said with a sigh, because I sensed she was growing weary of my questions, and my suspicious mind, and the nagging doubts that called me from my sleep and took me to the window to stare out without seeing – all the toxic questions that will not leave me alone. The questions that would do us no good.

And yet I could not stop them.

What the hell happened with Charlie? What did you do with him that makes him ready to give his life for you?

In those hours they shared together – from his gallant pickup on his boat when she sat alone on the slipway on the Polmouth side of the estuary, to the crucial hours in the cream-and-blue cottage, to the moment they walked into the lock-in at the Rabbit Hole and he lost her forever because he would not dance to the music.

What happened to make Charlie ready to sacrifice his freedom? Did she put her mouth on him? Is that what happened? Your mouth on him? I want to know. I don't want to know. I want to know.

'I'm going to sleep for a bit now,' she said, and I could hear in her voice that she was telling the truth – for once! 'Ask me anything,' she murmured again, giving me one last chance to hear the truth, her head so lovely on the pillow where she slept.

And so I blurted it right out, the only question I really wanted an answer to.

'Will you marry me?' I said.

LISA: *It just felt so wrong. Seeing them together down on the quay, eating organic ice cream when the world was falling apart. All's fair in love and sex, as they say. So fair play to her — she always got what she wanted, did our Clementine — or Tina — or whatever her real name was. But it still did not feel right. To see them so happy — holding hands, taking selfies, touching each other as if they couldn't wait to get back in the hay and have another go.*

A man was in jail. Two men were dead. There were journalists coming out of the woodwork, sniffing around, digging up dirt, wondering who had blood on their hands. And those two were swanning around St Jude's as if they were the greatest love story of all time. Yeah, right. Pass the sick bag, Romeo. You're too stupid to see you're only banging Juliet on the rebound. It just felt all wrong. Every part of it.

And it felt like somebody was going to have to pay.

40

It was the best of days, one of those days when your happiness is so exquisitely intact that it already feels like a memory, something that you will return to in the days ahead and wonder – was I really that happy? And the answer is and always would be – *yes, yes I really was that happy.*

The sky was a perfect blue, unbroken by a single cloud and the sun turned the water a molten gold, and it shimmered and shone, tickled by a gentle breeze from the open sea. Out on the rocks, a young seal was digesting his meal, so relaxed in his lolling that you could almost hear him sigh.

The sounds of high season drifted up from the esplanade and across from the quay and the old town. But today the children were happy and laughing, and the husbands were patient, and the wives were content, and the young lovers were wrapped in their happiness.

After the lunch trade, I hung the lobster in the top hat closed sign on the door, and began preparations for the night's party. And all of that – hanging the fairy lights out on the deck, putting up the black-and-white bunting, the colour of our Cornish flag, and blowing up party balloons – it all felt part of this perfect day.

I was sitting on the deck filling a pink balloon from a helium canister, pinching the nozzle to release the air into the balloon, the sun beating down, so hot that it was becoming uncomfortable, when I heard the gate from the steps to the esplanade. I expected my Clementine, back from her daily swim at Maggie's Cove, euphoric from the open sea.

But DCI Graves stood there, staring sweetly at the balloons that lay scattered all around me.

'Celebrating?' she said, and my thumb and index finger must have slipped because the half-filled balloon launched from the helium canister, and the rogue balloon began to whizz wildly around the deck, making me duck my head and just missing the detective, who did not flinch, before shooting beyond the gate and crash landing somewhere down on the esplanade.

We stared at each other and I realised DCI Graves was waiting for an answer.

'Yes,' I said, suddenly feeling ridiculous, sitting cross-legged there on the deck filling party balloons.

I began to rise with as much dignity as I could muster, the helium canister still in my hand. 'Yes, we're celebrating.'

Graves smiled pleasantly. 'I didn't realise that anyone knew.'

I stared at her.

'Your friend,' she said. 'Charles Farthing? We're releasing him. Dropping all charges against him. He's coming home.' She stared up at the black-and-white bunting. 'I didn't realise anyone knew.'

I licked my lips. They were suddenly very dry.

'But he confessed,' I said. 'Didn't he?'

'Nothing in writing,' she said. 'We had nothing signed and dated. Which makes the paperwork easier now. But the CPS – the Crown Prosecution Service – have decided not to proceed. The evidence fell to bits under primary examination. That audio file – the two voices on the phone – was run by audio forensics. Do you know what that is?'

I must have shaken my head.

'They're the professional experts in voice recognition. They do audio analysis, audio enhancement, audio transcription and then they stand up in court and say – yes, that chap in the dock is the same man on the tape, Your Honour.' She shook her head. 'But it's not Charles Farthing on that recording. One of the men is our Sergeant Monk, deceased.' I stared into her watery blue eyes. 'The other man is unknown.'

'But what about the other murder? What about Stephen Monk?'

'Charles Farthing spent the night Stephen Monk died in bed in Padstow with a woman who has come forward and signed a sworn affidavit. All a bit awkward because the lady in question is married. But perhaps not quite as awkward as a life sentence for murder.'

I understood instantly who it must have been.

Michelle, Anton's wife.

'I don't understand,' I said. '*Why would someone confess to something that he didn't do?*'

'They teach us that there are three kinds of false confession. One – the persuaded false confession – when the police beat it out of you. Two – the compliant false confession – when the accused innocent just wants the questions to stop, and believes justice will be done in the end.' She smiled wryly, as if we were still having a pleasant chat. 'Not always the case, by the way. And three – the voluntary false confession. That is the most complex. The accused may have mental problems, or a slippery grasp on reality.'

The gate at the top of the steep stone steps creaked as it opened and closed and Clementine stood there staring at us, her hair wet and a darker red from the sea, and a bath towel thrown over her broad shoulders. She wore a one-piece swimming suit, the costume of a serious wild swimmer. Graves and I both stared at her as she stood on the deck, drying her hair, and then Graves looked back at me.

'Or they may be trying to protect someone,' she said.

Clementine began crossing the deck towards us, and the sun was dazzling in my eyes, and I could feel the sweat on my brow, my upper lip, my lower back.

'I wanted to be the first to tell you that Mr Farthing is being released,' Graves told me. 'I know how concerned you have been about your friend.'

She took it all in.

The balloons that had already been filled with helium, the ones that waited their turn. The bunting and the fairy lights.

'But I see you have already heard,' she said.

Silence. There was something stuck in my throat. I coughed it out.

'That's not why we're celebrating,' I said. 'That's not the reason for the party.'

Her head flinched, as if someone had called her by some old nickname.

And then Clementine was – no, not in my arms, but rubbing against me, the long, wet length of her, pushing against me, something feline about it, and she slipped an arm around my waist.

'Tom and I are getting married,' Clementine said, and she held out her left hand, and the diamond glittered on her third finger.

And DCI Graves looked at me, as if seeing me properly for the first time.

41

Detective Chief Inspector Graves was coming for me now. She saw me true at last.

I would have to pay for my sins.

And I realised – with a sense of shame so deep it seemed to run in my veins – I had hoped Charlie would pay the price for all I had done to set Clementine free.

And it was not going to happen.

So I crawled across the kitchen floor of the Lobster Pot, and I ran my fingertip between the grouting of the tiles, and I stared intently at the dark stain on my skin and my heart leapt at what I imagined was blood.

Clementine watched me from the doorway, her arms folded across her small and perfect breasts.

'What are you doing?'

I was desperately trying to hide all traces of what we had done in this room. I was hoping against hope that there was still a way for me to evade DCI Graves and all of her decency and wisdom and justice. I was hoping that I could still have a happy life with the woman I loved as I had never loved anyone in my life, not even myself.

'Nothing,' I said, crawling across the floor, my fingertip still scraping between the tiles.

'Can you relax?' Clementine said.

'I'm fine,' I said.

'Because if you can't relax, I'm going for another swim.'

'OK. I'll just finish up here and then I'll do the rest of the balloons.'

I heard her turn away with something that wasn't quite a sigh, more of an exhalation of breath, full of exasperation, and walk out of the kitchen. I waited, and I heard the gate creak out on the deck as she took the steps down to the esplanade.

Then Lisa was there.

'I chucked three bottles of bleach on that floor,' she said. 'And I washed the lobster pick that I stuck in his thick neck and then I put it in with the rest of them. Then I decided that wasn't good enough and I threw them all away, every one of them, ordered new ones from Truro.'

'Threw them where?' I said, still on my knees.

She nodded towards some place far away. 'Polmouth side. One of the old fishermen's cottages is being renovated and there was a skip outside. All of our lobster picks went in there. They took the skip away. I checked.'

'What about the clothes you were wearing?'

'Burned them. Down on Maggie's Cove. There are fires burning on every beach in Cornwall at this time of year. My gear all went on one of those. What about your clothes?'

'Washed them. Stuffed them in with the rubbish. Bin men took them away.'

She raised a wry eyebrow. 'Better than nothing, I suppose.' She nodded at me down on my hands and knees. 'It's not the floor you have to worry about.'

My mind raced through those minutes in our lives when everything changed. I saw it all again. But Lisa was talking, interrupting the blood-soaked replay.

She glanced around the restaurant. 'Looks good, all the lights. The Cornish bunting is a nice touch. But I have a question – *are you sure it's true?* About the guy in London – Alex? He had a wife and kids – and she didn't *know* about it? Do you really buy that? Is it even possible these days, to keep a secret like that?'

I felt sick to my stomach. I had never doubted for one second that it was true. She went to him – she saw his family – and she realised that her future was with me. How could that be anything but true? But Lisa was still talking.

'If you get married – if she's your next of kin – then all this belongs to her. The Lobster Pot. The apartment. Whatever you have in the bank.'

'What's your point?'

'She seems a little unlucky on the husband front. They don't last long, do they?'

I laughed. 'You hate her, Lisa. You really hate her.'

'I don't hate her. I resent her. I'm jealous. But how could I hate her? Her husband beat her. Her lover turned out to be married with children. No, I don't hate her, Tom. She has been abused by every man she ever loved. And I just wonder . . .'

I waited.

'What you are going to do to her, Tom.'

'I am going to love her,' I said. It was simple and true, and I saw it turned Lisa's stomach. There was tuneless humming from inside the restaurant. 'Ryan's here,' she said. 'You better get up.'

But I was on my knees still.

Because there was something I had missed.

I saw it again. Down on my knees, it played out once more as if it could possibly end some other way.

Steve drunk, talking about the bill, leering at me, wanting to give me a tip – what tip did you have for me, Steve? – shirtless and powerful, sickeningly healthy, this man who had loved her. And Steve watching Lisa shuck the lobsters with her violent efficiency. A neat pile of pink and white knuckles, claws and tails lined up before her. And his cruel taunting, mocking her, the spite of it — making fun of her husband dying not tragically alone, but in the presence of the teenage girl in the denim shorts who she had hired to look after little Paolo. Steve goading Lisa as she rinsed lobster meat in the big industrial sink, laughing at her as she stuck a lobster pick deep inside a claw.

Laughing at her right up until the moment that she had stuck it in him.

And suddenly I remembered what I had forgotten.

We had cleaned the floor and burned our clothes and dropped all of our lobster picks — all of them! — in a skip Polmouth side. But there was something we had missed.

I remembered the takeaway bag with the lobster in the top hat, I remembered filling it with the bloody wads of tissue because Will Farthing had told me I was an idiot for wanting to put them in the rubbish bin. I could see it now — the takeaway bag on the kitchen island, stuffed full of enough evidence to lock us away for a lifetime.

'What happened to the takeaway bag, Lisa?'

'What takeaway bag?' she said, but even as the words were coming out of her mouth – she remembered. 'You got rid of it – didn't you?'

I shook my head. 'I didn't get rid of it. I thought you got rid of it.'

We stared at each other for a long moment. And then she called out a name.

'Ryan!'

The boy appeared in the doorway. I got up off my knees and pointed at the kitchen island.

'There was a takeaway bag just there,' I said.

'That didn't have a takeaway in it,' Lisa said.

Ryan looked from me to Lisa with his dazed surfer's eyes. Then he brushed the hair from his face.

'It was there when I came into work,' he said. 'Just sitting there. I wasn't going to put it in the rubbish because I thought you might get in trouble. And I wasn't going to dump it in the town because I thought *I* might get in trouble. And I wasn't going to just leave it there because I thought we might all get in trouble and the Lobster Pot would have to close.'

'So what did you do with it?' I said.

He nodded at a refrigerated glass case, full of bottles.

The wine cooler.

'It's in the back,' he said, and Lisa joined me on the floor as we quickly removed bottles of white and rosé and champagne from their racks. The takeaway bag with the grinning lobster was stuffed at the back, crumpled and cold.

'Should I have . . .?' Ryan said, and Lisa immediately went to him, and patted his back.

'It's OK, Ryan. You did good. Thank you. Let me help you with whatever it is you're doing.'

They left me alone.

I took out the bag.

The tissues inside were stiff with cold, the blood blackened by time. The bag was torn, the rip passing right through the lobster's speech bubble – *Take me home with you!*

I began to restock the wine cooler with the bottles we had removed.

'Tom?'

I looked up at Clementine.

I stood up, half of the bottles still on the floor, the wine cooler door open and starting to beep a warning signal for the day was hot and the door did not enjoy being open for long. The takeaway bag was in my right hand. And I thought she would say – *I never asked you for violence. I never wanted anyone dead. I just wanted them to leave me alone. I just wanted them to stop talking, to stop touching me, to stop thinking they owned me. I did not want murder. I wanted only freedom.*

But she said nothing.

I stood there uncertain what to do, or say, but she came to my side and she placed a kiss on my lips and I felt my hands reach for her, as they always would, in this world and the next.

'Burn it,' she said. 'Burn it and then come to our engagement party.'

42

There was an ancient fort on the outskirts of St Jude's, one of the small artillery forts built by Henry VIII to protect his kingdom from invaders after his break from Rome, and I thought it would be a good place to burn what must be burned. The fort stood at the very edge of the coastal path, and to reach it you walked out of the esplanade, and the road fell gently down to a tiny beach before rising steeply to the blackened ruins overlooking the point where the estuary met the open sea. But when I reached it, the takeaway bag in my hand, the opening folded over, and then folded over again, the old fort was full of tourists waiting for the sunset to paint the horizon. There was not much to see of Henry VIII's castle, but it afforded some of the best views in St Jude's. So the tourists waved their phones in each other's faces, and I walked on, down the coastal path. I thought to burn what must be burned on Maggie's Cove but, even at the end of a summer's day, there were still bathers who had not had enough sea, who had not had enough sun, and so I walked on. Perhaps there was another way, and a better way, for at this point of the season, even the bleakest parts of the coastal path, those spots where the wind seemed to pick up ferocity, and the path fell away dangerously from the cliff edge, there were still people, hardcore ramblers who were coming from further down the coast. And so I walked on, far beyond Maggie's Cove, until the only other sign of life I could see was a tiny figure far ahead of me, walking with the determination of someone who knew exactly where they were going.

And when I reached the Baulking House, she was waiting for me, her face flushed with unaccustomed exercise.

'Tom?' she said, and I cringed at the unearned intimacy. 'Remember me? Scarlet Bush?'

'Like the porn star,' I said. 'You're the journalist.'

She nodded, then indicated the bag in my hand. 'I didn't know you did deliveries.'

I felt my face flushing.

'Joke,' she said, losing interest in the bag. She indicated the Baulking House. The plain wooden benches inside the scarred white shelter, the shuttered cottage. 'Funny place for a bus stop.'

'Funny place to bump into you,' I said, more comfortable now that she had forgotten the takeaway bag.

She looked surprised. 'Really?' She glanced towards the cliff edge. 'But this is where they found him, isn't it?'

I said nothing.

'Sergeant Monk,' she went on. 'Isn't this the spot where he went over the edge?'

We were both looking at the edge of the cliff. There was nothing beyond it, a nothingness so vast it took your breath away, only the distant horizon, where the sea met the sky in a shimmering haze of heat. The sun was sinking low now, a hard red ball that was already painting the sky and would give the tourists back at Henry VIII's fort images to treasure.

Scarlet Bush was walking towards the cliff edge, chuckling to herself, and those last moments with Sergeant Monk came back to me so vividly that I felt I was with him once more.

It wasn't an accident, I had told him, and the memory made me swallow now, it made me choke something down.

Scarlet Bush was standing on the cliff edge. Like Sergeant Monk, she had her phone in her hand. She had asked me a question but I had not heard. And I wanted to tell him more, I wanted to tell him every-thing, I wanted to explain that I had never met anyone more deserving of my love than Clementine – a name he did not even recognise. But there was no time – that was what I remembered most of all, the total paucity of time – because he flew at me, and then I had to fight him.

Scarlet Bush was on the edge of the cliff, a strange look on her face. She was suddenly aware that I had not heard a single word she had said.

'I said – do you know why the rest of the media have shipped out?'

I shook my head. I had been aware that there were fewer journalists sniffing around St Jude's, trying to pick up the scent of murder.

'It's because the victims are not attractive,' she said. 'Stephen Monk and his stepfather – all these stories are starting to come out about them. They are almost a hashtag. And so we don't care. The media likes their murder victims to be cute. Or we lose interest.'

The wind whipped around her, covered her face with her hair. She pulled it away, but the winds were high now, they were always high at the Baulking House, and I saw her swaying on the spot, trying to keep her balance.

'But you're still here.'

She smiled. She wasn't a bad person. But there was a professional curiosity about her that made her seem like my enemy, and the enemy of everything I loved.

'Because I don't have an editor to tell me to move on,' she said. 'There's a freedom in that, a liberty.' She rolled her eyes. 'Even if the money is lousy. I heard they are letting your friend go, dropping all charges. A source told me. The police can't keep a secret. You must be happy.'

She turned back to the clifftop and edged a few baby steps closer to the point where it fell away to the rocks below.

That's what she was here for, that's what she was photographing. The crevice where the seagulls nibbled on the face of Sergeant Monk as if they were at an all-you-can-eat seagull buffet.

She leaned as far as she dared to lean in this wind.

And I held my breath, and I did not move.

And then she stepped away from the cliff edge.

'Well, that's me done,' she said, walking back onto the coastal path, chatting away in her cynical yet strangely merry fashion. 'Just wanted that for my records, for when I write my masterpiece. I think the world is ready for a modern *In Cold Blood*, don't you? Are you a fan of Capote?'

I was unable to move, unable to speak, and shaking with the moment that had come and gone forever. The moment when it would have been so easy to give that journalist a little helping hand, just a small shove in the back would have been enough. The thought sickened me, scared me, made me feel like howling with hysterical laughter. I had nothing against this woman. Not unless she wanted to tell the world the truth about me. Not unless she wanted to punish me for my sins. Then I did have something against her.

I was shaking quite hard now. But the wind covered everything, cloaked our voices and emotions in that blustery gale that never stopped in that lonely place.

She had asked me another question, and again I missed it.

'I said – are you walking back to St Jude's? We can walk together.'

I shook my head, gestured vaguely further down the coastal path, tried to think about a plausible excuse for walking further with a takeaway bag in my hand, but the gesture had been enough for Scarlet Bush.

She turned away with a pleasant smile, as if we were friends now, as if we were all in this together. I sat in the shelter of the Baulking House until she was out of sight.

There were a few false starts, for the coastal path back to St Jude's dipped and then rose, so that I lost sight of her and then she appeared again a few minutes later, and I felt like weeping for her, because she had been so close to death when she stood on the edge of that cliff.

But the coastal path rose and fell and twisted and turned, and in the end there was a moment when her tiny figure disappeared and I knew she would be able to see the lights of the town in the distance, and she would be close to Maggie's Cove, and there was no way she could see me.

There was less wind now in the shelter of the Baulking House. They knew what they were doing, those old pilchard-watchers of long ago. So I took out the disposable lighter I had brought with me, and put the takeaway bag in a corner of the shelter where the crumbled white rock formed a snug little hole, perfect for my purpose. I placed the takeaway bag in the hole and lit the bottom. It burned quickly, the bag with the grinning lobster burning to black ashes and then the bloody contents, all those wads of tissues that we had used to stem the bleeding in Steve's wound.

It all burned, and when I had kicked over the ashes, and I saw that it was all no more, I turned for home and I walked away from the Baulking House.

And I was watched.

The blood ran cold in my veins because I knew with total certainty that I had been watched, although I could not tell if I had been watched by the eyes of the living, or the eyes of those who had been dead for one hundred years.

43

CHARLIE FARTHING: *There was a party but it was not for me. There was balloons and fairy lights and special nosh — but none of it was for me. Me coming home from that place where there are locked doors surrounded by steel walls surrounded by razor wire was not the reason for their celebration. That stinking, airless prison, that place of cruelty and stupidity and bad breaks, where every breath you take is an effort. They had no idea. They didn't have a clue. They all smiled, and they hugged me, and they said — Welcome home, Charlie! But I was an afterthought, as I have been all my life, and the place where you grow up doesn't always feel like home. And I took the champagne when it was offered to me, and I raised my glass and smiled at them all. But they did not guess at the rage that was inside me. And that was the irony — that was why the mad laughter bubbled up inside me! I could hardly stop smiling. I felt like howling in all their happy faces. Because after coming back to St Jude's, I really did feel like killing someone. And I knew now that dreaming about leaving was never going to be enough. Not now. If I stayed in St Jude's, this little piece of paradise would eat me alive.*

The party had begun without me.

I paused down on the esplanade and high above me I could see the fairy lights strung out above the deck of the Lobster Pot, and I could hear their laughter, and their voices, and the music. It was that mad playlist that you heard at a lock-in at the Rabbit Hole, that weird eclectic soundtrack of pop, rock, dance and karaoke classics. As I stood there, Kylie's 'Can't Get You Out of My Head' segued so casually into Sigala & Ella Eyre's 'Came Here for Love' that it made me smile.

I moved towards the entrance to the steps.

Then I saw her.

She was a little further down the esplanade, and she was also staring up at the music and the lights of the Lobster Pot.

And somehow I knew who she was, and I knew that she was figuring a way to get up to the deck, for the entrance to the steps that climbed to the restaurant was easy to miss if you did not know it was there.

She was in her forties, much younger than I had expected, her hair very blonde and styled expensively, dressed smart – too smart for Cornwall, really, because unless I was mistaken her white jacket and dress with the gold bling was from Chanel. She was not quite as tall as her daughter, but I could see the ghost of Clementine in her striking face. She saw me coming.

'You're Tom,' she said, and when she smiled I could see her daughter even clearer, for there was something self-conscious about the way she tried to dial down her grin, as though it was too much, as though that smile was anything less than lovely. 'I'm Mary.'

'Clementine's mother,' I said.

She followed me up the steps to the party, her heels clicking on the granite, and if I had been worried about how the night would go – and I had – then that first sight of the party reassured me.

Clementine and Lisa were coming out of the kitchen with plates of grilled lobster, followed by Ryan with two bottles of Whispering Angel in each hand. The guests were gathered around the table.

Will and Bet Farthing, done up to the nines again, but happy now, because Charlie was sitting between them, a surprise guest, grinning with what looked like relief. He caught my eye, nodded and smiled.

Paolo sat next to Will, his fishing skipper, and on the other side of the table were Anton and Michelle with young Saskia Winter – another surprise guest – next to her. Sandy, an accomplished DJ after all those lock-ins at the Rabbit Hole, was fiddling with her phone, adjusting the volume of 'Sweet Caroline'.

They all turned to Mary and me as we appeared on the deck. 'I want you all to meet my mum,' Clementine said.

Clementine made the introductions, and we filled our glasses.

'Welcome to St Jude's,' Clementine said to Mary, and then turned to the Farthings. 'And welcome home, dear Charlie.'

We all drank to that, and Clementine squeezed my arm and smiled as we all took our places at the table.

'You can have anything on the menu,' Lisa said. 'As long as it's the grilled lobster. And you can drink what you like, as long as it's the rosé.'

'Caught these beauties this morning,' Will told Mary, always quick to impress a pretty face.

Mary in her white Chanel suit looked suitably stunned. 'You actually caught these lobsters?'

Will jerked a thumb at Paolo, the only one of us who was not on the Whispering Angel.

'Me and my crew mate here,' Will said. 'He can shoot the pots out himself now, can Paolo.

When he's big enough to haul 'em back in, he'll not need me.'

Mary took a mouthful of Will's lobster. She did not need to fake it. Will Farthing's day-caught lobster tasted like the best thing in the world.

'Dad finally found the next generation of fishermen,' Charlie said, and we all laughed, but then it needed some explanation for Mary – and for Saskia too, holding one of Ryan's hands under the table. And so the Farthings – Will and Charlie, but mostly Bet – told the story of how the Farthings had been fishing folk for generations until Charlie decided that he wanted to do something different.

'So what do you do?' Mary asked Charlie, and I was struck again by how totally different she was from who I had been expecting.

I had heard so many tales about the sixteen-year-old girl who gave up her baby that it was hard to connect this sleek, confident businesswoman in her white Chanel number with that desperate teenager and her baby.

'I have been away,' Charlie said, and an awkward silence fell over the table. 'At Her Majesty's Pleasure.' He grinned at the table and we smiled back as best we could.

'He didn't do anything,' Bet added.

Charlie smiled at Mary, but didn't look at me. 'All a bit of a misunderstanding. All sorted now. No harm done.' He took a long, languid pull on his Whispering Angel, as though you did not get that in HMP Dartmoor. 'In fact, it has been a bit of a wake-up call. I always fancied seeing the world beyond St Jude's. And now I think I am going to sell my boat and really do it.'

'Sell it to Paolo,' Lisa said, and we all laughed, and we were all happy for the chance to laugh.

'Oh, are you a fisherman too?' Mary asked the boy, and I saw the easy charm that Clementine had; I saw the way she could hold you in her hands with just a few words and a smile.

'Summer for lobster,' Paolo told her. 'Winter for mackerel.'

And Will happily played the Cornishman for Mary, showing her his intact hands.

'Still got all my fingers, see?' he said. 'Not many fifty-year fishermen can say that. She'll tell you,' he said, indicating Sandy, and I thought of all the smiling faces of St Jude's lost fishermen behind the bar of the Rabbit Hole.

Then Clementine was standing at the head of the table, me looking up at her, as she tapped the side of her wine glass with a knife.

'And Tom and I have an announcement to make,' she said, and I swallowed hard because I thought that our happy ending could put the kibosh on a party that was going so well.

But it did not. And Clementine told our friends and neighbours and her mother that we were engaged to be married, and somehow it lifted the party to new heights, and the women kissed me and the men shook my hand, and Charlie slapped me on the back and wished me all the luck in the world as if we did not love the same woman.

And against all the odds, he seemed to mean it. And also against all odds, I could tell the party was going to be a huge success.

These were both long shots, but sometimes the long shot wins. Because this community ritual was what we did best in our fishing village, and this collective coming together was the kind of moment when St Jude's revealed its genius. And they loved Clementine and they loved me too.

So we ate our day-caught grilled lobster and we washed it down with a crate of rosé and we celebrated our engagement, but we also celebrated Charlie coming home, and we celebrated meeting Mary, and we celebrated Ryan and Saskia staying together despite her father's objections.

It ended around midnight and it was good that it did not go on any longer. For Paolo was asleep in his mother's arms, and Anton and Michelle were charming to everyone except each other – they were ignoring each other the way only an unhappily married couple ever can – and Charlie had taken to glancing at Clementine with a stricken expression, and Saskia looked as though she was still too young to know how much she could drink without feeling sick, and Ryan was laughing as he told me that he and Saskia were shacked up in an empty second-home that he had broken into Polmouth side, and I was telling him to be careful, and Will Farthing had been knocking back the Whispering Angel like water. He cornered me as I was collecting the plates with their pink and white lobster debris.

'You know what we should have done?' Will grinned. 'We should have dropped him down an old tin mine. Cornwall's full of 'em. Quite an extensive choice. Then nobody would have found the bugger! Too soft we was, Tom!'

'Time to go home to your bed, old man,' Bet said.

And later, much later, when they had all gone home, we sat out on the deck, shivering in the night air, Clementine and Mary and I, and the rosé was all gone so we were all drinking Korev beer, and I held Clementine's hand and looked at the blue and orange label and the motto I loved – *The coast is our compass*, it said. *Born in Cornwall.*

And we let her mother do the talking, and I was aware of the giddy strangeness of it — to be a parent who missed all those years of their child growing up.

'Marry soon,' her mother was saying. 'I do hope you'll marry soon, you two.'

Clementine touched my face, and we had our moment, out on the deck, our shining moment under the stars, a moment that would never be lost, and would never come again.

'Have a child, have more than one if you can.' Mary had not touched her Korev beer, and it crossed my mind that she was possibly not the kind of woman who liked beer. 'That will bring you closer together than anything,' she said. 'It is the great project, having a child together, the only thing that really gives our lives meaning, the only thing that holds men and women together for a lifetime. The meaning of life is — more life, and to love and nurture that more life.'

Clementine laughed. 'She's telling us the meaning of life!' She raised her Korev in mock salute. She was a bit tipsy. 'Cheers, Mum!'

'I didn't do it,' Mary said, dead serious. 'I failed. I know I did. They took my child away. My baby girl. They took you away.' No tears, no self-pity. A cold statement of hard fact. 'I was too young, too stupid, not ready.' She thoughtfully sipped her beer, destroying my theory, and turned to me. 'But you and Clementine have the chance to do it.' She looked at both of us. 'You are a beautiful couple. And she has always needed a man to love her and not try to control her, to change her, to know everything that has happened to her.'

Clementine laughed with embarrassment, with delight, and with emotions I could not guess.

'A bit late for life lessons, *Mother!*'

I was a bit drunk. The music had stopped. Sandy had gone back to the Rabbit Hole and taken her party playlist with her.

When had the music stopped?

'It's never too late,' Mary said. 'So be kind to each other. And marry. That corny, old-fashioned ritual – do it. But do it soon. Before the sex wears off.'

Clementine and I stared at each other.

Then we laughed.

Because of course the sex had never worn off between us.

And it never even came close to wearing off.

44

DCI Graves was waiting for me.

I knew the moment would come. I knew that one day I would turn around and there she would be, small and slight and smiling politely. It was almost a relief when it finally happened. My heart fell away at the sight of her waiting for me – of course it did – but I also felt some nameless weight lifting from me. *Let's get it over with then.*

A month of summer days and summer nights had drifted by and it was now the height of the season. We were at Maggie's Cove. Clementine was out in the water, moving gracefully through sea as smooth as a mirror, the sun splashing it with gold, while I watched her from the beach.

And then there was DCI Graves, looking up at the shuttered beach house that stood at the edge of the sand. She indicated the abandoned building as I approached her.

'Somebody told me this is the beach in *Rebecca*,' she said. I must have looked blank because she elaborated. 'The Daphne du Maurier novel?'

'I saw the film,' I said. 'Alfred Hitchcock.'

'The book is better,' Graves said, looking at the beach house and not me. 'And someone in St Jude's told me they thought this was Rebecca's cove in the book.'

'I think that place is more Fowey way. Not far, but a bit further along the coast. They all like to say – ah, this is the place you are looking for. Have another pint. Have another pasty.'

She finally looked at me. She was no longer smiling. 'Will you walk with me?'

I glanced out at Clementine in the water.

She waved, and I waved back. She trod water, looking at us. She was still close enough to shore to recognise who I was talking to.

'I'm a bit busy right now,' I said. 'We've got to go back and get ready for the lunch trade.'

'I would like you to walk with me, Mr Cooper,' she said.

And I saw that it was not an invitation.

And so we walked, leaving the cove and joining the coastal path, steep and winding. I looked back once, to see Clementine on the beach, staring after us as we pressed on, the wind picking up the further we were from St Jude's. We met a couple of middle-aged ramblers on the path, going in the opposite direction, and we all wished each other a hearty good morning. But then we saw no one, not a soul, and I wondered how far we would have to walk before we stopped.

Then I saw the Baulking House ahead, stark on the high cliff before us. And that was where we finally paused, taking our seats in one of those little bus stops that was not a bus stop, that was never a bus stop, both of us staring out to sea as if this had all been arranged long, long ago.

'I know you did it,' she said, and then there was nothing but the wind and the gulls, trying to drown each other out.

I looked at her face as she stared out at the horizon.

'That's your voice on Monk's phone,' she said. 'I didn't think it was at first. But when you announced your engagement, it all made sense. I didn't need the audio forensics bods to tell me I was going after the wrong man.' And she finally looked at me. 'Motive is everything. Well, almost everything. Opportunity is the rest of it.' She nodded to the clifftop that seemed to crumble away to infinity just beyond the coastal path. 'My guess is that Sergeant Monk was dumb enough to bring you up here to plot some clever revenge – or you persuaded him to come up here on some cock and bull story – and he did not realise what he was signing up for until he was sailing through space. Is that about the shape of it?'

I said nothing. I could not find the words to lie.

'I know you did it because you love her,' she said. 'And because they were cruel men – Sergeant Monk and his stepson Stephen – who were beyond reason, who were beyond everything but violence. Cruel men, as I say. They should never have been police officers. They were the type of male human being who should have been chased, nicked and banged up by police officers. If there was any justice in the world – which I sometimes doubt!'

I thought of running. It would not have been the first time in my life that I ran away from ruin. But I could not move my legs.

There was no escaping DCI Graves.

'They don't have a lot of time for police around here,' she said. 'The people round here are a law unto themselves. Always have been. Anyway – after this case – I will be out of it. I spent most of my career in big northern towns but I'm from this part of the world, and I quite fancy retiring down here, finding the places that Daphne du Maurier based her books on. The real cove in *Rebecca*. The moors in *Jamaica Inn*. The secret river in *Frenchman's Creek* where the woman lay with her pirate lover.' She laughed, a little embarrassed. 'Does that sound silly? You see, I never married, never had kids. None of that ever happened. I had an experience as a young woman that put me right off all of that caper. It was – well, let's just say it never happened. So, looking for Daphne du Maurier – that's the plan once we have tied all this up.'

She looked at me steadily, and I saw the steel in her, and the hardness, and the lack of pity for those who broke the law.

And that was me.

'You ever heard of a copper called George Oldfield?' she said. 'You wouldn't have – but George Oldfield is famous in my game because he believed he had the Yorkshire Ripper in his sights. And he didn't. George had a confession on tape – a fake confession – from a man who called himself Wearside Jack. He confessed directly to George Oldfield, claimed he killed all those poor women. And because the man on the tape had a Newcastle accent, George Oldfield was convinced – totally certain – that he was looking for a Geordie. And he wasn't. He was looking at the wrong man. And do you know what it did to him, looking at the wrong man? Do you know what it did to George Oldfield?'

She was waiting for me to respond. The gulls were screaming high above us. The wind was howling in our faces.

I shook my head.

'It killed him,' she said. 'Getting it wrong. Chasing the wrong person. All that wasted energy. He died of congestive heart failure at the age of sixty-one. This job will kill you if you let it. And nobody cares. It killed George Oldfield because he worked long, long hours – in many ways he was a great copper, totally dedicated. But he never took leave, never took a break. And in the end he ran himself into the ground. The killer was right under George Oldfield's nose. And he missed him. I was looking at the wrong man too, wasn't I? But it is not going to kill me. I'm not going out as another George Oldfield. I know I got it wrong, too. Difference is – *this is not going to kill me*. I want to sit in the sun and reread *Frenchman's Creek* – Du Maurier's masterpiece, in my opinion. But this is not going to kill me. Because I have found the killer. Do we understand each other, Mr Cooper?'

I nodded. She smiled her sweet smile.

'Good,' she said. Then she sighed with satisfaction rather than despair. 'The Monks were typical of the modern cop. I wish that wasn't true, but all the evidence tells me that it is. Good riddance to bad rubbish. But I am afraid that is not enough to give you a pass. That is not enough to let you just walk away. The fact that they were a pair of bastards is not enough for you to go free. Do you get that, Mr Cooper?'

I may have nodded. She inhaled deeply, let it go slowly, stared dreamily out at the sea.

'What's out there, do you think? It looks like nothing – doesn't it? But I bet there's Nazi U-boats and pirate ships and fishing boats – generations of them. It looks like nothing, but it's – everything. Life. History. Oh well.'

I watched her take a phone out of her jacket. I realised it was Sergeant Monk's phone. I understood it was the phone with the audio file of his last words, our final conversation, heavily redacted by the wind.

She gave it to me. 'Evidence gets lost,' she said. 'Evidence gets contaminated in the chain of custody process. Evidence goes missing.'

She stood up. I stood up with her.

'I don't know how much you know about the Monks,' she said. 'Sergeant Monk was the famous one. Because back in the day he raped a young female police officer who was going after the same promotion as him. He got her in his squad car to talk about the job they were both after. And raped her. And the punchline was that he got the promotion and she was told to keep her mouth shut if she knew what was good for her. She was told to suck it up. She – this girl, this young naïve kid – was told nobody would believe her. She was told to stay silent.'

She looked out to sea and then back at me.

'And so I did,' she said.

She gave me the phone. Placed it gently in the palm of my hand, placed both her hands on mine, patted them twice.

'I wish you and Clementine a happy life,' she said, and I watched her walk away, a small solitary figure on the coastal path, taking her steps carefully in that high, lonely place.

And when the coastal path twisted down and away and I could see her no more, I walked toward the edge of the cliffs, my fist tightening around the phone as I aimed it at the place where the sea met the sky.

45

It was the time for goodbyes.

The Winter family had loaded their SUV, locked up their second home Polmouth side and fled back to Chelsea – or was it Notting Hill? Ryan did not seem too bothered, going about his chores in the restaurant lost in the music plugged into his head, and so we knew that he would see Saskia again.

Scarlet Bush had wheeled her suitcase to St Jude's tiny railway station, which would take her to Penzance and the sleeper train back to London and the uncertain life of the self-employed in a dying trade.

Clementine's mother, Mary, had returned to her family in an affluent suburb of Manchester, where there was a husband and two teenage children waiting for her.

And from the deck of the Lobster Pot, Clementine and Lisa and I watched DCI Graves leaving the little Airbnb she had near the quay, loading her suitcases into an unmarked car. Young police officers fussed around her, wanting to help, but she waved them away and hefted her own bags into the back of the car.

She looked up at us and waved.

We waved back.

Goodbye and good luck.

St Jude's smiled at us.

As our new life found its rhythm, this we found to be true.

Our village smiled at us. Our village was happy for us.

Clementine would rise before dawn to swim in the cool glassy water of the early day. She never again swam across the estuary from St Jude's to Polmouth, but she would take her first swim off the quay of St Jude's and swim halfway across the water before turning back.

I told her it was not safe. That in the high season the estuary filled with crafts of all kinds. There were the fishing boats of St Jude's, of course, but those salty old boys knew enough to avoid a lone swimmer. What she should fear were all the crafts of the incomers, that ragged fleet of sailing boats, dinghies, kayaks, yachts, even the odd jet ski, frequently going far too fast. For a solitary swimmer, the water was never totally safe, and especially not at this point of the season.

But nothing could dissuade Clementine from her sacred early-morning dip. And when I awoke, I would go out on to the deck of the Lobster Pot and I would watch her. She would always be well into her swim by then, edging towards the halfway mark between St Jude's and Polmouth on the far side, where she would turn back and head for home with the steady, effortless grace of her long-limbed crawl.

Clementine's swimming became a feature of the village, something to be pointed out and remarked upon and watched for, as if she was the lead character in that oldest of Cornish folk tales, the Mermaid of Zennor.

'Did you see our Clem this morning?' someone would say in the Rabbit Hole or down on the quay, and the others would smile with affection and respect.

She was *our Clem* to them now. Another incarnation in her life. Tina was no more, and she was our Clem in the village, but always Clementine in my arms and in our bed, the sea sighing beyond our window in our modest rooms above the Lobster Pot. We were never happier.

Mary had told us to marry quickly but we decided to see out the season. In St Jude's we all made the money that would have to last us through the coming winter, and the Lobster Pot was packed every night.

Clementine fit into the rhythm of the restaurant, taking over the hostess role that she had once performed at Le Poisson Imaginaire. Her early friendship with Lisa was restored, and some nights the pair of them would talk together – at the reception desk or in the kitchen or out on the deck long after last orders, and I would leave them alone.

And when the season was ending, Clementine began going online in the evening, out on the deck with her laptop, or sitting up in bed with her phone as I lay by her side stroking her limbs, still dumbfounded by my great fortune in finding this woman, as she looked for her wedding dress.

It wasn't wise, of course, to swim the way she swam in the morning – so far out, so alone, never knowing what idiot was going to come barrelling into the estuary – and I would watch her from the deck of the Lobster Pot, almost bursting with pride and anxiety.

For some nameless dread was gripping me during these last days of summer, a dread that our happiness was about to be snatched away by nameless, faceless forces. But Clementine soothed me, and told me not to worry, and asked me to think of DCI Graves waving goodbye, and getting into her car, and driving away from St Jude's forever.

Nothing was going to go wrong for us, she swore.

And we whispered in the darkness of the years ahead. Our life together. A child together, God willing. And we talked of other things – our plans for the Lobster Pot, our life in St Jude's. And how to make this feeling last forever.

'And what did he look like?' she asked me one night, when the darkness was full of the headlights of the incomers going home.

'Who?' I said, already knowing.

'What did Sergeant Monk look like on that cliff in the final moments?' she asked quietly. 'What did he look like just before you pushed him off that cliff? What was the expression on the rotten bastard's face just before you killed him?'

I lay there listening to the sea, feeling my heart thumping in my chest.

I cleared my throat.

'He looked surprised,' I said, for it was the truth, it was surprise more than anything that life was about to end, and she said nothing, and I waited for some long moments but she still said nothing, and she clearly had no further questions.

And I had nothing to add.

Then she squeezed me tight, and soon we slept in a tangle of limbs and love and that sweet, spent exhaustion that came after our sex, the best feeling ever, as if nothing could be better than this, as if nothing could ever come between us, as if there could never be an ending for us.

We no longer went to the cream-and-blue cottage up on the hill, and when the lease ended, it would not be renewed. The apartment above the Lobster Pot was home for both of us now.

But the night before our wedding day, we were up at the cottage packing some of her clothes that she wanted in the apartment now that the season was turning, and the old cream-and-blue cottage stirred something in both of us, and we fell into the comically sagging double bed, caught in a fit of nostalgia and madness and mischief, and we decided to stay the night there.

We slept together at the cream-and-blue cottage that night although we knew it was bad luck on the eve of our wedding.

We slept together although we knew we were mocking the fates, goading the gods, laughing in their faces, and cursing ourselves forever.

46

It was nearly our anniversary.

We had been married for nearly one hour.

'Everybody's waiting,' I said.

'Let them wait,' Clementine said. 'Just a little bit longer.'

We were standing on the beach by Le Poisson Imaginaire. We could see our guests inside the bright glass box of the restaurant, waiting for us. We were barefoot, Clementine and I, having walked back from the registry office in Padstow along the string of huge golden beaches that run along that stretch of the north Cornwall coast.

It had been a small wedding, with just Will and Bet Farthing as our witnesses. But we were going big on the party.

Everyone in St Jude's was invited – the fishermen and their families, the incomers we had got to know at the Lobster Pot, everyone we knew from the Rabbit Hole, all our friends and family we had left – which wasn't much family at all, just Clementine's mother Mary and her husband and their children.

But although we were short on family, we were not poor in people who loved us. And now they were all waiting for us.

But we stood in the water, Clementine with her high heels in her hand, me with my suit trousers rolled up to my knees, and we felt the cool sea on our legs and feet on the last of the warm days as the sea breathed and sighed behind us and we watched our guests from a distance.

And I looked at my wife – my wife! – and I felt I understood, because I could feel it too. This need to pause and savour this moment of pure and undiluted happiness, to hold it, and to store it away in memory, safe and sound and secure in our hearts, and to keep it close so that we could always take it out and re-member it in the years ahead, just in case we were never this happy again.

And I thought – *my wife*.

And I needed to make quite the effort to hold back the tears, because I really did not want to spoil this moment by letting my emotions get out of control.

But I loved her, you see. I loved her for the way she looked – I would never deny it – that slightly goofy grin, the limbs that I had stroked, slept by, stared at in wonder. The limbs that I wanted around me forever. But I loved her for the things that were not so immediately obvious. I loved her brave, defiant heart, the spirit that refused to bow down no matter what life had chucked at her. I loved her shining soul. And I loved her because I knew – with the total certainty that allowed no daylight in on the magic – that she loved me too.

And I loved her no matter what anyone said about her, no matter what they knew, or thought they knew. Because no one ever knew her like me.

But then there were faces at the big floor-to-ceiling glass walls of Le Poisson Imaginaire, and there were smiles and waves.

We were close enough to see them – Will and Bet, our witnesses, who we had put in a taxi after the service. And Charlie and Lisa and Paolo. And Sandy and the men and women we knew from the Rabbit Hole and the quay and the restaurant. And Anton and Michelle, our gracious hosts, gesturing for us to join them.

'It's so good in the water,' Clementine said, squeezing my hand.

'But we better go in now,' I said.

They roared when we walked into the restaurant.

This great big throaty cheer that touched me deeply, as though we both belonged here with these people, as though we were home at last. And as though they were happy for us – more than happy – delighted, proud, and wishing us well.

Champagne flutes were raised all around us, and a young waiter I did not recognise smilingly handed a glass to my wife and me, and the glass had just been taken out of the freezer – that classy Le Poisson Imaginaire touch – it was so cold that it burned my fingers.

Champagne and hugs and kisses and congratulations. Faces – Bet and Will and Anton and Michelle and Lisa and Charlie and Paolo and Sandy. Fishermen who were struggling to make a living with their wives and children, all wearing their best clothes.

We had the entire restaurant to ourselves today, the long tables covered in white linen and silver cutlery and glass vases of coastal wildflowers. There were ox-eye daisies, also known as moon daisy and dog daisy, like a daisy, only bigger. There was pink sea thrift to ensure we were never poor, red English stonecrop that grows among the black granite cliffs, fluffy blue flowers called sheeps bit scabious because sheep can never get enough of them, and small white flowers known as dead man's bells.

'It's beautiful, Anton,' Clementine was saying. 'Thank you.'

'Shall we begin?' Anton said.

The first course was lobster cocktail. Day-caught lobster landed at dawn by Will Farthing and Paolo out on the *Bonnie Bet* while we were all still sleeping.

There were, I now realised, a pack of young waiters waiting to serve us. They wore black and had been bussed in from some neighbouring city – probably Bristol – because it was so hard to get staff in our corner of the world these days. They were young, these boys and girls waiting with their trays of champagne and lobster cocktails. Almost certainly university students who needed to bump up their grant. And they were bright-eyed, willing, decent kids who could not stop looking at Clementine. Serving at our wedding reception was obviously just a weekend job to earn a few quid.

They stood there looking at my bride and I knew they would never forget how she looked that day.

And then there was the unexpected crash as an explosive noise broke the spell, followed by apologies and expressions of regret and a few mocking cheers.

A girl, late teens at the most. Small, pretty, black hair and eyes I had not yet seen. She was staring at the floor, the mess of broken glass and spoilt lobster and smashed plates. Other waiters, her mates, rushed to help her, to clear up the mess, to maintain the mood.

And then suddenly she looked at me. Eyes that were brown, large and shining. And I realised that all the waiters had been staring at Clementine from the moment we entered the restaurant. But one of them had been looking at me.

'Dad?' she said, her eyes wide with shock and horror.

That was me.

Dad.

Her dad.

She was staring at a dead man.

47

Manila was the best place to die.

P. Burgos Street is named after Padre José Burgos, a Catholic priest accused of mutiny and executed by the Spanish colonialists. It is the red-light district, teeming with all life forms in the hours of darkness, and it runs like a neon-lit river through Manila's financial district, Makati City.

If you know where to look, you can buy anything on P. Burgos Street.

And I knew where to look.

Walk from one end of Burgos – as the locals call it – to the other and someone will step from the shadows to sell you whatever you are in the market for – drugs, Viagra, a gun or a companion for the week, the night or fifteen minutes.

But I was looking for something that would last forever.

My death.

I needed a way out of the hole that I had dug for myself.

I craved the exit door on my life.

All my research had pointed to this country, this city, and this street. The search engines all directed me to a fourteen-hour flight on Philippine Airlines to Manila, and the services rendered on P. Burgos Street. All my research had screamed – they will sell what you are looking for in Manila.

You can fake your death in the Philippines.

London had had enough of me. London was sick and tired of me. London wanted me to pay my debts. And if I did not – and if I could not – then London was ready to break my heart, my legs, my neck.

It was not poverty that brought me low.

It was debts that had grown like a tumour.

Gambling debts – my problem was as banal as that.

Scarlet Bush was wrong – I was a journalist. That was never a lie. I wrote about sport. And I bet on it too, and I made money, and then when I started to lose, I played harder, for bigger stakes.

And one day I woke up to find the hole I was in was a grave.

Sometimes your problems are so insurmountable that only death can draw a line under them.

I had done my research, of course.

And I would have far preferred to make my dramatic exit on home soil. I had to wait for an excuse to go to Manila. In the end it came – an up-and-coming young boxer who was widely predicted to be the next Manny Pacquiao. I watched him spar, train. I even went running with him and his crew. We sat down to talk in a hotel where the air con made me shiver. I even filed a 2,000-word feature. I don't think they ever printed it.

I could not fake my death at home. The pile of clothes on the beach – or the lonely lakeside – had just been done too many times. That disgraced MP in the olden days, John Stonehouse. That man in a canoe. And Clementine, with her neat pile of clothes left on a rock in the Lake District.

None of them pulled it off for long enough, did they?

And when you are faking your death, only forever is long enough.

They even try it in the Philippines, funnily enough. Skipping out on their failing life after some pantomime of drowning. And it doesn't work there either.

Nobody buys that clothes-on-the-shore routine any more.

Stephen Monk didn't buy it. His stepfather didn't buy it.

Although of course – I can't be sure! I can't be sure that some lucky soul did not pull off the old clothes-on-the-shore routine. Because such is the nature of – technical term – *pseudocide* that the ones who never get caught are the ones who you never hear about. Because they pulled it off.

And then they remain happily dead forever.

I have, you will guess, inevitably made a study of the subject.

Men – like me – almost always do it to escape debt.

Women, like my Clementine, almost always do it to escape men.

The successful disappearing act takes elaborate preparation.

And perhaps one day the world will catch on that foreigners who die in the Philippines sometimes enjoy a strange afterlife – running a lobster restaurant at the far end of England, for example.

But the world has not caught on right now. Not quite yet, and not in my time.

Manila turned out just fine for me. No, that's not true, of course – because when a man walks away from his debts he also walks away from everything and everyone he ever loved. You tell yourself – as the years after death drift by – that they, the loved ones left behind, are better off without you.

On the good days, you even believe it to be true.

My top tip for faking your death – you have to be sure before you begin. Think twice. And then think a thousand times more. You have to be positive that you have the will to see it through to the bitter end.

What helps is if there is no other way out. What helps is when dying seems like a bloody good idea.

The initial contact was the hard part. I wanted something a bit more dangerous for all concerned than a bar girl, a gram of blow or a Beretta 92 clone from Turkey. One of the tech guys at my newspaper showed me how to access the Dark Web – research, I lied, for a piece about elite sportsmen buying performance-enhancing drugs. What I wanted was waiting for me on the Dark Web.

And I met a man in a bar called Stardust, at the unlit end of P. Burgos Street.

Stardust was a bit different from the other bars on the street because it was clean, there was a cabaret, and carefully choreographed dancing girls in elaborate costumes.

It was far more upmarket than most of the bars on P. Burgos. It was a lot less hard sell – you could drink a beer, for example, without someone sitting on your lap. Perhaps that is why, when I walked in, the place was completely empty apart from me, the guy behind the bar, and around fifty girls wearing either string bikinis or elaborate evening dresses.

And then he walked in.

Middle-aged, balding, no nonsense. He wore a barong tagalog – the traditional Filipino shirt for men, like a white dress shirt, long sleeved and buttoned at the neck, but worn outside his trousers. American accent. Educated. He told me he was a civil servant. We left it at that.

And he told me how it would be.

We ordered two San Miguel Lights.

And we began at the end as he placed my death certificate on the bar.

48

Republic of the Philippines
OFFICE OF THE CIVIL REGISTRAR GENERAL
CERTIFICATE OF DEATH

It was all there on one single yellow sheet of paper.

My name – my real name – my gender, my date of birth.

My date of death, my place of death, my cause of death.

Car accident. A hit-and-run driver on Roxas Boulevard.

My hand reached out to take it. The man in the barong shook his head.

'This is for your family,' he said. 'For your authorities. Don't touch it. It goes to the British embassy on Upper McKinley Road. And then back to your country.' He sipped his San Miguel, stared with some disapproval at the dancing girls on stage, smiling at the empty bar. 'It goes back with your remains.'

They want you to succeed. All of them.

The policeman who reported the dead tourist run down on Roxas.

The doctor who signed the certification of death, and the second doctor who reviewed and signed the document. The funeral director who signed the burial/cremation permit (I chose cremation, an unclaimed cadaver at the morgue providing the ashes – so much more final). The registrar who recorded my death. And the man in the barong shirt in Stardust, although he scared me more than anyone I had ever met. I was terrified of blackmail. I was afraid the one million pesos bill could become ten million.

Which I did not have. I was afraid – right at the end, as the girls at Stardust danced before an empty nightclub – that I was going to be betrayed, shaken down, carted off in handcuffs.

But they all want you to succeed.

Betray one death fraudster and the industry would never recover.

That's why it is possible. That's why it works. That is why it cost me everything I had left in the bank – one million Philippine pesos: £15,000, plus change.

The Philippines is a poor country. And that kind of money, it changes lives. And it changed mine.

The return to the UK presented problems.

I could not, for obvious reasons, use the return leg on my Philippine Airlines e-ticket. My passport stayed with my death certificate and the other paperwork. The official police report from the Manila Police District of the Philippine National Police. An authentication certificate from the Department of Foreign Affairs, as I was a foreigner.

But I had brought another passport with me in the name of Tom Cooper, acquired online – not even on the Dark Web! – before I left home.

But Tom Cooper is not my name. That's why Scarlet Bush could find no trace of me among the old hands of the newspaper industry. They would recognise my real name, they would remember me as a pretty good sportswriter, and not a bad bloke. He got pissed in Manila and hit by a bus, silly sod.

But once Tom Cooper was on home soil it was all remarkably easy. I knew where I was headed – the county where I had been happy as a child.

Did I say Manila had cost me everything I had in the world? That's not quite true, for there was a Cleto Reyes kitbag waiting inside a locker at Paddington railway station that contained cash – not a fortune, but enough to start a modest restaurant at the end of England that I was going to call the Lobster Pot.

I caught the sleeper train from Paddington to the end of the end.

There was no insurance policy to cash in – the quickest way to have the authorities on your tail. That's how they get you – asking them for money. Your death matters a lot less to the world if there is nobody holding out their hand for compensation.

I had no dying parents I had to see. I had no friends who I could not live without. My wife had tired of me, fallen in love with the single dad next door – who can blame her? – for I was preoccupied with my gambling debts. My untimely death on a business trip would, I strongly suspected, be a relief to a wife who was looking for her own way out.

But, ah, my little girl.

My daughter.

That's who I would miss.

And I would miss her forever.

But that was the price I had to pay.

The price I paid to the man in Stardust – that one million Philippine pesos – was not the real bill. I was leaving a woman who had loved me once – whatever she said now! – but what really cut me to the bone was leaving that beautiful, special child who I would not get to watch grow up, the girl who – I thought! – I would never see again.

So, yes – fear, regret, sadness, depression, all of that.

But mostly – *the shame*, like a birthmark you will never remove, like a wound that never heals, like a weight that can never be lifted.

That's what it ultimately does, walking away from your life.

It shatters those you leave behind.

But it kills you.

I stared with wonder at the daughter I had not seen for ten years.

Half her lifetime! How quickly the years fly, and how heartbreakingly out of reach they are when they are gone. All that precious time, and it could never come again.

I could see her mother in her. But I could see myself too – something about her mouth, and her eyes – and that was hard to look at. Because she was appalled by me, and by the level of deception.

By the weakness of the parent who ran away. And far worse than that – who pretended to be dead. All those years. All those lies.

My cruelty was unspeakable.

'I didn't do this to hurt you and your mother,' I told her now. 'There were some very bad men after me. I did it to protect you.'

'To protect yourself, more like!'

'Yes, that too. But to make a happy life possible. For you and your mother.'

Behind us, the wedding reception was struggling to know what to do. We were being watched. But they all melted away, even my bride, and there was just me and my daughter. She stood with her back to the glass wall, and the great expanse of the ocean was behind her, and that faded to nothing too.

'She remarried. Remember Joe? The man next door with the little boy? They're both very happy as far as I can tell. I think of *him* as my father. I think of *Joe* as my dad. And he is a good man. And do you know the greatest thing he does? *He shows up*. He's there. That's what a real father does. That's what a loving parent does. That's what *a real man* does. They show up. Get it, do you?'

She watched the hurt register on my face.

'I want to explain,' I said. 'I don't ask for forgiveness or understanding, I don't expect you to feel anything for me but contempt. But I want you to understand why I had no choice.'

'No,' she said, taking off her apron, throwing it in my face. 'Just – *no*. Drop dead, will you?'

It did not sound like the worst idea in the world.

49

WILL FARTHING: *You won't see Tom Cooper round here no more. Done a bunk after that maid saw him at the wedding. His daughter, turns out. Not much of a party after that, was it? Lot of tears. Lot of trauma. I don't think anyone even tasted my lobster. Our Clem — his wife — came to see me and my missus the next morning. She thought he might have bunked down with us until it all blew over. But we hadn't seen hair nor hide of him. Tom walked out of that wedding reception and he was gone. I have to say that at the party he looked — how can I put it? He looked as if he was at the end of everything.*

Shame. Bloody shame. Lovely couple they were. But he's gone now and I reckon he's gone for good. He looked like a man who had had enough of life. He looked like he couldn't stand no more. Run out of road, as the saying goes.

And what do you lads want him for? Money, was it? Like — a lot of money? Yes, that is a lot of money!

Well, good luck with that. Best not hold your breath. My bet is that Tom Cooper — or whatever his real name was — chucked himself down a tin mine. Those shafts are a long way down. If you want to top yourself in these parts — if you really want to see it through, if it's not a call for help — then you go to one of the old tin mines, and you step off the edge and you drop yourself down one of them shafts. You want to find Tom Cooper? Try looking down the tin mines. My hunch is that you will find Tom's body at the bottom of one of them.

How many old tin mines are there in Cornwall? Ooh, I believe there are around two thousand or so.

That sound about right, Paolo?

Anyway — me and this young man are going out on the second tide soon, so we can't stand around here yakking all day long. Yes, nice to meet you, lads. And good luck with finding Tom down a tin mine. But one word of advice for you.

The red-haired maid up at the restaurant — the Lobster Pot.

Steer clear of her, all right?

His wife. Yes, Tom's wife. My advice — don't go anywhere near her, hear me? Don't talk to her.

Don't ask her for money.

And don't even look at her.

Because if you ever do — if you ever do — then you will have the whole of St Jude's to answer to. That's what we are like around here.

We look after our own.

And we got tin mines galore.

Enjoy those pasties, lads. Come on, Paolo.

We're done here, son.

50

CLEMENTINE: *He should have stayed. I wish he had stayed! We could have faced it all together. I could have helped him. I was shocked to learn who he was — of course I was — shocked beyond belief. That poor girl. But — that poor man too. Poor Tom. But I understood — or at least I would have tried to understand. We could have got through it together.*

I loved him, you see.

Yes, I suppose I am a wealthy woman now. I am only now starting to think about it. There was cash in the bank, and this apartment, and the restaurant itself. The Lobster Pot was a little gold mine. Tom — and he will always be Tom to me — even had life insurance.

Our baby is due in six months. Thank you for asking. So St Jude's will still be out of season. Yes, I'm staying on. This is the place he loved, these are the people he loved and this is where we fell in love. It was home. It will be home. For both of us. Me and the baby, I mean.

No — nothing from Tom. Not a word. And I don't expect there will be a word beyond the note he left out on the deck of the Lobster Pot. The police called it a suicide note.

But to me, it was a love letter.

51

Dearest Clementine, love of my life.

Well, this is a bit awkward! What kind of idiot wrecks the best day of his life? An idiot such as I. Sorry, sorry, sorry. You looked beautiful, by the way. But then you always looked beautiful to me. So crazy to spoil it all. We should have had years together, decades, a lifetime.

But I got what I deserved.

The Cornish have a name for their version of justice.

They call it — rough music.

They have always thought of themselves as a separate country down here, removed from English laws, abiding by their own code of morals, or ethics, or honour, or whatever you want to call it. They don't have the law of the land down here in Cornwall. They have rough music.

And I have been on the wrong end of some very rough music, my love. And I know I deserved every last note.

You will hear bad things about me now. I imagine that much of it will be true.

But please never doubt that I loved you with all of my heart.

Love our child — I know you will.

She is lucky to have your love just as I was lucky too — the luckiest man alive.

It breaks my heart to leave you. To leave the pair of you.

But I had it coming, this rough music. I have had it coming for years.

I am going now, Clementine.

I love you all ways, and always.

I am yours, and only yours, in this world and the next.

Tom

52

TOM: *Funnily enough, I did think about ending it all down a tin mine. There are so many of them, and they are everywhere, and you just chuck yourself down the shaft, and the job is done. But it was the thought of never being found — never being found — and laying down there with the bat bones until the end of time. I couldn't say I fancied it much. Not a tin mine then.*

Which left the sea. There were boats aplenty Polmouth side — so many boats, casually left around by rich incomers. Kayaks, training dinghies, single-handers, double-handers, cruising boats and multihull dinghies, which were a kind of baby catamaran. I was no kind of sailor, but Charlie Farthing had taken me out on the water a few times in the early days of our friendship and, like everyone in Cornwall, I knew enough to sail a single-hander by myself. And the good news — I wasn't going to have to worry about the return journey.

So I found a pretty single-hander on the slipway Polmouth side — single sail, ultra-light hull, idiot proof. It

was a nice little boat. Just left there by some spoilt incomer for someone else to put away. Incomers! They have
so much of everything that they don't appreciate
anything.

I dragged it down the slipway and into the water and
I sailed it out on the ebb tide as the lights of St Jude's
and Polmouth shone on either side of me. I aimed the
bow — the pointy bit at the front of the boat — for the
mouth of the estuary. Henry VIII's ruined fort rose above
me on my starboard side and soon I was in the open sea.
Choppy, black, the spray sopping through my wedding
suit, soaking me to the bone, and making the floral
spray buttonhole in the lapel of my jacket all wilted,
soggy and sad. Terrified that I might capsize and be
rescued, I steered far out and then followed the coastline
to Maggie's Cove, deserted now, and then sailed on, no
doubts in my mind, but trying to call up my courage.

And then I was beyond a sharp bend in the coastline
and Maggie's Cove was behind me and it felt like I was
on another, rougher ocean, because the single-hander was
much harder for me to control, and then all at once it
became impossible. The swell lifted me and the rig and
dropped us with what felt like contempt. I stared at the
shore but there was nothing I knew, no landmark I recognised, just black granite cliffs covered in lichen, the
coastal path above them empty of life.

And then I saw it rising above me.

The Baulking House. The shuttered cottage on the clifftop with what looked like the old-fashioned bus stops on either side.

And just as I saw it a bigger wave lifted the single-hander rig and hurled it sideways, and then I was under the water and felt something crack hard against my back, and it must have been a hidden rock because when I broke the surface the rocks were all around me, and the capsized rig was beyond my reach, sliding upside down out to open sea, and I reached for the rocks but the jagged black granite was like trying to hold razor blades.

A wave punched me full in the face and I swallowed a sickening gutful of seawater.

I sank below the surface, rose again, but felt my sodden wedding suit trying to drag me down.

Dear God, I thought. I don't want to die.

But the sea was wild now, and the rocks slashed at my hands and sliced through my waterlogged wedding suit, and the weight of those clothes and my life dragged me down for the final time.

And just before I went under, I looked up at the Baulking House and I imagined I saw them, the dark figures watching from the clifftops, and I called out to them for help but they were busy lighting their beacons, and the last thing I remember were their fires roaring and blazing in the darkness of the coastal path, as if the moment they had waited so long for had come at last.

53

A bonfire burns on a Cornish beach in the middle of the night.

The fishing village rises steep and timeless above me.

The fort, the church, the surf shop and the pub.

The sea whispers its secrets, sighs and then forgets.

The tide is going out.

I am on a beach I have never been on before. My hair is wet. My clothes are damp. The sea is black glass, dead calm, glazed with moonlight.

Bloody hell, it's cold.

So I have lit this fire from driftwood. It crackles and burns in the darkness. I know that if someone is awake and watching the beach, they will see my fire.

But it can't be helped. I crave the heat. I yearn for the light.

There is the total silence of deep night apart from the sounds that are always there. The sea breathing, as if it is a living thing, and the gulls crying, pining for the small ones about to leave the nest, and mourning the time to say goodbye that always comes in the end.

I hear the sleeper train moan as it makes its journey through the night, passing moors and meadows and granite cliffs and the sleeping fishing villages still lost in their dreams.

I stare to the east waiting for the rising sun to break up the darkness. It hasn't happened yet.

And then there are footsteps approaching.

One moment they were not there, and now they are.

Heading for my fire, my light.

Stepping softly on golden sand.

Coming for me.

And I stand on that beach at the end of the end, anxious to learn if I am about to be invited home to warmth, sweet tea and buttered toast, or if I am to be dragged off to pay for my many sins.

About the Author

Tony Parsons is a bestselling novelist and an award-winning journalist. His books have been published in over forty languages and his multimillion-selling novel *Man and Boy* won the Book of the Year prize in 2000. Most recently, he created the Max Wolfe crime series. *The Murder Bag*, the first Max Wolfe book, went to number one on the *Sunday Times* bestseller list and in 2023 was voted one of the 100 best crime books of all time by the readers of Dead Good Books. Tony lives in London with his family.

Max Wolfe is back!

The long-awaited seventh instalment in the
popular crime series from the number one
bestselling author of *Man and Boy*.

Read on for an extract from

MURDER FOR BUSY PEOPLE

by
Tony Parsons

Old dogs rise early, as if to make the most of the time that remains, and so it was that Stan and I were already wandering on Hampstead Heath when the sun came up and turned the string of ponds to molten gold.

Once, there would have been three of us on these walks, but somewhere along the line Scout had lost the habit. So now there were just us two, and as I watched him the old dog paused in the new daylight, as if remembering.

Or maybe not.

Possibly Stan was just staring blankly into space, with not a single thought between his extravagant Cavalier ears.

Now that he was knocking on a bit, our boy sometimes got distracted, and lost all sense of time and sight of me, even when I was standing next to him. But lifting that button nose — once as shiny and moist as a black olive, now parched and dry — could also mean that he had picked up the scent of a rabbit or fox that had been late going home to its burrow. A dog's sense of smell is the last thing to go. And it was still so early that the night was not really gone yet on Hampstead Heath.

Then I saw the dog, the dog Stan had smelled, and I paused too. Because he was the kind of dog that would stop anyone, two- or four-legged, dead in their tracks.

A big dog, a very big dog, unmoving in the treeline. A giant head of black and tan. And more than very big – massive. Even from this distance, he could only be one breed. Rottweiler. He watched us without expression. A Rottweiler that is brought up well can be as calm as a Buddhist monk. There was no aggression in him. Because there didn't need to be.

Stan rashly trotted off to say hello.

I cursed, calling his name even though I knew he would not hear. A decline in his hearing was another of Stan's growing list of ailments.

So I slowly followed, looking around for the Rottweiler's owner. A lone runner in the distance was the only other sign of life. So I stopped to listen for someone calling out the name of their lost dog. But there was only birdsong.

And then, as Stan and I got closer to the Rottweiler, I saw why the owner was not calling for his dog.

There was a man on his back, unmoving, almost buried in the long grass, directly in front of the dog.

I edged closer, then slowly knelt by his side.

The Rottweiler watched me all the way.

A Kennel Club tag glinted under his face. MY NAME IS BUDDY, it said.

'Good boy, Buddy,' I said. Buddy was unimpressed.

I watched Buddy and Buddy watched me as I leaned closer to his master.

This was not a young man. I placed two fingers to the carotid pulse point on the side of his neck, just under the jaw and beside the windpipe. Nothing. Then I placed the same two fingers on his radial pulse, where his thumb met his wrist. Again nothing. His chest was not rising and falling. I listened for his breathing for the standard ten seconds, but I already knew by now that I was never going to hear him draw breath.

On his wrist was what looked like a no-brand smartphone with a white strap. A heart rate monitor.

I stood up, deciding it was his dodgy ticker that had killed him.

There was no sign of violence.

Murder was the last thing on my mind.

I stared at him, that pause that comes when the living contemplate the dead, and I tried hard to see the man he had been.

His thinning, silvery hair was shaved very short in what they once called a number one crop, and he wore a green MA1 flying jacket with a vivid orange lining. There were Doctor Martens boots, muddy from the Heath, and his jeans were faded Levi 501s. The skin on his hands was so dry it resembled paper. He was a former Jack the Lad, a skinhead or a mod back in the day, who had lived long enough to collect his Freedom Pass.

And then I saw that he had a prison tattoo.

It was one of the classics. Five dots, arranged like the face of a dice – a quincunx, they call it.

I have heard a dozen different interpretations of what the quincunx means, but the one I always believed was that it represents one lonely human soul, surrounded by four walls.

Whatever else it stood for, the tattoo meant that the dead man had done time.

And what was unusual about this particular quincunx was that it wasn't on the dead man's hand between his thumb and index finger, which is where HMP alumni usually get their five-dots body art.

This one was engraved just below his right eye, staining his pale skin like five inky teardrops.

And it is possible that there are multiple old jailbirds out there who have made the rash decision to have the quincunx tattooed on their face.

Perhaps there are prisons where once upon a time having the five-dice inked on your face was all the rage.

But I had only ever known of one old con with a quincunx tattooed under his right eye.

'I know you,' I said to the dead man. 'Don't I?'

And finally the Rottweiler lifted his handsome head and growled at me, as if to give me a warning.

Bringing a book from manuscript to what you are reading is a team effort, and Penguin Random House would like to thank everyone at Century who helped to publish *Who She Was*.

PUBLISHER
Selina Walker

EDITORIAL
Joanna Taylor
Charlotte Osment
Emma Berrill

DESIGN
Jason Smith

PRODUCTION
Helen Wynn-Smith
Faye Collins

AUDIO
James Keyte
Meredith Benson

INTERNATIONAL SALES
Anna Curvis
Linda Viberg

PUBLICITY
Sarah Harwood
Klara Zak

MARKETING
Hope Butler

UK SALES
Alice Gomer
Olivia Allen
Kirsten Greenwood
Jade Unwin
Evie Kettlewell